THE OUTRAGE

THE
OUTRAGE

WILLIAM HUSSEY

USBORNE

For Dad, who always loves a good story.

First published in the UK in 2021 by Usborne Publishing Ltd., Usborne House,
83-85 Saffron Hill, London EC1N 8RT, England. usborne.com

Usborne Verlag, Usborne Publishing Ltd., Prüfeninger Str. 20, 93049 Regensburg,
Deutschland, VK Nr. 17560

Text © William Hussey, 2021

The right of William Hussey to be identified as the author of this work has been asserted by
him in accordance with the Copyright, Designs and Patents Act, 1988.

Face © shutterstock/elenabo

The name Usborne and the Balloon logo are Trade Marks of
Usborne Publishing Ltd.

A CIP catalogue record for this book is available from the British Library.

ISBN 9781474966184 05346/2 JFMAM JASOND/21

Printed and bound in Great Britain by CPI Group (UK) Ltd, Croydon, CR0 4YY.

TRIGGER WARNING

This book is set in a future England, following
a takeover by a far-right government.

The following text contains homophobia and
homophobic language, references to ethnic cleansing,
self-harm, references to suicide, and scenes of violence
that some readers may find distressing or offensive.

FOREWORD

BY JAY HULME

Until 1967 it was illegal to be gay in England and Wales.
Until 1981 it was illegal to be gay in Scotland.
Until 1982 it was illegal to be gay in Northern Ireland.
Until 1992 it was illegal to be gay in the Isle of Man.
Until 2001 it was illegal to be gay in the British Virgin Islands.

If you were born in the UK before the Equality Act was passed in 2010 it was legal to discriminate against LGBT people in your lifetime. If you went to a state run school or used a public library in England or Wales when Section 28 was in force, between 1988 and 2003 (2000 in Scotland), it was illegal for any of the teachers or library staff you encountered to speak positively of LGBT people.

Having grown up in the 1980s and 1990s, William Hussey witnessed much of this first hand, and this book is his warning to us all. We cannot be complacent about our rights. We cannot assume the victory is won.

A future like the one depicted in this book may seem impossible, but today, in 2021, you can be executed for being LGBT in eleven jurisdictions. In over 70 countries being LGBT is criminalised.

By comparison, the UK seems like a safe place to be LGBT. The idea that the UK could legally persecute LGBT people can seem inconceivable to those who grew up with such laws in action. But those laws are recent victories, and our status as equal citizens is still fragile. Between 2019 and 2020 reported homophobic hate crimes in the UK rose 20%. They have risen every year for a decade.

We see the warning signs everywhere; in the rising numbers of LGBT hate crimes, the publicly acceptable face of transphobia, and the regular insinuations in the media that, perhaps, LGBT rights have "gone too far". The more rights and visibility a marginalised group gains, the louder those who hate them become.

LGBT people in the UK are living through a very dangerous moment in time. Our rights ostensibly protect us, but rights are as thin as paper. Rights are agreements, voted in and out at political whim. One need only look at countries which have passed laws making LGBT people equal citizens, but are now, only a few years later, implementing LGBT-free zones.

Without tackling hatred, and the root causes of that, our rights are nothing at all; easily torn down, or pushed aside, ignored amidst a rising tide of hatred, and a reversion to a past that is all too recent.

Anyone would do well to keep this in mind as they read *The Outrage*.

Jay Hulme is an award winning transgender performance poet, speaker and educator. Visit www.jayhulme.com to find out more.

NOW

1

A constable sweeps the classroom, taking names, searching bags, dragging kids out of their chairs and slamming them against the wall. I sit towards the back, ankles clamped around the bag under my desk. It can't end this way, can it? Not like this. Not after everything we've been through.

June is hauled upright and pinned against the big bulletin board behind Miss Calloway's desk. She grunts, and in the same moment Eric does this half turn in his seat. He searches my face for any special reason why we should be fearing for our lives. Eric doesn't know about the disc in my bag. Probably wouldn't even suspect that I've taken one of the banned films from the library. Except he knows me better than anyone, so he really ought to be able to guess that I've done something apocalyptically stupid.

June's shoulders squirm as the constable gropes inside her blazer.

"Nothing in the pockets," he says at last.

His superior shrugs. I know Huxley, the sergeant of Degenerate Investigations. His green jacket – the uniform that gives these maniacs one of their nicknames – is so smeared with the sergeant's breakfast you could make a pretty decent meal from the spillage.

"Then move on," Huxley yawns. "All a waste of time anyway. No little degenerates in this pack – isn't that right, Miss…?"

"Calloway. Esther Louise."

The constable volunteers her name before Miss Calloway has a chance to speak. He has a frozen face, his mouth constantly smiling as if his lips have been painted on. Turning away from our teacher, he reaches inside his tunic and takes out a tape measure, which he unspools against the side of June's head.

"Stay perfectly still," he says, as he gauges the length of her hair.

At the desk behind June's, Liz sits with her fists tightly clenched. Meanwhile, my thoughts are swamped by the ticking time bomb inside my gym bag. If the constable is being this thorough then he'll find the disc, no question, and then? The secrets we discovered in the abandoned library will finally be exposed and we'll all get a trip to Re-Purification. Maybe our families will get to see us again one day, living zombies staggering out of the camps, a pink cross on our shirts to mark us out. Maybe they won't.

The tape zippers shut.

"Quarter inch into dyke territory." The constable cuts back to Huxley. "That's to say, hair of a length likely to indicate female degeneracy, contrary to the second Declaration of the Public Good."

Huxley nods and scribbles inside his notebook. "Your parents ought to know the restrictions on female appearance, young lady." He tears off a slip and hands it to June. "Pay the fine, grow it out and we'll say no more."

"Regs state that we should make a record of her identity, sir. For future reference."

"If we must. Name?"

"Juniper. Ryerson."

"What?" The constable's calm, coaxing voice shocks a tear onto June's cheek. She rubs it furiously, and I swear I can feel the heat of her embarrassment pulsing through the room. Like Liz, my own fists tighten under the table as fear and anger knot my stomach.

"Ju-ni-per," she repeats slowly. "Ry-er-son. I-D num-ber 2-5-0-8-1-9-/3-9."

The punch isn't unexpected. Okay, so we might be in Special Educational Exemption, excused from national service and all the paramilitary joys of two years' marching, folding uniforms and having the unholy hell kicked out of us, but we've witnessed our share of brutality. When I was

13

seven years old, I saw a shop assistant dragged over his counter and beaten bloody because a constable had overheard him moaning about the new ration books. Last year I came out of the post office to find an officer holding a little girl in a headlock, all because a neighbour suspected her parents' descendancy papers weren't in order.

But that driving fist to my friend's stomach? I don't know. Something inside me breaks.

I rise, and Eric rises, and I can't help it, I feel this swell of pride. The Eric of seven months ago would have stayed silent in his seat. But before either of us can intervene, Miss Calloway is helping June to her feet and offering apologies.

"I'm sure she didn't mean any offence, Constable. Juniper's a very upright girl. Very intelligent. We're fast-tracking her into the Protectorate's medical science programme, which I needn't tell you is crying out for clever young minds. I'd hate to think her placement in SEE has been endangered by—"

"Why don't you shut that silly mouth?" The constable's advice comes with a smooth serving of smile. "Unless you *want* to be listed for a Section 28 visit?"

Eric and I sink back as the blood runs from Miss Calloway's face. Section 28, one of the most chilling powers any officer can execute; named, so my dad says, in "honour" of some ancient law from the 1980s that forbade the teaching of degenerate lives and relationships in British schools. The new Section 28 allows an officer to search homes and workplaces for any evidence of "immorality". There have been whispers: Esther Calloway and that nice lady from the canteen living together on the outskirts of town. Maybe the Green Jackets have had their sights set on that lonely cottage for a while. But, then again, teachers are pretty hard to replace these days. All I know is that the fear in Calloway's eyes – immense and infectious – reminds me of the terror I once saw in Eric's.

"Juniper?" the constable muses, turning back and twirling his finger in front of June's face. "Sounds a bit ethnic, no? Maybe we should refer the whole family for a full background check."

"Nothing ethnic about it," Eric mutters. "*Juniperus communis*. The native juniper tree. You used to see them all over Britain until they went extinct about a decade ago. In fact, it's a perfectly patriotic name."

The constable's head snaps around. "Well, isn't that just fascinating?"

Losing all interest in June, he makes a beeline for Eric. And although I know he's the safest person in the room right now, still my heart slams into my throat. Eric doesn't look up. He keeps his gaze fixed on the open geometry book in front of him.

At almost the last moment, Huxley takes an interest. "Rakes."

Something new in the sergeant's tone. Something dangerous. Constable Rakes glances round and Huxley shakes his massive head.

"Open your eyes. That's the chief's son."

Rakes smooths down his immaculate jacket, adjusting the monogrammed armband on the sleeve: *PO-DI* (Protectorate Officer – Degenerate Investigations). He has a moustache, a hilarious yellow caterpillar quivering across his top lip. Maybe that's the joke that keeps him grinning.

"Eric. Of course, you have your father's way with words." He ruffles Eric's permanently untidy hair. "I don't know if you're aware, but I've recently taken over the local branch of the Young Lions. Interesting, you not being a member. Perhaps we'll see you at a troop meeting one day?"

"Move it along," Huxley advises.

Rakes disentangles his fingers and glides on to Albert. This is pure good luck, for me at least. I usually sit next to Eric but this morning Albert had one of his dizzy spells and asked if we might switch places so he could be closer to the window. It's one of those typical late-March days, ferociously hot, and Mosley Grammar's air-conditioning units rattled out their dying gasps three summers back.

Of course I said yes. Albert and I have been friends pretty much since for ever, though switching seats killed me a little. Thing is, I usually finish Miss Calloway's geometry problems well ahead of Eric, giving me a few precious moments to steal glances at that adorable face, screwed up in quiet concentration. But Albert had looked seriously queasy, so I agreed, proving the Protectorate wrong about one thing at least: us hell-bound degens *can* be decent human beings.

But Albert is only a stay of execution. A pit stop before the gates of Re Purification close behind me. As I watch Rakes grapple Albert to his feet, I suddenly realize that a lot of my ideas about the camps are based on playground rumours: *I heard the guards use the pervs for target practice; Don't be daft, they give 'em a chance to change first – electric shocks, my uncle says. Fry the dirty thoughts right out of their heads; Nah, you're both wrong. They just shoot the filthy gits stone dead. BAM! One shot. Well, the Lord Protector doesn't like wasting bullets, does he?*

I have asked my dad if he knows anything about the camps, but he just shakes his head and changes the subject. One thing I do know: in the great Protectorate of England and Wales, the reality is always worse than the rumour.

"What are these?" Rakes's voice brings me back to the room.

He upends Albert's bag and a rain of metal clatters onto the desk. The Adam's apple yo-yos in Albert's throat. He's small for seventeen, barely as tall as my shoulder. With his slightly spooky grey eyes and that sweep of pale hair, Albert reminds me of these characters from a fantasy board game we used to play together when we were little kids. The wood elves of the forest. I'd forgotten about that until this moment. Strange to think those Saturday sleepovers were only six years ago. Strange, too, how much we've drifted apart since then.

"Albert has a knack with mechanical stuff," I say, drawing every eye in the room. "Fixing broken junk is his thing. He even got some old car working again. Some piece of crap they made way back before the Outrage. What was it called, Albert?"

Okay, so this is classic Gabe Sawyer: right at the moment when I ought to be busy thinking up some brilliant plan to keep me out of a Re-Pure camp, I'm shooting my mouth off. Meanwhile, that shiny silver disc in my bag? It's as if I can feel it throbbing between my ankles, a treacherous volcano that will devastate not just my life but the lives of my family, my friends, basically anyone I've ever said hello to. Most of all it will destroy Eric, and I can't let that happen.

"It was a saloon," Albert murmurs. "Mercedes E-Class. 2030 model."

"Corrupt foreign machinery," Huxley grunts, as Rakes starts sorting through Albert's collection of spanners and wrenches. "We'll allow you to keep these items, but your father must bring the appropriate licences to our office. As you know, unlicensed tools can be a serious matter.

18

The explosives planted in parliament by the Resistance last summer were put together with—"

His voice is lost against the blood drumming in my ears. I've run through every possibility and there's no way out. I can't claim the disc isn't mine without having the entire school dragged in for questioning.

Once a year, Protectorate Investigations all turn up for their annual scare-the-shit-out-of-the-kids assembly: the Green Jackets from Degenerate Investigations, Yellow Jackets from Political, Black Jackets from Alien, and Grey from General Crime. And I have to hand it to the Filth-Finders, their slide show is always the most stomach-churning. So yeah, there's no way anyone I love is going to end up at the mercy of these mad sadists.

I'm sweating. My glasses are starting to fog. Snatching them off, I clean the lenses with my shirtsleeve before catching sight of Eric. He's clearly caught on to my panic.

What? he mouths at me. *What?!*

Good question. Although it's against the law, I don't believe in God. Never have. So I don't exactly pray, I just wish really hard. I wish for a fire alarm, for the disc to magically disintegrate, for Huxley to keel over dead of a heart attack. Right now, I honestly don't care. But my most fervent wish is directed at Eric: *When it happens, let it happen. Don't try to fight them; don't go running to your dad. Remember what you told me that day at the river bend?*

He'd watch his whole world burn for the Protectorate.

Suddenly I'm aware of Albert again. His gaze flickers between me and Eric, and whatever messages we think we're transmitting to each other, Albert is listening in. Those disconcerting grey eyes go to the bag under my desk. He swallows hard.

And then Albert does something incredible.

2

Constable Rakes is still writing out the citation for his tools when a dark patch blooms across Albert's crotch. The officer looks up, stops writing, and a second later the room erupts. Honestly, it's like the best and brightest of Mosley Grammar have regressed a decade and we're all back to chasing each other around the playground and laughing at willy jokes.

Which is exactly what Albert wanted.

"Christ's sake," Rakes mutters. Technically a blasphemy offence, but I doubt anyone is going to report him.

He throws his notebook onto Albert's desk and tries to call for order. But his authority is gone, for the time being anyway. Even a Green Jacket can't compete with the sheer joy of half a pint of piss sliding down a kid's trouser leg. Two dozen chairs scrape back and a mob forms around the tiny figure of Albert.

"What the hell, Albie? Had too much juice at nap time?"

"Whoa! Are you going to cry now? Heck! Guys, I think he's *actually* going to cry."

"No way. Then he'll be leaking at both ends!"

I can barely see Albert now. One moron who's only in our school because his mum's something high up in the Wellbeing Protectorate is flicking at Albert's groin with a wooden ruler. It's depressing, but I suppose there's no mystery here. Out on the street, us SEE kids are fair game, so venting a little by eating one of our own can sometimes feel good.

As I watch, Eric slips from behind his desk and takes up position in the circle, his back to me. Shoulders hunched, he looks like the most reluctant bully ever, but all six-foot-three of him is blocking me from Rakes's and Huxley's view.

My hands shake as I grab my gym bag and wrestle with the drawstring. It feels like I'm wearing mittens, my fingers are so clumsy. After a few frantic, fumbling seconds, I plant my chin on the desk and dare an upward glance. The insults are still flying but I know Rakes won't tolerate this much longer. Actually I'm surprised he hasn't already taken out his baton and started smashing in a few exceptional skulls.

Miss Calloway is covering her mouth with her hands. Huxley rests his head against the doorframe, a picture of boredom. Eric glances back and makes a hurrying gesture.

Okay, Jesus, I'm trying!

And then a shadow falls across the desk. I look up, certain that I'll find that pathetic excuse for a moustache looming over me.

"Need this?"

Ben Dempsey slides my geometry compass across to me. Meanwhile Grace Everard hops up onto the edge of my desk and loops an arm around her boyfriend's shoulder. I feel this stupid rush of jealousy – not directed towards Ben and Grace, who might just have saved my sorry arse, but because that simple loving gesture will never get *them* hauled off for interrogation. Shielded by Grace, I dig the pointy end of the compass into the knot, all the while wondering if my place in SEE is really deserved. After all, it took a friend to point out that the solution to my problem was an instrument I'd been using all afternoon.

The knot comes loose just as Rakes decides to end Albert's humiliation. I'm tugging the bag open and thrusting my hand inside when his voice blasts through the insults.

"Back to your seats, all of you. And thank the Lord Protector I'm not writing some of you up for profanity."

The name-calling stops.

Seconds now.

But I can't find the disc.

My fingers flinch over a crusty gym sock, bump against my rations box, discover a ten-thousand pound note, which might buy me a chocolate bar if I'm still a free man at four o'clock.

"I said, take your seat."

"I will," Eric says. "I just want to see if he's okay first."

Three or four students remain huddled around Albert. Ben shoots me a look over Grace's shoulder, a desperate plea to finish whatever insanity I've embarked on. Meanwhile Eric circles slowly around until he's almost facing me, pulling Rakes's gaze in the opposite direction. He knows he's practically untouchable, but even the chief inspector's son can only push this so far before the Filth-Finder smells a rat.

"What do you mean, 'if he's okay'?" Rakes grunts. "Clearly he isn't. The little pansy just pissed his pants in front of the entire class."

"And?"

This seems to baffle Rakes. "I'm sorry?"

"You intimidated him, he reacted." Eric shrugs. "I reckon my dad would be pretty proud of you for provoking that sort of response. Don't you think so, Carl?"

Still planted in the doorway, Huxley chuckles. "I reckon you're right, Eric. And it's not like we can arrest the little weirdo for making a puddle. Not yet anyway." The chuckle turns into a belly laugh. "Then again, you never know what the next Public Good directive might bring."

My fingers brush the disc. It had slipped itself inside

the pages of my pristine copy of *Protectorate Oaths and Regulations*. Ironic really, that something the government sees as so dangerous should be hiding in the very book that bans its existence.

I'm pulling the disc free when Rakes barks, "Wait. What do you think you're doing over there?"

The disc is in my hand, its rainbow reflection cast on the ceiling like a spotlight. I close my fingers around its edge, dig the groove into my skin, and feel my world fall away.

Not the world of Westwick or England or the great Protectorate itself, but *my* world: the snug bungalow I share with my dad, and the kitchen with its beat-up table where we read and drink tea and just sit, comfortable in our silences; the river where I swim almost every day, even when it's ice cold and my breath bruises the air; the valley with the tree that overhangs the drop, and the promises and secrets that were shared in those drifting branches. And the library, of course. Our place, mine and Eric's and our friends' – Ben and Grace, Liz and June and Albert. The place where we came together, where we were set free by the old movies we found there, and where I finally decided on my ambition to become a filmmaker. All gone now, like childish dreams whispered to the dark.

"What's the problem?" Ben asks, his voice snapping me back to reality. "We were only kissing."

"Don't be rude to the officer," Grace says. "I'm sorry, sir, we didn't mean anything. It's just, with everything kicking off, we didn't think anyone would notice…"

I don't hear any more. Grace and Ben are still parked on my desk, drawing focus. Hidden behind them, I spin around and hope that my memory isn't cheating me. I've sat in this classroom for the past four years, ever since the rest of our year graduated aged thirteen, either to do their national service or take on some kind of factory or labouring work. Surely the image I have of the clapped-out air-conditioning unit isn't just some desperate fantasy?

No. It's here, dented and rusty and freaking gorgeous. I don't waste any more time. I post the disc through one of the vents and hear the deafening *ching* as it hits the bottom of the unit. Fortunately, at the same moment Rakes loses his temper and orders Ben and Grace back to their seats. By the time they've hopped down from my desk, I'm sitting serenely, facing the front, a cartoon halo surely hovering over my head.

"Constable, I, uh…would it be possible for Albert to go to the bathroom?" Miss Calloway murmurs. "There are spare uniforms in the office and—"

Rakes takes Albert by the shoulder and throws him back into his seat.

"He'll sit in it for the rest of the day, and he'll walk home just as he is."

Albert stares dead ahead. He looks so small. So vulnerable. My heart slows, the euphoria of escape evaporating. All I want to do right now is walk down the row and pull my friend into the biggest hug. But even that would get me arrested. I glance over at Eric and see that he's also watching Albert, his mouth set hard.

Fuck Rakes. Fuck him, and fuck Huxley, and fuck every Filth-Finder who ever pulled on a green jacket.

"Something the matter?"

The constable holds out his hand for my bag and I shove it towards him.

"Why so eager?" he smiles.

"Why so amused?" I shoot back. "I guess it must be the comedy moustache thing, right? Don't get me wrong, it *is* quite entertaining."

The smile tightens. "You four-eyed little..."

He drops my gym bag and draws back a gloved fist. *Here we go.* I lift my chin, mirroring his grin.

"Leave him," Huxley rumbles. "He's a friend of the boy."

Rakes pulls up short. He works his jaw, as if he has a dozen threats bubbling behind the gateway of his lips, but all he says is, "Take your bloody hands out of your sleeves. You ought to know hands and faces must be shown at all times in public."

With that, he shoots me the mother of all stink-eyes and turns on his heel, marching out of the room like some

27

psychotic toddler. Huxley tips Miss Calloway a nod and leaves too.

After a few minutes' silence the bell jolts everyone into action. Students blink and laugh and start rearranging their inspected bags. A couple of hands pat Albert's shoulder on the way to the door. I'm about to check on him myself when he grabs his bag and bolts. Liz tries to intercept him but he slips past her and is gone.

"All good?" Ben asks.

"Yeah." I get to my feet, my hand resting on the rust-scaled hulk of the air-con unit. "Thanks, mate."

June and Liz join Ben and Grace at my desk. June is still grimacing with pain and Liz is rubbing her back. It's a simple, friendly gesture, but the tenderness is unmistakable to the few of us who know what these two mean to each other. Despite everything, this makes me smile.

"Do we want to know what that was all about?" Grace asks. Her fingers are twisted through the buttonholes of her cardigan.

I blow out my cheeks. "Honestly? I'm just glad he didn't ask me my name."

June breaks into a rueful smile. "Agreed. If he wasn't cool with 'Juniper Ryerson' then he'd have totally lost it at 'Gabriel Garcia Sawyer'."

I nod. June and I are probably the only kids at school with "exotic" sounding names. More than thirty years in charge of this disintegrating nation, and the Protectorate still encourages its citizens to wallow in nostalgia, as if that will make everything better. "Traditional" names are just part of the deal.

"You okay?" I ask her.

"Pffft." She shrugs. "My grandmother punches harder than that."

"I bet she can grow a more convincing moustache, too."

"At least he didn't start questioning my career ambitions," she says. "After Miss Calloway mentioned fast-tracking me into medical science? You know they only ever take a couple of women a year. And we have to perform ten times better than any male applicant." Her look sours. "Science, industry, the law – not fit jobs for the little women of the Protectorate."

Liz whispers that she's talking too loud and June closes her eyes and takes a deep breath.

Finally Eric comes over. He shakes his head at me, but he isn't the same boy he was seven months ago, and that big broad smile comes easier these days.

"Gabe," he sighs. "What the hell?"

3

All right, I'll admit it – even after seven months I still get dizzy every time I see Eric Dufresne. And I see Eric Dufresne every freaking day. Okay, so because I'm an idiot it took me a few weeks to realize that Eric's surname isn't spelled how it sounds, and so like some dozy kid with his first crush, I spent several nights writing *Dufrain* in my notebook, drawing excruciating hearts over a non-existent "i".

Yes, I am seventeen, and I am that ridiculous.

Now I float with my nose just above the surface of the pool, waiting for the same old dizziness to hit. I think the anticipation might be as good as the thing itself. But then he steps out of the changing rooms, that shy smile on his lips, and of course the real thing is way, *way* better.

So here we are, two boys alone, sharing a moment. Anywhere else this could raise suspicions, but at the municipal pool? Guys, knock yourselves out! In fact, why don't you get naked and shower together, maybe even swat the occasional buttock with a wet towel? Just know that everything must be undercut with a joke, and that a misplaced glance could easily destroy your lives.

Not that we have anything to fear right now. Except for us, the pool is empty, and because I've been swimming here longer than just about anyone, Dennis the lifeguard has slunk off for a crafty cigarette.

Eric slides into the water, ducks his head under and comes up grinning, droplets spilling from his cheekbones. He licks his lips, blood red against the marble of his skin. I remember when I first saw him, pale and frightened at the front of the class, and how I thought those lips looked almost like a wound.

He swims towards me and we float in a circle, hands reaching and retreating, aching to touch and to be touched. Finally, Eric sighs and drifts over on to his back.

"Will you ever take anything seriously?" he whispers. "I swear you do that sleeve thing on purpose."

"What sleeve thing?" Floating beside him, I cast a sidelong look, wrinkling my nose.

"Every single time you see someone official, you deliberately hide your hands up your sleeves. You shouldn't mess with them like that."

"Yeah, my mum hated that too." *Hates.* Why do I always talk about her in the past tense? "When I was little, I'd be wandering around the bungalow with my hands down my trousers and she'd tell me, 'If you don't stop doing that the Yellow Jackets will come and take you away.' Because clearly I was hatching a political masterplan to bring down the Protectorate, and not just five years old and naturally obsessed with my dinky."

Eric grins up at the ceiling. "Some things never change."

"My dinky's changed!" I object. "It's changed quite considerably. And anyway, you're wrong."

"Wrong how?"

I roll over onto my front. "I do take some things seriously."

"Is this about your dinky again?"

I launch myself at him, grabbing his head and plunging him under. From the poolside this would look totally non-degen. Just two red-blooded males wrestling in the water. Okay, so maybe my fingers are lingering a little too long in that wavy dark hair. And the tickling that spills from dopey laughter into eager and encircling arms? Well, isn't that just a bit of brotherly affection? And when the laughter hiccups into silence, and we move closer, and the back of my hand rests against his face?

"I take *you* seriously," I tell him. "Always."

He reaches for my wrist and removes my hand. "Not everything's a joke, Gabe. If they ever find out about the library? If they found the films?"

"They won't. I promise."

He glides backwards. "You take too many risks."

"Well, if *you* hadn't taken that first risk with me, we wouldn't be here right now. And I wouldn't be doing this." I kick towards him and squeeze his cheeks between my palms, then smooch his lips with a theatrical *mwah!* Only kids messing about. Surely only that. "Dude," I whisper, "has anyone ever told you, you have an extremely sexy fish-face?"

Eric doesn't say anything. His skin is flushed red and I can't tell if he's annoyed. He ducks under the water for a long time, bobbing at the bottom with his eyes closed.

I check the digital clock at the end of the pool: *16:25*. We've only a few minutes before the popular afternoon sessions begin, and I don't want him still mad at me when the hordes descend.

I turn and cut quickly to the edge, pulling myself up onto the coping. When Eric surfaces again, I drop to my haunches and barrel sideways along the pool, swinging gibbon arms and gibbering. He bursts out laughing as I execute a perfect belly flop and thrash my way over to him.

"Monkey funny?"

"Monkey idiot," he says, and the smile slides from his face. I told him about the disc on our way over and I can see he's about to start in on it again. "Honestly, a *complete* idiot. I just don't understand how you could be so careless."

I push the hair out of my face and try to match his seriousness. "We've been through this. I stayed late last night, packing everything away after you all left. The disc must have fallen into my bag. By the time I found it this morning there wasn't time to take it back to the library before school. It was just bad luck."

He frowns. "Daydreaming, more like." And then the frown evens out and he gives me an indulgent grin. "Still, I suppose being a dreamer isn't a bad quality for the next Steven Spielburn."

"*Berg*," I correct huffily.

I know he meant it playfully, but in a way that's what makes me grumpy. When I talk to Eric about my stupid fantasy of becoming a director, it almost feels as if it could happen. But we both know the truth. The only films made under the Protectorate are the propaganda bullshit they show on TV every Sunday – cheap, shoddily made rubbish about the loyal officers who guard our brave little island against the foreigners and traitors who threaten it.

I'd rather die than make films like that.

Eric's hand touches my shoulder. "Hey, I'm sorry. I was only teasing."

"It's okay," I say. "But you know, those movies we've watched together, the possibilities they've shown us? They've given me so much. I always knew it was okay, being what we are, but those films made me more comfortable in my own skin than I ever thought possible. They did that for me, Eric, and one day I'd like to do the same for people like us... Only it's never going to happen, is it?"

He sighs. "Is that why you haven't told the others?"

"I know they wouldn't laugh," I say. "Wouldn't tell me I'm being stupid. But when it's just us talking about it, the whole idea feels like it could actually happen. If I shared it with the others, though? I don't know. Somehow it *would* seem more ridiculous. Does that make sense?"

"Gabe," he says softly. "I..."

Voices echo out of the changing rooms. Blunt, indecipherable bellows. There isn't much time left.

"Anyway," I say, "we've got bigger problems than my stupid daydreams. We need to get that disc back."

He swipes a jewel of water from his chin. "Agreed."

"And I think I have a plan."

"You have a plan." He puffs out his cheeks. "Well, that sounds ominous."

"Hey! Have my plans ever failed us yet?" Eric has to admit my plans are pretty incredible. At least, that's how I choose to interpret his silence. "I'll fill you in later at the library. By the way, I meant to tell you – I found a couple of new films last night after you guys left." I speak quickly as we drift towards the steps. "These discs must've worked their way behind a flap at the bottom of the box. I suppose they might be the last films we'll ever get to see, unless we happen to stumble across another random treasure chest in some other ruined library."

"Did you watch them?" He narrows his eyes. "Gabe!"

"Sorry," I say, laughing and batting away his hands. "I couldn't resist."

"Okay, you traitor, so what are they called?"

"The first one is *Pride*." I pause, because suddenly there's this huge lump in my throat. "Eric, it's so incredible. The story's all about this lesbian and gay group collecting money and supporting miners during this strike in the 1980s –and it's based on something that *actually* happened, way before the Outrage! And some people are prejudiced, but mostly it's just people, joining together to help one another…"

I struggle, knowing I can't explain the inexplicable, but desperate to share some idea of how I was left after watching the film, sobbing with joy and grief and gratitude.

"It's why I love movies," I say at last. "Because maybe they help to define something you already know."

"What did it define for you?" He reaches out under the water, brushing his fingertips against mine.

"You'll have to watch it," I say. "But it's us, and it's everyone, even now, even here. And it's mind-blowing." I laugh, and Eric laughs too, shaking his head because he doesn't know why he's laughing.

Shadows loom across the wet walls. We drift further apart.

"Changing the subject – I don't think much of your dad's new Rottweiler," I say. "The way he treated Albert was sick, even for a Green Jacket."

"I know. I guess we should be grateful Huxley was there to rein him in."

"But why no heads up?" Eric has given us advanced notice of every scheduled inspection since last October. "Was it a last-minute idea from the chief?"

"I don't think so. And Huxley hasn't had an original idea in his life. I'd guess it was Rakes's initiative, maybe trying to impress my dad on his first day."

And just like that, our time's up. Kids come hurtling into the pool, dive-bombing, cartwheeling, shoving each other off the sides. Dennis is back, blowing his whistle, but no one takes any notice. It's understandable. If you live in the Protectorate, your life is one long list of rules: what to eat, how to dress, where to go, how to get there, what to say, who to say it to, even how to think is the prerogative of the state, or so they'd like to believe. And so, when you have a space like the Powell Municipal Pool, where you can't be marched off to a Re-Education camp just for disobeying the no-diving policy, rules can go to hell.

Eric heads for the steps. He's come a long way since last September, but he won't stay when there's a crowd. The cotton shirt sticks to his chest as he climbs out and he immediately tugs at the wet fabric, billowing it out.

What did he tell me on that second date? Eczema? The fact he ever trusted me with the secret of his scars – about how he got them, about why – makes me feel both valued and awful, all at the same time.

Swimming over to the lanes, I start ploughing up and down. This calms me. It always has: the pull and stretch, the rhythmic groove, my shadow ghosting across the tiles below. All afternoon my heart's been like a loose door in a gale, slamming and screeching – now finally it feels as if the storm has passed.

I swim until I'm forced to twist my head for air. That's when I see Eric standing by the changing-room door, a group of kids gathered around him. My feet hit the bottom.

"Hey, Dufresne, how's your old man?"

The group's leader steps right up to Eric and gives him a "playful" shove. Eric staggers back, his laughter bright and hollow. I'm starting for the steps when he shoots me a warning glance. And he's right, I've had a close call today. I can't invite any more attention, especially from the Protectorate's youth organization – those schoolyard bullies who sign up for a smart uniform and the opportunity to push other kids around. So I force myself to sink back into the water and watch as the Young Lions have their fun.

4

"This man's dad is the best perv-finder in the business. Ain't that right, Dufresne?"

Patrick Gilligan. Even back in primary school he was a little thug, so I guess growing up to become area leader of the Young Lions was pretty much inevitable. Like every loyal moron who joins the Protectorate youth wing, Patrick's been fed all kinds of steroids as well as benefiting from extra rations, so he's seriously built. Unfortunately for Gilligan there are no miracle pills to bulk up the brain nor, by the look of his trunks, any other vital organ.

He loops an arm around Eric's shoulder. "How is the chief? You know I'd love to hear some tales sometime. Stories about epic fag-hunts or how the Filth-Finders do their interrogations."

Eric shrugs under Patrick's bicep. "My dad doesn't talk about stuff like that."

"Good man." Patrick thrusts out his chin. "Can't give the degens any clues about how we find them, am I right?"

Like their namesake, the Young Lions can smell weaker prey but they're cautious too. Although this skinny kid they've cornered is no match for them physically, the power behind Eric is real, and so they make tender jabs.

"Can I just say something?" Patrick holds Eric at arm's length and looks him up and down. "You should really come with us on a training day. Man, there's nothing to you! Just scrag and bone. It's all that book-reading they make you do with them other SEE kids. You know, too much thinking is what almost ruined this country in the first place. That's what my uncle says. You spend too long reading and trying to figure out other people's ideas and points of view and you're gonna start sympathizing with them. Then, before you know it, you've got fags running the country. Even in the military."

"Sod. Right. Off!" one of Patrick's buddies laughs. "Pansies in the *army*?"

"Mate," Patrick takes on a teacherly tone, "forty years back, they even used to have degen generals. Then the Lord Protector took charge and all that bullshit ended."

"Oh God, I think I'm gonna puke."

"So, Eric," Patrick continues, "time to man up. When you gonna join the YLs?"

Eric scratches an eyebrow. "Well, that depends."

"Yeah? On what?"

"On whether you want me ordering your sorry arses about."

For a minute it looks like Patrick might forget who he's talking to. He rolls his head shoulder to shoulder, unkinking a thick wedge of trapezius muscle. Meanwhile I drift back towards the steps. Whatever happens next, I'm beyond proud; there's no way the Eric Dufresne of last September would have stood his ground like this.

"Fuck do you mean by that?" Patrick grunts. "Order *us* around?"

"Just what I said."

"Kid, if you're trying to mess with me—"

"Think about it," Eric says. "I'm the son of the great John Dufresne, best Filth-Finder in the history of the Protectorate. Do you really think that if I join the Young Lions they'll put me at the bottom of the class? Forget it. This guy, Rakes? The constable who's taken over your platoon? He's new to Degenerate Investigations. Wants to make his mark and get my dad's attention. So where in the ranks do you think he'll put me right on day one?" Eric extends a finger and prods Patrick's chemically inflated chest. "Somewhere above you guys, that's for sure. And do you think I deserve that kind of preferential treatment?"

Patrick looks like an early primate who's discovered the

gift of fire. Sure it's nice and warm but it also burns, so that's confusing.

"Well, I don't think it's fair." Eric shrugs. "You've put in all the work, marching around in circles and doing pull-ups for three years, and in I waltz and get it all handed to me on a plate, just because my dad's the degen chief."

Very slowly Patrick's frown evens out.

"This is a good kid," he declares, and the pack nods its agreement.

Eventually the YLs wander off in search of less baffling prey, and Eric shoots me a wink. I grin, snap him a cross-eyed salute, and return to ploughing the lanes.

By the time I'm done, most kids have launched their last dive-bomb and now it's only me and a few pensioners puttering up and down. I give old Mrs Lebbon a wave and head for the showers. I've timed it right. No one in the changing rooms and the water's strong and hot.

Towelling off, I rub an oval in the steamed mirror and put on my glasses. Okay, so I'm no Patrick Gilligan but you don't swim every day and not pile on some muscle. Otherwise I have these fairly ordinary mud-brown eyes and a flattish slab of a nose, although some people say my hair is cute. It's tight-curled and corn-coloured. This is a double-edged sword. Eric's a fan, which is nice, but so are quite a few girls, and I won't be able to keep refusing dates without someone noticing. Honestly,

I don't like to think about it, so I try not to.

Outside, I swing my gym bag onto my back and make for the bike stands. That's where I run into Patrick again. The Young Lions are huddled over some kid, laying in the boot pretty viciously. A Grey Jacket from General Crime wanders by on the other side of the road and, catching sight of this, reaches for his baton. Then he spots the YL uniforms with their flashy ceremonial belts and hesitates on the kerb, looking down at his baton as if he's never seen it before. Some Young Lions come from influential families, and so a side glance from Patrick is enough to send the constable scurrying on his way.

Meanwhile, I twist the drawstring of my bag around my fist. The swim did me good but now all my old anger is back, singing like wires in the wind. Including Patrick it'll be six against one, and I'll definitely get my arse handed to me, but here's the thing: admiring your muscles in a mirror (muscles I haven't exactly worked for, that are really just a by-product of my way of dealing with the world) then refusing to use said muscles when some poor kid is getting his teeth booted down his throat? Well, that just doesn't sit right with me.

I start towards them when suddenly Patrick's calling a halt.

"Fag's had enough," he announces.

The pack breaks apart, laughing and high-fiving as they

drift away. It's then that I see two horrific things almost simultaneously: it's Albert cringing and bleeding on the floor, and it's Albert's twin sister, Lana, who executes the final kick to his ribs.

"Hey, I said enough," Patrick says, grabbing her around the waist.

Lana has a little play wrestle with her Young Lion boyfriend before throwing her tongue down his throat. Then, coming up for air, she casts a last look at Albert.

"Someone told me he pissed himself in class today. And, you know, that's not even the worst thing he's ever done. He's a disgrace to our whole family."

She pulls back her head and a slash of spit ribbons her brother's cheek.

I watch them go. I don't want to just watch. Honestly, I'd love to drag Patrick back and make him apologize. Instead I head over and help Albert to his feet. He looks up at me. His lip is torn and a vessel has burst in his eye, flaming the ghostly grey of his iris.

"Sorry." He cuffs a runner of snot from his chin. "I'm a state, I know."

"Albert, you're fine."

On his feet, he rocks slightly, as if there's nothing to him, as if the baking breeze might pick him up and take him where it likes. Then he turns his face away and heaves out this huge, juddering sob. I check the street before pulling him into a hug. We haven't hugged like this since we were little kids and Albert showed up at my house one day, hysterical from a beating his father had given him.

"Don't let them see," I say, pushing him gently away again. "Don't give them that satisfaction, okay?"

He rakes fingers through his pale, sweat-soaked hair and treats me to a lopsided smile. You know, Albert is pretty cute. He has this sweet upturned nose and delicate bone structure, a bit like a porcelain doll. But although he's standing here hurt and tear-stained, I know he's not delicate. Not at all.

A memory, bright as a paper cut: it's the night after my mother left us, and Albert has shown up for our regular Saturday sleepover. I'm ratty and miserable and tell him I'm not in the mood. Albert dumps his stuff on my bed and pulls the chessboard from the shelf. He sets up the game and sits cross-legged on the floor, fiddling with the pieces until I finally stomp over and nudge a pawn into position. It's a long game, played in almost total silence. After a while my pissed-off grunts and huffs disappear and I lose myself in the contest. Looking back, I can see how skilfully he stretched it out, allowing me to win in a way that was almost convincing. Albert always won at chess. But he knew I needed the win that night, and that I didn't necessarily need to talk. Not right away.

Later, snuggled top to tail in my bed, he starts telling me this awesome ghost story until suddenly he breaks off.

"Gabe?" he asks after a pause.

"Yeah?"

"Are you okay?"

I reach under the covers and waggle his foot. "Course. I'm always okay."

"Yeah," he says. "Except, you're not."

That's when I buried my face in my pillow and cried and cried until Albert pulled off my sock and started tickling my foot. At first, I was annoyed but pretty soon I was screaming with laughter and begging him to stop.

When the hysterics subsided, I said, "Thanks, mate."

"Anytime," Albert yawned.

That was one of our last sleepovers. I guess we were eleven, and maybe we were getting too old to share a bed.

But I kept asking him over and Albert kept making excuses until, eventually, I gave up. Honestly, I don't know what happened between us. We didn't fall out, didn't fight, and I've continued to trust him, absolutely. I guess our friendship just changed as we grew, as childhood friendships often do, with no real reason either of us could identify. And we've stayed close – sort of – in the years since; always there when the other might need something, practically at least.

Still, I'd be lying if I said I didn't miss the way things

used to be. That easy way we'd talk and laugh together. Now the references to old jokes seem clumsy and forced. I think we both feel the distance between us, but a kind of fear, or maybe it's shyness, keeps us from addressing it. What if we insist on answers and all it does is push us further apart?

He scoots down and collects his bag. "Thanks, Gabe."

"Don't be silly. Thank *you*, Albert."

"For what?" He looks genuinely curious.

"For what you did this afternoon."

"Oh, that?" He shrugs. "That wasn't anything. I don't have much pride anyway, and—"

"Albert," I wince.

"What was it, by the way?" he says, deflecting. "The thing in your bag?"

"One of the discs." I hold up my hand. "I know, I know. I'm an idiot, Eric's already told me."

He smiles and makes his way to the road. "Eric's a good judge of character."

I start to call after him. And stop.

There's something wrong here, I can feel it. Something Albert maybe wants to say but can't.

You develop these instincts living under the Protectorate – *if* you want to live, that is. I should chase after him, take him somewhere, make him tell me, for old times' sake if nothing else.

But, as always with Albert, the right words won't come, so all I say is: "See you at Rebels later?"

He turns and rubs his good eye.

"Sure. After I've got cleaned up. It's been a messy kind of day."

5

I hand over my ten-thousand pound note and my ration book, both with the Lord Protector's idiot face on the front, and Mr Godfrey passes me a hot sausage roll. Clamping the pastry between my teeth, I wave my thanks and head on out, the shop bell jingling behind me.

Godfrey's has been Godfrey's for as long as any kid around here can remember, but you don't have to look far to see it wasn't always this way. Although the sign above the door has been painted over a dozen times, the old name keeps reappearing through the layers: *Banerjee's*. Hardly anyone ever talks about what happened to the Banerjees or, if they do, they simply say the family "went home". That's the Protectorate line, as if people who had lived here for generations, or who had recently come to lay roots and contribute to this nation, had welcomed the idea of returning to places they had never known or from which they had only just arrived. The pause that follows is almost always filled with downcast eyes. We know the truth but most of us can't live with it, so we accommodate the lie.

The "repatriation trains" that took the Banerjees "home" are a memory from my dad's youth. Sometimes when he screams in his sleep, I wonder if it's their screams he's echoing. The ones he heard from outside overcrowded stations or from the air slits in the sides of windowless carriages as they passed. Sometimes I wonder how my dad sleeps at all. The world we live in now is bleak enough, but what a nightmare it must have been to watch them make it. And yet the people the authorities wanted gone – the ones we know in our hearts never left, but lie buried in unmarked graves – are still with us. No matter how much the Protectorate tries to paint over them, their presence keeps shining through.

I mount my bike. It's late afternoon and the streets are teeming with kids, dirty faces popping out from the rubble of tumbledown houses. Most are pretending to be the heroes and villains from their favourite British Protectorate Broadcasting TV shows: brave Investigation officers keeping the neighbourhood safe from degens and traitors and spies. I swerve my bike to avoid a boy as he pretends to check the descendancy papers of his friend.

The houses peter out as I plunge into the industrial area of Westwick, making for the abandoned library. A horn blares and men shuffle out of factory gates, their faces worn green by exhaustion and fumes. Some catch my SEE uniform and cast me hostile looks while one bent-up old guy smiles as if he knows me. It's only after another street or two that I realize he was a few years ahead of me at Mosley. His name's Michael Harrison. He's twenty-two.

Beyond the factories lies Westwick Old Town, hidden away like a secret no one wants to share. Not even the poorest live here now – the houses were too badly damaged in the fighting after the Outrage. Ancient shopping trolleys sparkle darkly in the canal and as I hurtle along the towpath, I try to imagine the days when my grandparents might have filled those baskets to the brim. The idea seems ridiculous.

Posters flutter in my slipstream. Most are just photographs of Hilary Martin, the Lord Protector himself, smiling paternally and promising us that everything we endure is for "the Public Good". Uncle Marty never changes. He's still the same old bastard he was a decade ago. No one has seen our blessed leader in all that time, and although some people whisper that he's either dead or has gone gaga, his image still holds power. I flip him the middle finger and race on.

Other posters come and go: a picture of our tiny island surrounded by storm clouds, hideous faces emerging from the murk, captioned *WE PROTECT YOU FROM THE*

ENEMIES OF THE PEOPLE: Be alert for Fanatics, Spies and Foreigners; an angelic child holding up a cut finger while her mother looks on aghast – *WE PROTECT YOU FROM INVISIBLE ENEMIES: Infection is a killer! Report all injuries!*; a skeletal man with weeping sores and hollow eyes lunging towards the viewer – *WE PROTECT YOU FROM THE ENEMIES OF THE PAST: Degenerates spread disease.*

My palms squeak around the handlebars. How many rows have I had with my dad about this crap? It seems like every week I lose it with him, especially when I catch the latest poster taped to his drawing board. What pisses me off most is that he sits there and takes it, just like he sat back and did nothing when Mum walked out on us. But always later, when I'm lying in bed and my heart's cooled a bit, I admit he has no choice. My dad's a talented artist, and all talent must be used in service of the Protectorate, unless I want him to end up in a Re-Education camp.

I skid to a halt in the bombed-out shell of what was once the town square. Above one of the buildings a tattered fragment of the Union Jack snaps in the breeze. I often wonder why it hasn't been taken down and the new flag of the Protectorate – a blood-red cross on a stark black background – put up in its place. Maybe because no one ever comes here.

I hide my bike behind a heap of rubble and walk as casually as I can around the wire-topped fence. Before hunching down to the loose board, I stop and listen: birds squabble in the ribs of scooped-out rooftops; the wind moans through engineless cars. Not a soul but me in the ghost town.

A tiny tag, like a blooming flower or a curved scythe, marks the loose board. The symbol of the Rebel Alliance. We chose it as our emblem after watching this amazing movie called *Star Wars*. It's basically about a gang of freedom fighters waging war against an evil empire, so the symbol felt sort of appropriate. In fact, it was just after I'd been blown away by the film that we decided to invite the others to share our discovery.

Not an easy decision. Of course we trusted them, they were our friends, but those two months of just Eric and I sharing these amazing treasures had felt so special. Now it's hard to think of life without the Rebels. It's just a shame the film that brought us all together – *A New Hope* – is the fourth in the series and that we'll never get to see the other *Star Wars* movies. I bet Episodes I–III were brilliant.

I slip under the loose board and, now inside the perimeter of the fence, cross to the steps of the library. It's an impressive ruin of ivy-curled columns and tall, mostly broken, windows. Straight away, I feel this completely irrational sense of freedom. The seven-foot fence that surrounds it makes the library an oasis, right here in the heart of the Protectorate. I climb a couple of the steps leading to the double doors and spread my arms. This is our place, mine and Eric's, and no one can touch the memories we've made here.

My mind moves through the spaces before me: the entrance hall with its weed-cracked floor and its huge painting crowded with forgotten authors; the main library with its toppled shelves and the giant scorch mark at the centre of the room; the alcoves and study tables on the floor above, where kids etched their initials a lifetime ago.

My dad once told me that they came for the libraries first. "Not smashing and burning, not in the beginning," he said, "but claiming no one used them and closing them down, one by one. You see, Gabe, when they take away the places that help people think, sometimes people stop thinking altogether."

My mind moves on, to the secret space high above me and the treasure that Eric and I found there. Opening my eyes now, breathing in the stillness, I let the memory take me.

THEN

SEPTEMBER – SEVEN MONTHS AGO

Some new kid is introducing himself to the class. It's such a sick form of torture I used to think it must have been invented by the Protectorate, but no, my dad says this particular evil goes *way* back. So I guess the world was always at least a little fucked up.

I gave the newbie a quick glance when he was ushered into Patriot Studies – tall, messy hair, head down – before sinking my gaze back to the book in front of me. *After the Outrage: The Birth of a Purer Britain.* We all know the origins of the Protectorate backwards, but Mr Joyce gets his weekly hard-on by reading out his favourite passages –

Thirty years ago, a bomb was planted at the Merripit Hotel. It killed forty-three men, women and children, including several members of the Public Good Party – that noble group of patriots who later went on to form our glorious Protectorate. On the very day of the bombing, Hilary Martin, future Lord Protector, condemned the action as an "outrage against civilization". He vowed that the alliance of foreigners, fanatics and degenerates who planted the device would be punished and…

Yadda yadda yadda. I have Joyce's rants practically memorized. But today he seems more interested in the newbie. Meanwhile, I have other things on my mind.

I drop my aching arms to my sides. I've seriously overdone it this morning. Four miles in the pool before school, and I'm still raging about last night. Honestly, I didn't even want to see my mum, but Dad insisted. Why is he so fucking reasonable all the time? She betrays him, abandons us, treats us like shit, and what does he say? "*You need to see things from your mother's point of view.*"

Okay, Dad, fine, but you *can* insist on being treated with the tiniest molecule of respect, can't you?

The last three days have been hellish. Example: sitting in the Majestic Hotel while the Farmer shoved hunks of steak into his face and Mum worked her way through the wine list. The whole thing actually made me feel kind of sick. Everyone I know is almost constantly hungry, and there I sat, daunted by a huge plate of ration-free food. I guess that's one of the perks of being the stepson of the Deputy Protector of Agriculture.

I don't even like calling him the Farmer: that's his own fake-meek nickname for himself. The truth is, if it wasn't for our real farmers we'd all have starved years ago.

"You really are a mystery, darling," my mum mumbled into her Merlot. "So big and broad and yet you hardly eat a thing. If only you had some good home-cooked meals, heaven knows what you'd grow into. We might even have an Olympian in the family, don't you think, Roger?"

Roger took a ten second break from devouring slabs of cow to glare at us both.

"Protectorate hasn't entered the Olympics for decades. Too much chance of racial contamination. You ought to know that, Mags."

Mum drew the back of her hand across her mouth, smearing her lipstick. "I only meant—"

"Stop beating about the bush," her husband grunted. "Tell the boy."

Mum put down her wine, so I knew straight away this was serious. "Darling, Roger and I have been talking—"

"Not my idea," Roger said. "But whatever makes your mother happy."

Red-taloned fingers reached across the table and grabbed my hand. Overhead, the electric chandeliers fluttered. Even the Majestic isn't immune to the now daily power cuts. Yes indeed, our resources are running dry, but you better believe that all is good in the glorious Protectorate! You just *better*.

"We'd like you to come and live with us!" Mum trilled. "It's horrible how little I see of you, and you're growing up so fast. I've thought it all through. Roger can get you into the best schools in London, can't you, dear? And you can spend all your weekends with us at the estate in Yeovil. The house has a magnificent library, even a few books that aren't completely legit." Her theatrical wink was immediately checked by Roger. "Now look, I know you're very attached to your father," she continued, slightly flustered, "and I'm sure he does his best, but the truth is, he simply can't provide you with the opportunities Roger and I can. And that bungalow. Well, really it's little more than a hovel—"

That's where the conversation terminated. Shoving back my chair, I thanked the waiter, threw whatever money I had onto the table, ignored my mum's parting shot, and got the hell out.

Now I plant my elbows on the desk and rest my head in my hands. Fortunately my "tantrum" persuaded Roger to rescind their invitation, but what infuriated me even more than Mum trying to assume control of my life was Dad's reaction when I got home. He listened in that oh-so-reasonable way of his, while I stomped around the kitchen, then asked if I was sure I didn't want to live with my mother.

"You are actually kidding me!" I exploded.

"Well, you have to admit she has a point. You wouldn't want for anything."

"I don't want for anything here."

"I didn't realize I ran such a house of luxury." Dad blinked at the cosy, cluttered room, then held up his hand when I started ranting again. "She's right about the education side, you have to give her that. You graduate from Mosley next summer, and then what? You might get a job in administration or maybe as a factory overseer. Is that what you really want?"

"Or I get adopted by the Farmer and graduate to boot-licking duties in some government department. I wonder what my first job'll be – carrying bags for the Deputy Protector of Wellbeing? Hey, we might even get to visit a Re-Education camp and gawp at all the political 'traitors' having electrodes wired to their baby-makers."

Dad looked at me over his glasses and pushed away the poster he'd been working on. "There are ways out for clever people," he said quietly. "But first you need to get to the top. And yes, that might mean sacrificing your principles."

I knew what he meant. We'd all heard whispers of spies and diplomats on overseas missions defecting to foreign countries.

"Gabe." He laid a meaningful hand on my shoulder. "Being the way you are, this could be the only way to keep you safe."

I shrugged him off and headed for my room. Problem is, my dad's right, it could be the only way to keep me safe, and so of course I'm furious.

Gradually the newbie's voice brings me back to the room. He has a low, hesitant way of speaking, a kind of awkwardness that somehow inspires a smile. I glance up.

"We moved here last week," he murmurs. "It, uh…it seems okay. My dad, he travels back to London almost every day. Personally, I'm really interested in—"

"Your father!" Mr Joyce squeaks. "Tell the class what your father does."

The kid looks like he wants the ground to swallow him up. Even if it did, I'm pretty sure Joyce would dig up his corpse and insist it finish the presentation. The newbie's very tall, gangly really, and until now, with his chin on his chest, his face has been hidden under a tangle of long brown hair. Almost too long. I'd be surprised if the Green Jackets haven't handed him a caution. A sigh ripples through the kid and he looks up.

He has this beautiful heart-shaped face. Honestly, it's kind of captivating, really wide across the cheekbones, tapering down to a proud jut of a chin. Stark against his pale skin, his eyes are vast and dark and his lips… His lips are this dizzying shade of red.

The next thing I know, I'm catching a suggestive smirk from June. She opens her mouth, places a finger under her jaw, and snaps it shut. I shoot her a glare and return to the newbie.

I feel myself reeling. Which is ridiculous, I know, I

know, but when he starts speaking again, all I can do is watch those trembling lips. His mouth is like a wound and it's as if the words are actually hurting him.

"My dad. He works for the Protectorate. His job… He's a chief of…"

Mr Joyce can't contain himself any longer. "Mr Dufresne is a chief inspector at Degenerate Investigations!" He claps his hands as if the newbie has just pulled a rabbit out of his arse. "And although he'll be based in London, Mr Dufresne has also taken over all local cases in the Westwick area, so you might well be seeing him out and about. Isn't that thrilling?"

A couple of students look fascinated, most don't react at all. Not reacting is often the best tactic for survival. Me? I jolt back to reality. Fancying the son of the chief of the Filth-Finders? Only you, Gabriel Sawyer. Only you.

"Questions!" Mr Joyce demands.

A hand shoots up. "Have you ever been on a perv raid?"

The kid bows his head again. "No. No, that wouldn't be allowed."

"What are the Re-Purification camps like?"

"I've never been inside one."

"Okay, what's the sickest thing your dad's ever seen? Like, has he ever caught two degens kissing?" A chorus of disgusted groans. "What? It's a legitimate question. And at least I didn't say fu—"

"Why did you leave London?" Ben cuts in. There's no side to Ben's question, he's just curious. The Protectorate likes to keep travel between areas strictly limited – much easier to control the flow of ideas if communities seldom mix – and so anyone who has been to the capital is always an object of fascination.

The kid swallows. "My dad wanted a fresh start for us."

Liz raises her hand. "Not a question. I'd just like to say welcome to Westwick. I hope you like it here, Eric."

I don't even realize I've taken out a pen, let alone that I'm writing in the hallowed pages of *After the Outrage*. Not until June throws me another quizzical look. I glance down. There, at the bottom of page 246, I've scrawled *Eric Dufrain*. I quickly scribble it out.

"Well then," says Mr Joyce, clearly disappointed in what he had hoped might be his star student, "you'd better get yourself settled. Free desk there, next to Mr Sawyer. Please don't mind the glasses, he gets it from too much reading."

I don't know where Mr Joyce gets the idea that I read too much. I've never checked out a single sanctioned book from the school library, even though one a month is technically compulsory. June covers her back by continuing to borrow *The Fountainhead* by Ayn Rand, though she says reading even a single chapter is like inserting a swarm of wasps into your skull.

Eric takes his seat. He pushes his copy of the big book of

bullshit to the far corner of his desk while Joyce launches into his usual praise of Uncle Marty. The kid's wearing this fern-green tie, probably because the school hasn't sorted his uniform yet. The colour complements his eyes somehow. He glances at me, opens his mouth to speak, swallows instead.

"Hi." I hold out my hand. "Gabe."

He swallows again and those dark lashes flicker. He makes a mess of taking my hand, shaking my fingers once before pulling back. First day nerves, I guess.

"*Cassida viridis,*" he whispers.

"Okaaaaay." I frown at him. "I thought your name was Eric."

He licks those red lips and turns in his seat. Then he reaches across and scoops a trembling finger along the page where I've just erased his name.

"The green tortoise beetle." He lifts this tiny, lime-coloured bug from the spot where it had just landed on my book. And his smile suddenly becomes radiant. "Pretty rare."

He lets the bug trundle along his hand and I notice his fingertips look really sore from where he's bitten his nails to the quick.

"Hey," I murmur.

He looks up, adorably cross-eyed from staring at the bug. "Oh… Hey."

Now it's my turn to hesitate. What was I about to say? Even I'm not sure. I suddenly flash to my mum's parting words as I took off from the Majestic, just before she started popping the little white pills from her handbag: "*You should be careful, Gabriel. One day that big mouth of yours will get you killed. And maybe not just you, either.*"

"Nothing," I mutter. "Just... Welcome, I guess."

Eric nods, places the bug on his desk, and turns to face the front.

NOW

6

I kneel inside the big scorch mark in the middle of the library, my fingers tracing the stain on the bare stone floor. They thought they'd burned it all. Immolated it. Yeah, that's the right word – *immolation:* to burn as an offering or a sacrifice. It's what they were trying to do in the months and years after the Outrage, building their bonfires, piling up all the books and movies and ideas the old world had to offer and sacrificing them to the new.

Except there were pieces they missed.

A shadow falls through the open doorway and I jump up. Eric laughs as I rush the last few steps and throw my arms around him. We spin on the spot and the old dizziness hits, as it always does. When we stop for breath, I press my lips to his. Eric closes his eyes, but I never do. I want to see him, always.

"Hey."

He pokes my cheek. "Hey."

"So, I don't think I said it earlier, or if I did, I probably didn't say it properly. But I'm sorry, Scarecrow. About the disc. It was careless, bringing it to school. Forgive me?"

He lets me hang for a few seconds until I tickle an answer out of him.

"All right! I do! I forgive you, Monkey."

"And you'll always forgive me for my stupidity because I'm so incredibly gorgeous, right? C'mon. Admit it, you think I'm gorgeous, don't you?"

A blush erupts across his skin. It isn't hard, making Eric blush, but it is a lot of fun.

"You're pushing it," he says.

"And you're beautiful." I nuzzle my nose against the underside of his jaw. "You're beautiful and I love you."

"Shut up, you idiot," he laughs.

"I may be an idiot, but I also know that one day you're going to say it back."

I mean it playfully but he catches my eye and shakes his head, pulling me close and planting a kiss on my forehead. "Idiot."

After a while we break apart and wander together among the deserted shelves. A breeze scurries in behind us, whipping up dust, chasing a faded flier around our feet. I bend to pick it up and find myself facing Uncle Marty again – *DO YOUR LOVED ONES WHISPER DISCONTENT?*

PATRIOTS REPORT ALL TREASON! – and a picture of a happy family on their doorstep, beaming with pride and saluting as their father is dragged away by a team of Yellow Jackets. Eric takes it from me, tears it into strips and throws it back to the breeze.

"The power these things have," he mutters. "But just imagine what someone could do who really understood film and imagery. What a difference they could make."

I kick at the scorch mark. "Eric, stop. It's never going to happen."

This receives a cheek poke. "Not with that attitude."

"So you want me to join Protectorate Broadcasting and make film versions of that bullshit?" I jab a finger at the shredded flier as it disappears behind a shelf. "Honestly, that would feel like betraying every film and filmmaker we've ever experienced here."

"I agree," he says. "And I didn't mean that."

"Then what?"

He touches my face, cups my jaw. "I don't know exactly. Only that I think, if anyone will ever get to tell the story of what goes on under the Protectorate, it'll be you, Gabe. You'll show the world. You'll make them see."

It's an absurd, unachievable dream but Eric's faith makes me smile anyway. I shake my head at him. "What put you in this good mood?"

He screws up his face, all adorable concentration.

"I don't know. Maybe it was the song Beatrice was singing this morning. It made me think of you. She was making Dad's breakfast and she must've forgotten where she was for a minute. Bea's got to be about a hundred, but right then? I don't know, Gabe, she looked really young. I can't remember the title. Something about sunlight." He clicks his fingers. "Sunshine... *You Are the Sunshine of My Life*. It was a really beautiful moment – until my dad asked Bea where she'd heard it, said it was culturally contaminated music. Basically scared the crap out of her. But then he got called into work and after he left, I found her crying in the pantry. I told her not to worry, that he'd probably forget about it by tomorrow. She said..." He tries to look away but I draw him back to me. "She said I seemed really happy these days. Happier than she'd ever seen me, and she asked why."

"But you didn't tell her?"

"No."

"Will your dad forget about the song?"

"I hope so."

"How did it go?"

"Oh Gabe, I don't know. She was only singing it for a few seconds."

I shoot him a sceptical glance. Eric has a great memory for these things.

He sighs, closes his eyes, and after a while, he starts to

sing. A couple of lines in, he loses the words but finds the beat, humming and tapping his fingers against a dusty shelf. The rhythm is smooth, lush, and hearing it, you can't help grinning.

I take his hand and pull him into the middle of the room.

He blinks, stops dead, but I tell him to keep going. We start to dance. It's mad, neither of us knows how to move to this ancient tune, and yet we feel our way. His hands go to my hips; I rest my forearms on his shoulders. As Eric loops back around and starts the melody again, I brush a drift of hair from his face. His eyes are tight shut and he looks perfect. My Eric. My Scarecrow. How much of this have we missed? The movies and the music and the books and the paintings and the poetry? All the stuff that could have been and never was. And all for what?

Eric slows the tempo and laces his fingers back through mine. He stops humming. "Thank you, Gabe."

"For what?"

He shrugs. "For making me want to dance."

The squeak of the loose board echoes from outside. I squeeze Eric's hand and we part.

"Before the rest of them get here, I should tell you something," I say. "It's about Albert."

As he listens to the story of how Albert was attacked by Lana, Patrick Gilligan and the Young Lions, I can see the fury building inside him. Just seven months ago, when we first met, he wouldn't have expressed any emotion at all. But maybe fury's the wrong word. Rage is my department; perhaps indignation is more Eric's thing. Anyway, when I get to the part about Albert's sister laying in the final kick, his lips form a tight line.

"Animals." He shakes his head. "No. Animals would never... Poor Albert."

"Something's going on with him," I say. "I don't know what, but it's like when we were kids – I always knew when he wasn't telling me the whole story." I glance over to where the Rebels have started to file through the doors. I guess the truth is, this isn't a new feeling. I've had this instinct about Albert for a long time now: that he's holding something back, that maybe this is why we've drifted apart. I turn back to Eric. "Let's keep an eye on him, yeah?"

Eric nods. "Definitely."

And so our co-conspirators have returned again to the scene of the crime. Naturally, June leads the way. June and I go *way* back. In fact, my mum has a photo of us together at some birthday party, me going in for a sticky-lipped smooch. Funny, how things work out. June says she can't remember a time when she didn't know about me, whereas I had to have her secret spelled out in blazing neon, basically because I'm a moron.

She comes forward and waggles my head between her hands.

"How's the tummy?" I ask.

"Bit sore." She flicks her head. "But today's hair inspection has been an inspiration. I'm thinking about a buzzcut. What do you reckon?"

Liz breaks off her conversation with Eric. "Seriously?"

"No, not seriously," June sighs. "It's a shame, though. I think I could really reclaim the look from those Young Lions dickheads."

She could. June has these incredible green eyes that almost overwhelm the rest of her features; a buzzcut would complement that intense focus.

"Hey!" a voice calls from the doorway. "Make way for the norms."

Ben and Grace head in, Ben hugging everyone because he's Ben and Grace feigning jealousy until she gets her own hug. When this threatens to turn into actual snogging, June calls a halt.

"Enough! Look, I'm as liberal as the next degen, but this display of hetero debauchery is too much. Aren't we supposed to be the Rebels? Will someone remind me what this macho star of the hockey field and the nicest girl in school are rebelling against?"

We all exchange an eye roll. Fake tirades are trademark June.

"Well, first of all, I'm glad you think I'm so nice," Grace says.

"And that I'm macho," adds Ben, flexing a bicep.

"I was speaking relatively. You're macho compared to the rest of the SEE boys." June gives me and Eric an appraising glance. "Which really isn't saying much."

"Moving on," Grace says, before I can roll up my sleeve for a total gun show. "We are in fact the most rebellious Rebels of all. We don't need to be here, the whole Protectorate is our playground, but we stand with you nonetheless. Norms and degens united."

Ben throws an arm around me and June, and kisses us both on the cheek. I kiss him right back and, after a second's hesitation, June relents and plants a theatrical *mwah* against his brow.

"Norms and degens united," she echoes. "Okay, I guess you can be honorary freaks."

"Nothing honorary about it," Ben grins. "We've got our own freaky-deakiness going on. C'mon, June, let me tell you all about it. You see, when my parents are out, Grace comes over and we—"

"Lah-lah-lah!"

June blocks her ears and hurtles for the stairs and the library's second level, Ben in pursuit. Grace gives us a weary shake of the head.

"In his dreams."

While June turns the tables and starts chasing a squealing Ben around the upper level, Liz heads to her sewing room. She returns moments later, throwing each of us our Rebel jackets: amazing creations, all vibrancy and big, bold stitching and fabulous flamboyance. If this weren't the Protectorate, Liz would be this crazy-talented fashion designer, celebrated the world over. As it is, she's found a haven here, just as much as Eric and I have – her room with its pedal-powered sewing machine and the pre-Outrage scraps she's salvaged over the years. Our normal clothes are as grey as the rest of our world – flamboyance raises suspicion – but here, in the library, Liz defies that world in her own unique way.

As we pull on our jackets, she brings us back to the grimness of the afternoon.

"Do you guys think the Filth-Finders will really go after Miss Calloway?"

Everyone turns to Eric, as if he has the answer.

"If I hear of any plan for a Section 28 visit, I'll let her know," he promises.

Not for the first time it occurs to me how we all do this: look to Eric for reassurance when the Green-Jacket world closes in around us. It worries me. Sometimes I think they forget the shy boy who arrived at Mosley Grammar last September and see only the young man he's become. But there are scars, physical and emotional, that Eric chooses to hide. Wounds that might easily reopen.

Grace's head snaps towards the main door. "Albert?

Oh God, Albert, what's happened?"

She rushes forward and brings him into the circle.

"I'm fine," Albert says. "Please, don't make a fuss."

Despite his protests, he gets a *lot* of fuss. A huge bruise discolours the right side of his face while the broken vessel in his eye flares like a dying sun.

Just then, June and Ben come clattering down the stairs, laughing and joking together until they catch sight of Albert. Hearing how he was jumped by Patrick and the other Lions, their expressions turn dark and they soon start plotting an epic payback, before Albert returns them to reality. Attacking a youth wing member is a crime against the state, punishable by Re-Education, and anyway that kind of revenge isn't really our style.

"But you're sure you're okay?" Ben asks, holding Albert by the shoulders and giving him an appraising look.

"Yeah. Anyway, I brought it on myself," Albert says. "I didn't want June getting all the attention, did I? Now please stop looking so worried and let's get on with this."

"Okay." I rub my hands together. "Everyone brought snacks?"

Six ration bags rustle in the air.

"Then follow me. It's showtime."

7

Indiana Jones punches a Nazi and the room goes wild.

"Yes! Take that, you evil bum-face!" Grace shouts; Ben tells her he loves it when she talks dirty.

Grinning, I glance over at the busted armchair just to the side of our overcrowded sofa.

Albert sits alone, as always, his poor eye glowing red in the flickering TV light.

What's going on inside that head? I wonder. Is Albert a degen like the rest of the Rebel Alliance (honorary norms excluded)? Of course, this isn't the first time I've wondered, and he's never said anything outright, but my instinct – my dad says they used to call it "gaydar" – makes me think he must be. So is that the reason he's been pulling away from me these past few years? Staying friends but with this distance between us? Because he thinks…what? That I wouldn't accept him? But that would be crazy, right?

All I know is that when Eric and I first discussed forming the Rebels, Albert was first on my list. Not because of my assumptions about him but because I *knew* he could be trusted and that he'd get something special out of the experience. And I was right. It hurts to admit it, but I think Albert responds to these films on an even deeper level than Eric. That complete, quiet absorption while the movie plays? It reminds me of those sleepovers when we'd share our ghost stories after lights out, Albert breathless in the dark.

I turn back to the screen. Underneath the old TV set with its built-in DVD player sits the cardboard box. In its own way, it's a bit like the Ark of the Covenant that Indy is trying to rescue from the Nazis. A chest full of ancient wonders. By now, I've watched every film it contains at least half a dozen times.

This one is directed by a genius called Steven Spielberg. He has two other films in the collection – a beautiful movie about an alien marooned on Earth and the true story of a man who saved hundreds of Jews from the Nazi death camps. Films about difference and defiance. A message, I am sure, from the librarian who originally hid the box away.

We have lots of time tonight for a long movie marathon. Those Rebels who have parents who care about such things have told them we're involved in the school's plans for the upcoming Outrage Memorial Day festivities. As the consequences for not getting every part of the annual celebrations right can be severe, it's expected that even student meetings might run long into the night. This was Albert's idea, and it really is the perfect alibi. No parent would even dare to question it.

I remove *Raiders of the Lost Ark* and slip this film called *The Kids Are All Right* into the slot. It's about a family where there's two mums, who have their kids using a sperm donor. The kids are teenagers in the film, and they contact their donor dad and it's so funny and warm. At no point does anyone make a big deal about the fact that these kids have two mums. It's just a film about a family trying to stay together.

"Wow," June whispers. "I can't believe we used to make films like that."

"I can't believe we had *lives* like that," says Liz.

"And they're so open and relaxed, talking about sex and stuff. With their *parents*," says Grace.

Next to me, I feel Eric tense, and I place my hand on his. We sit there in silence, taking it all in.

Albert stands up and stretches, and then everybody begins to stir. I eject the disc and stow the film carefully away in the box.

"Thanks for tonight, Gabe," Ben says. "That was really special."

Grace reaches over and grips my wrist. "It was." Her

eyes are bright. She looks around at the rest of us. "I just wish… These films. It's horrible to think that this was all possible once and now it's been lost."

"Not lost, not completely," Eric says, catching my eye. "Forgotten for a while maybe. And yeah, that hurts, but it's also inspiring, isn't it? That they used to make entire stories about us? That gay people got to be the main characters in films and books? And who knows, something like that could happen again one day…"

"Not in our lifetime," says Liz, throwing back her head and staring at the cobwebbed rafters. "Not here anyway. You have to wonder, though, did they ever think back then that everything could change in a heartbeat?"

"Probably not." June loops her arm around Liz's shoulders. "No one likes to point out the storm clouds when the sun's shining, do they?"

"But it's not only your stories." Ben sits forward, elbows on his knees. "Gay people got to *make* these films too. You guys had real power back then. Politically, culturally, you were a force to be reckoned with. It's like Eric said, I don't think that power has been lost. We might not know about it, but I bet there are people out there continuing the fight in their own way.

"And we're learning how to do that too. These movies? They're teaching us how. I mean, I'd like to think Grace and I would always have been allies, but seeing it right there on the screen has made it more real for us. It's teaching us how to be better."

I can't help grinning. This *is* what the films have given us: not just the energy and will to be true to ourselves but also the chance to understand who we are in a system that has taken our history and language away from us. Rediscovering these ways to think about our lives has empowered each of us.

But now there's something I need to say, because the old world we see in these movies, the one we've all been cheering on and idolizing? It wasn't some perfect shining beacon. Not for everyone.

"Representation was important," I say, pulling the box towards me. "*Is* important. To see yourself reflected as a human being, with worth and dignity? I really think that has the power to change minds. Even save lives. The problem is, even back then, not everyone got to see themselves represented. Not well, anyway."

I slip a blank disc from its sleeve – the second movie I watched on my own last night – a documentary that tells a story I'd never seen before. Eric shoots me a questioning glance while Ben and June check their watches.

"Please," I say. "I think it's important."

The film is called *Disclosure*. Watching it had been a revelation. It had shown me that, even in a freer time, this medium I'd come to love hadn't only opened minds and challenged prejudice, it often had a dark and damaging influence too. I'm still not really sure how that makes me feel.

I pop the disc into the player and we all settle back into our seats. Through interviews and movie clips, the film charts the lives of transgender people and how they were represented – or *misrepresented*, I should say – throughout the history of cinema. The Rebels and I have discussed trans and non-binary people before. From banned books I'd read and conversations with my dad, I'd understood something of their experiences. *Thought* I'd understood. But how they were perceived by society? The challenges and hostility they'd faced every day of their lives? It was this film that showed me all that for the first time.

No one speaks during the movie and there's another silence, heavier this time, as the credits roll. Finally, Albert breaks in.

"They were there," he says. "Right from the beginning of cinema, trans people were there."

"They were." I nod, turning to the busted armchair. "But what a mess. Hundreds of films depicting them as weird or predatory or mentally ill, or just the butt of some stupid joke."

"Or all those things at once," Liz says, her voice tight.

"Serial killers or clowns." June gets up and ejects the disc, looking down at it for a moment.

"What gets me most is how many gay people were hostile to them." There's anger in Eric's eyes. A kind of shame too, I think. "Like they weren't even accepted by people who faced all the same sorts of rejection they did." He throws his hands out towards the glowing screen. "It doesn't make any sense! I mean, in the film it's clear that trans people were right there in the fight for our rights. They were actually the ones who first led us into battle, and then what? We just disowned them?"

I think back to the footage of Sylvia Rivera, a trans activist being heckled and harassed by crowds of gay people at the 1973 New York Pride March. How her voice almost broke – *"I have been beaten. I have had my nose broken. I have been thrown in jail. I have lost my job. I have lost my apartment for gay liberation, and you all treat me this way?"* – but how she stood there, defiant. She'd risked her life for the principle of equality and here she was being repaid with contempt. Like Eric said, it makes no sense.

"And even sympathetic people seemed to objectify them," Grace says. She looks almost as pissed off as Eric. "Only talking about their bodies, their surgeries? Never seeing them as complete human beings, just as sexualized objects. I mean, we can relate to that – right, Liz, June?"

"Their lives looked so hard." There's a tremor in Ben's voice, and I love him for it. "Abuse. Homelessness. Unemployment – sex work. And that's all anyone saw on

81

screen, without any explanation as to why that might have been their only choice."

"But it was changing," I say. "It says near the end, just before the Outrage – movies and TV shows, they were starting to get the representation right. Trans people were writing and directing and playing themselves onscreen. But then the world changed again. Or at least it did here."

I wonder, like I often do, about the outside world and its attitudes. Living under the Protectorate, most of what we know is only rumour. Are there places now where trans people live without fear? I hope so.

"It went backwards," I continue, "and those old negative, ignorant representations? What's the betting the Protectorate used all that in its propaganda? I mean, it fed right into their narrative about LGBTQ people being perverts and predators. So yeah, film wasn't always a friend to people who were different."

We all begin to make a move, stretching cramped limbs, gathering our things, heading for the door. Albert brushes his fingers against the screen as he passes.

"They hardly ever got to be the hero of their own story," he says.

Returning the disc to the box, June gives him a sad smile. "Oh honey," she says. "Who does?"

8

Moonlight bleeds through gaps in the boarded windows, caging the main library. Downstairs, we move through bars of light and shadow and hand our jackets back to Liz, who stores them away in her sewing cupboard. When she returns, she has this look on her face.

"Hey." I drop my head to her shoulder. "Be nice to wear them outside one day, wouldn't it?"

She ruffles my hair. "It would. But wearing them here? It's enough. For now."

It's only when we're all outside again that I see we're missing a Rebel. I say my goodbyes to the others and start to head back into the building when Eric pulls me up short.

"Gabe, wait." He catches my sleeve and turns me around. "About this Rakes guy? I've been thinking. He didn't like being humiliated today. Trust me, I know these people, humiliation *always* turns into suspicion."

"What do you think he'll do?" I ask.

Eric shrugs. "Maybe convince my dad to order a full inspection? That'd mean taking the school apart, quite literally. And I don't think he'll wait too long either. We need to get that disc back."

"All right," I say, "then I'll go to Mosley tonight."

"*We'll* go."

"Eric—"

"Don't argue. We're in this together." He takes hold of my shoulders. "And anyway, if we're caught you've got a better chance if I'm there with you. So what's the plan?"

The plan is simple and agreed in moments. I say "agreed" – I don't like it, and I try to argue him out of being involved, but this isn't the Eric of last September, and he has a point. If some Grey Jacket does catch us breaking into the school, we can claim it was a dare and Inspector Dufresne will probably get us out of it. He might even be secretly proud that his once timid son has done something reckless. And so we agree to meet at Totes's cabin at three a.m.

Eric touches the back of my neck and we share a brief kiss before he heads off.

Still fretting about the plan, I almost jump out of my skin when Albert shuffles into the cramped space beside me.

"Jesus, Albert! I've had a scary enough day without you giving me a freaking heart attack."

"Sorry," he murmurs. "Well. G'night then, Gabe."

"Hey, hold on a minute."

He turns that elfish face towards me before cutting his gaze away. I take a breath. I reach for the words. I actually don't know what to say. The days when we shared all our secrets seem like a long time ago.

"Are you okay?" I ask lamely. "That stuff earlier with your sister—"

His eyes remain rooted to the ground. "I'm fine. You don't have to worry about me, Gabe."

"What? Of course I worry about you! We worry about each other, right? That's the deal with us Rebels. It's just, are you sure there's nothing bothering you?"

His nod isn't convincing, so I try again for the right question that will bridge this space between us. In the end, I admit defeat and, closing the big double doors, follow him to the broken board. Albert's about to step through when I ask if I could borrow some of his tools, just for tonight. He finally looks at me, concern etched in those moon-grey eyes.

"Is this about the disc? If you need any help—?"

I shake my head. "Two idiots should be more than enough."

He tells me he'll drop the tools outside my door later, then hesitates, his hand gripping the board until his knuckles stand out, sharp and white. "Thanks again for tonight," he says quickly, and disappears before I have a chance to catch my breath.

* * *

Back home, I find Dad working at the kitchen table. He blinks at me through the telescopic lenses of his spectacles and waves a glue brush at the stove.

"Stew."

"Thanks," I say, dumping my bag onto a chair. "I've already had a sausage roll from Godfrey's."

He leans back over his book, tongue between his teeth, carefully applying adhesive to the peeling spine. "Stew."

I light the hob and heat up the saucepan. When I finally sit down opposite him and spoon the thin ration stew into my mouth, I realize how hungry I am. Dad looks up as I help myself to a hunk of black bread and a knob of butter.

"What's that one?" I ask between mouthfuls.

He sighs and places the book between two house bricks so that the glue will set. "*Wuthering Heights*. I can't for the life of me understand why they banned this and not *Jane Eyre*. They're both stories about strong young women who defy the patriarchal rules of their society. Still, it's not like anyone in the Culture Protectorate actually reads the books they outlaw."

Dad creaks to his feet. He's forty next year, and although he has what many people think is a cushy job, in a country with virtually no healthcare, not many men live past fifty. He tries not to use his wheelchair if he can help it. Tonight, he props himself on his sticks and moves slowly across to

86

the window where his drawing board stands.

"Your mother called," he says over his shoulder.

"Huh," I grunt into my bowl.

"Sounded like she could do with a chat."

"Yeah, well, it's late."

"There's ten more minutes until they close the lines for the night. Time for a quick natter, eh?"

Sometimes I wish he'd just order me to do what he wants. I'm a kid of the Protectorate, I'm used to following orders. Mostly. What gets me is this soft, sensible cajoling. It almost always provokes a row, during which he sits there blinking up at me like this patient old owl. But I'm too tired for an argument.

I rinse my bowl in the sink and pull the telephone from the sideboard. We're the envy of the neighbourhood, having our own phone, but with Dad mostly working from home it's deemed an official requirement. I track my finger through the dialler and look down at the primitive device. Nostalgia used as a weapon. Again. The Protectorate says you can't beat good old-fashioned British-made tech. The truth is, tech like this is easier to monitor, and anyway, England simply can't afford anything more advanced.

I hear the telltale click as the call connects.

"Huhmm-hello?"

I sink into a chair. "Hi, Mum."

"Ga-habriel?"

I shoot my dad a look: *Drunk. Again.*

He gives a little shake of the head: *Be kind.*

And so she stumbles on, lurching from one subject to the next, hardly a connection between them. At one point she pauses and I can hear the snap of her pillbox. Eyes closed, I give the usual responses while my mind drifts back to different days. I can't say they were happier – other people's happiness isn't exactly my mum's forte.

I'm six years old and it's summer at the river bend. Shivery reeds float around my ankles. The green water is refreshing in the blazing heat, but who knows what monsters lurk in these depths? My mum waits. She splashes water into my face, tells me not to be a wimp when I wince, then laughs to show she isn't mean. Eventually I take a big-boy breath and make the plunge.

And suddenly there's no fear, only my mum's strong hands under my arms, and we're face to face, laughing madly. Hour by hour she teaches me, under the arc of the willow tree, and in that single afternoon I come to love my mother, maybe for the first time in my life.

It was five years later when she left us.

I'm snatched away from memories.

"He did tuh-terrible things…" she says. "Even b-before. Way back. In the uh-early days before any of it started. I know that now."

88

I can't say I'm surprised that the Farmer has done terrible things. Terrible things are what the deputies of the Protectorate do. But I've never heard Mum criticize Roger before.

"Hey," I say, "maybe you should get some sleep. It's late and—"

And I don't want her talking like this. Not on an open line. But she plunges on.

"I should've guessed. It was ob-obvious. He…"

The line crackles. I press my ear to the receiver and hear only static. Then—

"He was *there*…found it all…hiding behind the swimmers."

"Mum? Mum, I can't hear you."

Another static burst. "Smiley. That's what we called him. Smiley in Red. He was *there*."

The line goes dead. I spend a few seconds staring at the phone in my hand before replacing it in the cradle. The swimmers. *Smiley*… I tell myself to stop. It's not like this is the maddest late-night conversation we've ever had. Once, about two years after she dumped us, I endured half an hour of ramblings about the bugs crawling across her bedroom wall and the fact the maids were stealing her clothes.

"How was she?" Dad asks.

"Out of it," I tell him. "So pretty much normal."

He's made himself a cup of tea. Putting down the mug, he gives me a weary stare.

"Gabe. Don't."

I slump back against the wall. "Don't what?"

"You should forgive her," he says. "For your own sake, if not for hers. You have a big heart, son, but it's much too easily bruised, and that's a dangerous thing in a world like this."

Something stirs in the back of my mind. Eric said something similar to me once. I push off from the wall and head for the corridor and my room.

"Thanks for the wisdom, Gandalf."

I try to put some snark into it but that's pretty much impossible with my old man. He just waggles his eyebrows and goes back to his book.

"How's our Eric?" he calls after me.

I stop and smile despite myself. "He's good."

"Good," my dad echoes. "You know I'm very proud of you, don't you?" I look back at him through the open doorway. He's never been a big man, but tonight, under that single electric light, he looks horribly frail. "I'm proud of you both."

And I don't know, those words... When I step into my bedroom I can't see for tears.

THEN

SEPTEMBER – SEVEN MONTHS AGO

Mr Joyce has kept me behind. He believes my engagement with Patriot Studies is "less than one hundred per cent". No shit. Anyway, he's making me write out the entire chapter from *After the Outrage* on the bombing of the Merripit Hotel and the beginnings of the Protectorate, as punishment for my "attitude".

By the time I'm done, school's practically empty. Dropping my work onto Joyce's desk, I bust through the main doors and head for the bike stands. I'd usually be royally pissed off about being kept back – all bunched fists and anger scratching behind my eyes – but today other emotions – confusing ones – tumble inside my brain.

All through detention, the only thing I could think about was the newbie. That heart-shaped face. Those striking lips… For about the thousandth time, I bat the image away.

The *actual* son of a chief inspector of Degenerate Investigations, Gabe! I must be losing it.

At the stands, I crouch down, spin the wheels of my padlock, and pull my bike free. Normally I'd stop at the pool for a swim before heading home, but today I'm all kinds of exhausted, and anyway I really need...

He's there. Eric Dufresne, alone at the gate. As if he's been waiting for me. Which is ridiculous. Of course he hasn't. He's probably just... He's staring at his shoes, his long hair hiding those big dark eyes. I could almost swear he's pretending he hasn't noticed me. He's tense, shoulders hunched, arms taut as he grips the handlebars of his bike. He looks – I don't know – excited and scared, all at the same time.

Okay, stop it. He's a stranger. Whatever he is, it isn't your concern.

I lean into my bike and force my gaze beyond the gate, buzzing past him with a fixed smile. Except I can't help it. Just when we're level, I turn my head and find him looking back at me. He makes this tiny gesture, not quite a wave, but it's enough. My foot hits the ground and I skid to a stop.

"Hey, Eric. Everything okay?"

His bike – some expensive Chinese racer – is propped against his hip. It makes my old bone-rattler look practically prehistoric. He takes hold of the saddle with both hands.

Then he looks up with a sharp nod, as if he's made a decision.

"Yeah. Thanks. I was just wondering though…could you do me a favour?"

The late-summer sun ripples in his hair, finding streaks in the jet black that look almost blue. I pedal slowly back towards him. It's as if I can feel the tug of a current between us, a pull I know I should resist. I bump my front tyre playfully against his and he flinches.

"What do you need?" I prompt.

"It'll sound stupid," he says, wheeling his bike back and forth. "But I…" He lets go of a long breath. "Okay, so I don't know my way home. My dad dropped me off this morning, *meandmybike*, and I'm not sure I know how to get back to our new house."

Meandmybike. Added so quickly the words ran together. So I wouldn't, what? Wonder if he'd actually cycled to school and was making up this excuse so that he could talk to me? Crazy, right? So why do I feel the blush on my cheeks?

"Where do you live?"

"Arnold Leese Walk?"

I whistle. "Fancy. Okay, so it's fairly easy to find from here."

I pull up next to him, our forearms almost touching, and plot his route out on my palm. At one point he leans

93

closer and I can feel the warmth of his breath on my neck. It smells like peppermint. When I look at him, he fixes his attention hard on my open hand.

"Think you'll find your way?"

"Um. Yes. Thank you." He goes to pull away. Stops. "Or maybe you could give me the tour?"

"The tour?"

"Of Westwick. Help me get my bearings? I mean, if you're not doing anything?"

"Oh. No. I mean, I'm not. Doing anything. So." I shrug. "Sure."

Sure, Gabe? Sure?! The son of the most important Filth-Finder this side of London, and you say "*Sure*"? You are a fully fledged, five-star degen! What the hell do you think you're doing?

It isn't even as if I'm some confused teenager clumsily trying to work out who he is. I *know* who I am. I've known since I was eleven years old. And it's not like I'm naïve or inexperienced or anything. In the end you can't scare people out of their first fumbles, no matter what the Protectorate might think.

My first fumble. God. It was Liz's fifteenth birthday party. Her parents had gone to some friends' for the night and everyone had pooled a few ration coupons to trade for a jar of homemade cider from this kid who worked at the army base. So there we were in Liz's basement, all wearing paper party hats and playing spin the bottle. By the time my turn came, I was feeling all warm and glowy and basically in love with everyone. Lurching to my knees, I took my spin. Round and round the bottle rumbled, until eventually it landed on this Adam kid. Everyone laughed, I spun again, I pecked lips with Liz, and that was that.

Only.

I didn't know Adam had left the basement until I stumbled upstairs to the bathroom. He hadn't locked the door, and when he glanced over his shoulder, he smiled, like he'd been expecting me.

"Oh. Shit. I'm sorry," I said. "Too much freaky apple juice."

"S'okay," he said, grinning. "Hey, no, don't leave. I'm almost done."

I rocked woozily on the threshold, all my survival instincts trying to blare through the fog of evil cider. But Adam? He was cute. And he didn't go to our school. Some cousin of Liz's, I think. Anyway, he had this short strawberry-blond hair and these mad freckles that made me feel very odd and fluttery.

"I think a rat fell into that cider and died horribly," Adam said.

He moved to the sink and started washing his hands.

"Yeah. Ha. Probably."

Turning to the bathtub, I began randomly playing with

the shower curtain. I liked the way it squeaked between my fingers.

And then he was there, right in front of me, pulling my hands from the curtain and pressing our fingertips together.

"Weird how that bottle landed on me."

"Yup." I nodded. "*Puh*-retty weird."

"Do you believe in fate, Gabriel?"

"Um. Don't know. Not sure I want to."

"Because fate is usually shitty?"

"Usually."

"But not always."

He tilted his face – God, those freckles – and closed his eyes. And of course I lunged forward like a total amateur and smashed our teeth together. Hissing, we both drew back, and I immediately felt the urge to roll myself up in that squeaky shower curtain and never come out again. But in the next second Adam was laughing and asking if we could give it another go. It worked out a little better on the second try, and by the time Liz shouted up that June was projectile vomiting over the garden wall, my teeth had stopped aching and my technique was pretty solid.

There have been a few more fumbles here and there, some more intense than Adam, but I guess you always remember your first. Not that everyone is lucky enough to have a first. Sometimes a kid can be hauled away on suspicion only, before they ever get a chance to test out those funny, troubling feelings.

But as I say, with Eric Dufresne I'm not some giddy, know-nothing kid. Except it sort of feels like I am.

His face lights up when I agree to the tour. I tell myself this is because he's the new kid and he's just happy he's found a friend.

"Okay," I say, turning my bike and pushing off. "Get ready to be *seriously* underwhelmed."

Honestly, there isn't much to see: the grassless park with its single rusted swing; the town dump, overflowing with skeletal rats; the little parade of shops with their almost-empty shelves and peeling paintwork. Everything tired; everything just about hanging on. We zip past Godfrey's, me shouting a few "interesting" local facts over my shoulder when Eric suddenly skids to a halt.

"What's this way?"

I make a tight arc and swing back to him. He's pointing down to the cobbled towpath and the stagnant canal. Beyond, shattered rooftops stab into the sky.

"Westwick Old Town," I grunt. "The bit they didn't rebuild after the Outrage fighting ended."

He reaches out and snags my sleeve, the side of his hand brushing mine. "Can we see?"

"It's a free country." I shrug. "So they say."

I see him stiffen a little but he doesn't say anything.

97

We're forced to ride single file along the towpath, and it's crazy, but I keep looking back. I need to check that Eric hasn't had second thoughts and raced off to tell his dad. But tell his dad what? This was his idea, wasn't it?

We emerge from a side street and enter the demolished town square. Old bullet holes pepper some of the shopfronts while a vast black powder-burn haunts the side of one wall; ghosts of a final battle before the Protectorate claimed victory. I bounce my bike over the rubble while Eric carefully steers his racer around snarled cables and yawning potholes. I'm desperately trying to think of something to say.

"So, uh, did you have loads of friends back in London then?"

He appears to be concentrating very hard on steering. "Um, no. Not really."

"Right. I suppose your dad probably frightened them off? You know, him being a Protectorate officer and everything?" I make a mock-stern face. "Might be a bit intimidating."

"I guess. He has very definite ideas, my dad. About the kind of people I should be friends with."

"And what about you?" I ask.

Eric shrugs. "New school, fresh start, you know."

He cuts his gaze back to the sky above the new town, where threads of green poison from the factories vein the blue.

"My dad's a very powerful man. But I'm his son, not his constable. I don't have to follow all his orders."

I grin. "Good for you. And is it just the two of you at home?"

"Yeah. Why do you ask?"

"No reason." Have I offended him? I can't see how, but my big mouth plunges on, as usual. "It's cool, I'm practically motherless too." *For the love of God, Gabe.*

We dip in and out of shadows. A shop dummy slumped against a glassless window watches us pass. Her clothes were stripped from her long ago and she's missing an arm. Behind her, a crowd of other mutilated mannequins seem to leer at us, their milky eyes swimming in the dark. I shiver and Eric asks, "Are you cold?"

It's a ridiculous question because we're both sweating. Eric's shirt keeps sticking to his body and he seems obsessed with plucking the fabric away from his skin. Still, I glimpse the flat plane of his stomach and a thatch of black hair around his belly. It's difficult to look away. I start to say something else – some lame joke about school – when he rests his bike against this tall, wire-topped fence.

His gaze roams around the square, until it reaches above the fence, to the rooftop of some forgotten building. Eric's palm hovers momentarily over a sign attached to the boards: *UNSAFE AREA – DO NOT ENTER – BY STRICT ORDER OF THE PROTECTORATE.* I watch his fingertips trail downwards, playing over the cracked and warped panels until one board creaks aside at his touch. His head snaps back to the sign. He licks his lips.

"C'mon." A slash of colour cuts across his pale cheeks. "Let's take a look."

I kneel beside him. "Are you sure?"

A beat. "Why not?"

He swings back the loose board and we both peer through the gap.

"It's like a secret entrance," I say. "Like Narnia...or something."

Crap. Is *The Lion, the Witch and the Wardrobe* a banned book? It's hard to keep track sometimes, what with my dad's secret stash under our floorboards.

"Narnia..." Eric grins. I think this is the first time I've seen his full neon smile. It banishes the haunted look around his eyes and I can't help it, I laugh. "What?" he says. "I loved those books when I was little. Mr Tumnus and the beavers, and Prince Caspian and the Dawn Treader. My mum..."

He stops. He has this rising and falling way of speaking, like he's reading a poem. Before I can say anything, he pushes the board as far as it will go and steps through. I follow to find him standing in front of a huge, abandoned building, soaring columns choked with ivy. Carved into the stone above the big double doors are the words: *WESTWICK*

PUBLIC LIBRARY. As Eric leads the way up a set of stone steps and into an echoing vestibule, I feel my heart expand inside my chest.

All these years living in this crummy town and I never knew this was here. A library. Just imagine! Oh sure, I've read about these places, and our school has what it calls a "library" – two shelves of approved books so full of lies and hatred they ought to be issued with a sick bag – but a real *library*? Somewhere you could roam for hours among aisles of books, sit and read to your heart's content, learn about different lives and histories and opinions, without fear of your curiosity being punished? Even now, standing inside one, they seem like mythical, magical places, so unlikely that I have to touch the crumbling plaster to make sure that it's real.

An immense painting covered in decades of dust almost covers one wall of the vestibule. It's grimy as hell, but I manage to glimpse a few familiar faces – Dickens and Wilde, King and Blackman, Orwell, Angelou and Atwood – maybe fifty authors, almost all of them now banned as dangerous, degenerate or both. If Eric recognizes them, he doesn't say anything.

Even before we move into the main library, I know my hopes for acres of forbidden books are ridiculous. Still, it hurts when I see the miles of empty shelves. It hurts even more when we notice the big scorch mark at the centre of the room. Eric stops at its outer edge. He's quiet for a while, then—

"My dad. He says they had to do it." For the first time since we met at the school gate, I see of a flicker of uncertainty. "A lot of the books written before the Outrage, they just confused people. Too many voices... Dad says no one could think straight any more." He drops to his haunches and touches the burn mark, then pulls back his hand as if, after all these years, the floor is still hot. "They had to clear away all the confusion. Didn't they?"

It's the same old Protectorate propaganda, but he says it while twisting his fingers and asking the question. I squat beside him. His shoulder trembles against me. The way he pushed through the fence, the way he initiated all this?

I feel like he's caught between something.

"Come on." I nudge his shoulder and, jumping to my feet, shout, "Tag!"

"You're not serious?" he calls after me.

"Rarely," I call back.

I'm not sure what those old librarians would have thought about two ridiculous seventeen-year-olds racing around their library, leaping over shelves, wriggling under desks, shrieking their lungs out like a pair of little kids, but I'd pay any fine just to hear Eric Dufresne laugh like this. The cage he seems to carry around with him disappears and his whole face becomes joyous.

We've been hurtling around for about ten minutes when we crash into each other. Limbs hopelessly entangled, we trip and land in a flailing heap on the stairs that lead to the second level. We lie there for a moment, groaning at the pain of the impact and laughing hysterically. Until suddenly we aren't. A handful of seconds stretch away. He's so close I can feel his heart pound against me.

"That wasn't... That didn't count as a tag," he says in a shaky voice. Then, pushing me aside, he sprints up to the second level.

I start to my feet, head reeling. Before I can even begin to think about what's just happened, I hear a hollow splintering sound from the floor above. I call up, asking if he's okay. All is silent when I reach the second level. I begin searching under desks and around alcoves, saying I've had enough, that we should...

"Gabe."

It's the first time Eric's used my name. I turn to find a boy whose eyes shine full and bright with terror. I run the length of the room, right up to the librarian's issue desk at the far end. A slant of cobwebbed daylight catches Eric's face.

"What's the matter?" I ask. "What's happened?"

"I fell." He turns to the wall behind him. "My shoulder went right through. I...I was getting up again when I saw it. I just pulled it out. Didn't even think."

I look from the ragged hole punched into the mouldy plasterboard to the cardboard box now sitting on the desk. One of the flaps has been pulled back and inside I can see row on row of slim plastic cases. Eric moves in beside me. I reach into the box, take out a case and snap it open. Inside, there's a single silver disc, shining like a jewel.

"What is it?" he asks.

And I smile.

"Treasure."

NOW

9

Reaching across the bed, I pull Albert towards me. He bites his lip as I glide my fingertips between the sweep of his hips.

"Hello, Elf," I whisper.

"Hello, Monkey."

I frown at that. It isn't his nickname to use. But then he's cupping the back of my head and kissing me, his mouth urgent on mine. Taking his hands, I lock my fingers around his wrists and spread his arms over his head. Then I roll him onto his back and, sitting astride his chest, lower my face.

"I told you it would be better, just the two of us," he sighs.

I kiss his throat.

"Better without that broken scarecrow boy."

"What?" I look up. "What did you say?"

"Doesn't matter. We can forget about him now."

That impish face stares back at me. One grey eye is filling up with blood.

"That little patchwork pansy," Albert laughs.

Except it isn't Albert any more. The body beneath me is transforming, widening at the hips, swelling around the chest, the white-blonde hair growing down to her shoulders. My heart slams into my ribs as I tug the sheets around me and stumble from the bed.

"What's the matter, Gabey? Don't you want me any more?" Lana Heck crawls across the mattress, chuckling as she goes. "No, I s'pose not. But you know, you ought to be careful with that brother of mine. He lies. He—"

Her head snaps to the window. Behind the glass, a face stares back into the room. Such fear in that face. Fear like I haven't seen since our first afternoon in the library, when we discovered the box. I run to the window, try to pull it open, but the sash has been nailed shut. A few stray nails litter the sill and there's a hammer lying on the floor. I reach for it, thinking I'll use it to break the glass, but then I see the name printed neatly across the grip – Property of Albert Heck – and for some reason I flinch away.

Back at the window, I start tearing at the nails with my fingers, but it's no good. I can't free the sash. And so I push my palm against the pane and Eric presses his lips to the other side. At first I think he's kissing the glass, but when I remove my hand it's misty and there's a single word scrawled in his breath.

HURRY

"They're coming for you, Gabe," Lana croons from the bed.

"They've always been coming for you. In the light and in the dark, there isn't a minute they're not watching and listening. But now it's not just you they're coming for. You should never have taken him on that little tour of Westwick. Should never have bound him to you with promises neither of you could ever keep. He's going to die for your hopes, Gabriel."

A huge painted smile shines out of the dark. Constable Rakes – Green Jacket, Filth-Finder – throws his arms around Eric and starts dragging him back into the night. In the distance beyond them, black gates erupt out of the earth while shapes in white coats mill around, waiting for their latest victim. Eric's mouth splits into a scream. As the gates of the Re-Purification camp close around him, a vortex of tiny silver leaves bursts from between his lips and rushes towards me, battering the window where I—

take a sharp breath and sit up in bed. The house is dark, quiet. No Eric at the window, no leaves on the pane. I grab my glasses from the nightstand and check my wristwatch: 2.25 a.m.

I push the dream away. I'm too fuzzy to think properly about it, and anyway, I've never been big on the whole dream-analysis thing. So I had a nightmare about Rakes threatening Eric. Well, that *is* a concern. *Aaaand* I dreamed about sleeping with Albert. Well, he *is* kind of cute – though honestly, I've never thought of him in that way before – but anyway, dream-cheating isn't real cheating, is it? Okay, so the Lana transformation bit was pretty unexpected, but I guess, like life, your dreams rarely make total sense.

I get up and push the light switch. Nothing happens. Power's out again, probably for the whole area; fifth time this week. Rummaging in a drawer for a candle, I dress quickly and head for the hall. I want to be on my way, but down the corridor I glimpse the flicker of a lamp. I tiptoe as quietly as I can into the kitchen, where I find Dad slumped over the table, his head pillowed by one of the books he's been repairing: *The Road to Oz* by L. Frank Baum.

Seeing that title, I experience this vivid flash: my dad and me when I was little, snuggled up on the sofa for story time, Dad using different voices to bring to life a strange land of heartless tinmen, brainless scarecrows and timid lions. Curled into her armchair on the other side of the room, my mum puts down some important book she'd been reading and a rare, affectionate smile plays across her lips. The memory almost winds me. I haven't thought about that moment in years. Maybe because, since she left us, it's been easier to focus on the bad and banish all kind memories of her. I grab a blanket from the linen cupboard and drape it carefully around my dad's thin shoulders.

Outside, I find the bag containing Albert's tools, dropped off on my doorstep as he promised. I put them into my own backpack and, turning away from the road, stride into the forest that sweeps around our garden. Strictly speaking, there's a ten p.m. curfew, but nobody patrols Hamilton Woods.

Dark greens flash by: moss on tree bark, lichen in a pond. The forest around me seems eternal, constantly changing and yet always the same. But people aren't like that. We're not allowed to stay in one place for ever. So how much longer have we got, Eric and I? Next year we graduate and, however well we do in our final exams, it's unlikely we'll end up in the same job, let alone the same part of the country. It haunts us both, I know, and so we don't talk about it.

I march on. This is why I can't indulge in stupid fantasies about becoming a director. When I'm not even allowed to hold onto the person I love, how could I ever make the kind of films I need to? Films like *Pride*, documentaries like *Disclosure*: I want to create stories that rage against the reality of this prison we live in. Anything less than that, I'm not interested. I've seen now how movies are like a knife: they can be used as a tool to feed and nourish or as a weapon to hurt and destroy. If it turns out I have any talent at all as a filmmaker, I won't use it to serve the Protectorate. I can't.

I take a deep breath. Just like I can't live without him. I've known that for a while now. Life without Eric by my side… I ball my hands into fists. What am I even thinking?

It's stupid to say I *can't* live without him. What's the alternative? We tell the truth and maybe we get to ride the same train to Re-Purification. Except of course that would never happen. The minute the secret left our lips, we'd be separated, tried by different enforcement courts, sent to different camps. Then, when and *if* our treatment of aversion therapies and forced chemical castration were completed, we'd be released and assigned jobs in different cities, with only the pink cross on our shirts to remind us of what we'd once been. We'd never see each other again, and if we ever tried…

No. I can't think about a world without Eric in it.

I march on. My dad kindled my love of books, and the box in the library gave me new ways to dream. Whether or not I become a director, I *am* a dreamer, and so here's a dream to accompany me through the wood…

Two young men pass in the lobby of a grand hotel somewhere far across the sea. One is an assistant to a diplomat, the other works in the Protectorate's trade mission. They pause for a moment, exchange a smile, and half-remembered names come to their lips.

Scarecrow?

Monkey?

Their mouths clamp shut because even here, far from England, the walls have ears. But still they pause, and one holds out his hand. They laugh and shake, feeling somehow ridiculous. The pale one with the red lips blushes and the other remembers how his fingers would once trace those blooming, fading continents.

They say it's been years, and they reminisce about childhood days while skilfully avoiding everything that made them who they were. Who they are. But they are both still young men, and their hands are still pressed together, and in that moment all the hollowness of the years between then and now is understood and mourned.

The man with the corn-coloured hair starts to say something, and the man with the red lips wants to listen. So much. So much. There's a border somewhere, a car or a plane or a boat ride away, if only they dare. But it's been so long since Westwick and the old school and the library, and they are strangers now. The fearlessness of youth is like a shadow. And so the man with the red lips shakes his head, and the man with the corn-coloured hair shakes his, as if it was all a joke. Which it was, wasn't it? All a big joke. And so they nod and wish each other well and say that one day they'll have to meet up again and talk about childhood days.

Just two old friends.

And their wives.

10

"Hello to you too, Totes."

I drop down into the warm, dusty straw of Totes's cabin and let the little monster jump all over me. We have no idea how old Totes is, but the black and white mongrel is still as playful as a pup. He is also powerfully adorable. I know this because, despite his general scruffiness, he has managed to melt every Rebel heart.

Eric likes to teach Totes tricks, like hide the ball and… Well, if I'm honest they haven't got past hide the ball. Eric won't have it, but our mutt is a dog of very little brain. Still, he has a pretty cool house for such a tiny doofus, and we love him very much.

I sit back against the wall of the old stone-built shed. Heaped in the corner is the vast collection of toys the Rebels have brought Totes over the months: rubber bones and tug ropes, a hockey stick from Ben, and his favourite, a raggedy squirrel that used to be June's bedtime buddy. I hug the furball to my chest. It sucks that we have to leave him out here alone, over a mile from my bungalow, but Dad is allergic, and Eric's dad? Well.

"If that was anyone else, I might be getting jealous right about now."

Totes leaps out of my lap and starts dancing around Eric's feet. Eric blocks the gate with his leg until it's properly shut, then slides down beside me and we share the mutt between us.

"Nothing in *Protectorate Oaths and Regulations* about men kissing dogs," I reply with a shrug.

"Yeah." Eric rolls his eyes. "They're not total monsters."

Totes bounces from lap to lap, nipping fingers to get attention.

"So, you got out okay?" I ask.

"Nope. I'm still tucked up in bed, dreaming of sexy Beatrice."

"Your hundred-year-old maid?"

"Heh. At least it's legal."

"You know, I like this sassy new Scarecrow. You should bring him out more often."

"Well." Eric pokes my cheek. "Who else would I be dreaming about?"

Because I don't want to tell him who *I've* been dreaming about, I change the subject. It's something I've been thinking over for a while, and it kind of chimes with the thoughts that have dogged me through the forest.

"Okay, so you won't believe this, basically because it's me saying it, but I was wondering if it's time we started acting responsibly?"

Eric scratches an eyebrow. "Yeah. I understand these words, but they're coming out of *your* mouth, which is… weird?"

"It's the mutt I'm thinking about," I say, ruffling the scruff under Totes's chin and sending him into raptures. I glance at Eric; he won't hold my gaze. "He's gotten a lot bigger and it's not fair to keep him cooped up out here. My neighbour, Mrs Lebbon, she lost her spaniel Brewster last Christmas. I know she'd take good care—"

"Why are you being serious?" he breaks in. "I mean, *you*?"

I rest my head against the wall. "I'm sorry, Eric, I am. But you always knew this was coming. We've got a year before we finish school, and it would be good to get the crazy hound settled by then."

"Yes, I know," Eric snaps. Totes looks up from his finger-nipping, clearly worried that he's done something wrong. "I know," he repeats, softer now. "But can we not talk about this tonight? When it's all over, when we've got the disc back, we can discuss it then."

"Sure." I nod. "No, you're right. I'm sorry."

He pokes my cheek again. "*I'm* sorry."

Our surprise three a.m. visit is over and, for once, Totes doesn't seem all that sorry to see the back of us. He gives this full-on yawn and trots away to his little bed in the corner, dragging June's squirrel after him. Turning out the lamp, I follow Eric to the gate.

"Night, boy."

Totes yips, and we link hands.

Three a.m. hand-holding is all kinds of beautiful. Okay, so Eric's a bit antsy at first, darting looks over his shoulder, but no one's going to be lurking in the forest at this time of night, and he soon starts to relax. I swing our arms and hurry him on. My backpack bounces against my tail-bone and my glasses bump my nose, and suddenly I'm grabbing both his wrists and swinging him around, and I'm singing.

So yes, I'll admit, my singing voice is awful. Not a patch on Eric's anyway. But he doesn't wince. He just laughs and swings with me. The song – I Have a Secret Love – is from some old cowboy musical we watched a few months ago, and I haven't been able to shake it. The main character sings it about this dude she's pining for, and I guess it's kind of schmaltzy, but its meaning is as true as anything I've ever seen or read.

Spots of rain bat the branches overhead. After a few more paces, Eric delves into the pocket of his anorak and presses a curfew pass into my hand.

"I told Dad you had to help me with a nature project,"

he explains. "Identifying the nocturnal habits of *Limenitis camilla*. The white admiral butterfly. Black wings with white bands, noted for its distinctive flight pattern. Not to be confused with the purple emperor, which we made extinct about five years ago. As a species, we really put the sap in *Homo sapiens*, don't we?"

"On so many levels," I agree. "And your dad bought that ridiculous story?"

Eric shrugs. "He always turns off when I start talking about the other ninety-nine point nine-nine per cent of life on planet Earth."

I give his hand a final squeeze. I'll never get why his father's approval still matters to Eric, but maybe it isn't my place to understand.

We come out of the thick woodland onto Mitford Street and our fingers unthread. Cottages face the road up to the school, and who knows if some loyalist snoop might be looking out of their window.

When we reach the wall, Eric cups his hands and gives me a boost. It makes sense, he is approximately nine feet tall. I scramble up and he passes me my bag, which I lower as far as I can into a bush on the other side. It makes this tiny clanging noise as it drops, loud as a siren in my ears. I reach down and pull Eric up after me. He's almost made it, his feet scudding the brickwork, when his eyes cut to my bunched-up bicep.

"Hey," I hiss. "Not the time to be checking out the merchandise."

He grins and we scramble down the far side. Retrieving my bag, we make our way across the sports field to the dark hulk of the school. My heart's battering inside my chest like one of Eric's white admirals, so I sketch out the plan again, just to settle my nerves.

"Kids are still breaking into the school for food, even though they've burglar-proofed the canteen," I whisper. "So, one broken lock shouldn't arouse much interest. And as nothing obvious will be stolen, and the Grey Jackets are overstretched anyway—"

"No investigation," Eric says. "Gabe, I really do get it."

I nod and lead the way to the gym. We're out of direct moonlight so Eric shines the torch while I remove the largest of Albert's screwdrivers from the bag. The padlock that secures the gym door rattles as I slide the tool into the rusted loop.

"You're sure he was okay lending us this stuff?" Eric asks.

"He said he was." I test the screwdriver against the lock a couple of times. "I think he wanted to help."

"That's nice of him, but if we're caught? Rakes only saw this gear a few hours ago."

"Albert knows the risk."

The screwdriver strains, the loop snaps, and the padlock

hits the ground. I dig my fingertips around the door and ease it open. Eric collects my bag and we both step into the cathedral vastness of the Mosley Grammar gymnasium. Gigantic pieces of the latest exercise equipment loom out of the dark. The rest of the school might be falling to pieces, but you have to hand it to the Protectorate, they really do invest in keeping their underfed children fighting fit.

"So," I whisper, "I've been thinking."

"This seems to be becoming a dangerous habit."

"Ha ha. But seriously, what do you think about Albert?"

"You mean, what you said today? About something going on with him?"

"No, not that. Except, well, maybe there is. But it isn't something new that's just popped into my head. I just started thinking and—"

"Gabe." Eric touches my arm. "What are you trying to say?"

"I don't know. I wonder, though – do you think he's like us? Because he's never actually come out and said that he's a degen."

Eric stops dead, his hand on the door that connects the gym to the main school.

"Don't say that."

"Don't say what?"

"Degen." He gives me one of his old sad smiles. "Gabe,

that's how *they* define us. Degenerate. Disgusting. Twisted and inferior and rotten and ugly. It was you who showed me none of that's true."

"Oh, Eric." I pull him into a hug. "Eric, I'm sorry. So yes, okay, what are we, then? Pick a word. Something amazing."

He shrugs. "Gay. That was the pre-Outrage word, wasn't it? Before they said they were reclaiming it and making it pure again. I like it." He strokes my face with his fingertips and his smile loses its melancholy. "We're gay."

I nod. "Gay it is… And Albert?"

"Gay," Eric laughs. "Most definitely. Don't you see the way he looks at you?"

He pushes through the door and, after a dumbstruck moment, I trot to catch up.

"What?" My voice grenades down the hall and Eric turns on his heel, pressing his hand to my mouth. "*Whuh?*" I mumble into his palm.

"Honestly, Gabe, you are the most oblivious human being ever."

"But…Albert?"

"Definitely gay," Eric confirms. "And definitely into you. During Rebels, I swear he watches you almost as much as he watches the movie."

"Oh." Did I know this subconsciously? Is that the reason behind the Albert dream?

So here we are, strolling through our school at the dead

of night, armed with a burglar kit, intent on liberating a degen – *gay* – movie from an air-conditioning unit, and suddenly a host of new worries start to crowd in on me.

"Listen," I say, dancing around Eric as we walk, "you know I haven't encouraged him, right?"

He arches an eyebrow. "Gabriel Sawyer, please. Yes, I know."

"Right." I puff out my cheeks. "Good. But… Wow. *Albert*."

"I'd take it as a compliment," Eric says. "He is pretty cute."

"So, do you think this might be what's going on with him?" I can't help a slight swagger, even though my brain's feeling a bit like a pinball machine. "He's got this perfectly understandable crush and he's just trying to get his head around it?"

"Yes, Gabe, you are the sun around which he orbits." We stop outside Miss Calloway's room and he gives me a pitying pat on the shoulder. "But don't worry, I'm sure it's only a temporary bout of insanity."

I am very tempted right now to tease Eric about my obvious irresistibility, but we have work to do. Through the window in the door, I can see the old air-con unit sitting in a band of moonlight. Time to retrieve our treasure.

THEN

SEPTEMBER – SEVEN MONTHS AGO

"I think maybe we should go."

I turn from the hole in the wall to the boy crouching beside me. The carefree Eric I chased around the library – the kid who defied a Protectorate notice and pushed his way through the fence – is fading, and his invisible cage is back in place. I swear I can almost see him staring at me through the bars. Who put you in there, Eric?

"It's okay," I say. "We haven't done anything wrong."

He stands abruptly and looks to the stairs and the library below. For a minute I think he'll bolt, but instead he nibbles an already raw thumbnail and rocks on his heels.

"Hey," I say, nodding towards the hole. "You see this? This bit of wall above where you knocked through the plasterboard? C'mon." I bob my head and he slowly nudges in beside me. Sweat from the tag game has plastered his shirt to his torso and he starts picking and pulling at it again. "See that faint line, just there? I think someone deliberately sawed through the plasterboard then fixed the whole thing back up again. Must have repainted the wall too, so the join wouldn't be too obvious."

"Okay. But why?"

I get to my feet and we go back to the issue desk and the cardboard box resting there.

"They must have thought this stuff was worth saving." I cut my eyes to him. "From the fires."

Eric gives a careful nod. "Like conservation. Of an endangered species."

"Maybe."

I pick up the silver disc and its case from where I left them beside the box. The case is blank but the disc has a title printed in black: *Love, Simon*. Eric peeks over my shoulder.

"So what are they?"

I open all four sides of the box and begin popping cases. After a while, Eric starts picking up one or two discs himself. I recognize a couple of titles from banned books, though most read like a foreign language: *The Hunger Games, Pride, The Miseducation of Cameron Post, Blinded by the Light, Carol, Erin Brockovich, Platoon, God's Own Country, The Way He Looks, 120 Beats Per Minute, Star Wars, Moonlight, It's A Sin* and so many others.

"They're films," I reply, grinning. "Movies from before the Outrage."

Eric drops the disc he's been holding and takes a step back. "This...this needs reporting. My dad's department, they can incinerate them. There's a blanket ban on all pre-Outrage films, Gabe, you know that. Section 78 of the..." He rubs his cheek. "It's cultural contamination."

I take him by the shoulders and make him face me.

"We're just looking, okay? We've found something possibly – possibly – illegal and all we're doing is checking it out. I don't honestly know what these things are." This is premium bullshit: I know exactly what these silver discs are and, unless I'm forced at the point of a gun, there's no way I'm giving them up. "Isn't it our duty to at least investigate?"

He scratches an eyebrow. "What does that even mean, 'investigate'?"

I turn back to the box. There's nothing random about these films. There's a message here, I'm sure of it. Why else were they all boxed up together and hidden away so carefully? And if there is a message, then our long-ago librarian must have left a way for that message to be read. My gaze drifts back to the hole in the wall.

Without thinking, I take Eric's hand.

"Oh."

I look back and my throat almost closes up.

"I'm sorry." I bark out this weird dry laugh and pull my hand away. "Me and June, we're always holding hands and I guess I just—"

"June? Is she your girlfriend?"

The idea is so hilarious I can almost hear June cackling in my ear: *Oh, Gabey, this super-deadly date is just so you.*

"Um, no," I say, mentally banishing her. "But we've been friends ever since she was old enough to get me in a headlock. Anyway. You coming?"

Here's the moment it could all go wrong. I'm halfway through the opening, and it's a tight squeeze, so I can't look back to check on him. But still I get this feeling that he won't disappear on me. I have no actual basis for this belief. I've known Eric Dufresne for all of six hours, we're currently in possession of some Grade-A hazardous material, and he's jittery as fuck. And yet, when I pull myself through and into the secret room, I'm not surprised to find him crawling in after me.

We both rise, spluttering on dust. The space we've entered is pretty roomy; even Eric can stand fully upright. Webs drift from the roof like phantom bannerettes and the only light comes through the hole in the wall. It feels like we're archaeologists exploring some forgotten tomb, except I'm pretty sure no pharaoh was ever buried with a four-person couch and a flat-screen TV. It makes perfect sense, though. Here's how we decode the librarian's message.

I move over to the television. Even the shoddy Protectorate-manufactured TVs that sit in almost every home are more advanced than this antique model. Still, it has an in-built DVD player with the remote control resting on the arm of the couch. I bunch up my shirtsleeve and use it to clear the screen. That's when I see the battery pack plugged into the back of the unit. It's one of those early 2030s saline "sleeper cells". If the remote has similar technology, then it's possible…

The screen blips into life at my touch.

"Okay," Eric breathes. "So the Stone Age TV works. Let's just take the box back to town and—"

"You are literally the worst detective ever," I laugh. "You know, you'll never be a big brave Green Jacket like your dad if you don't follow the clues."

I've said the wrong thing. Again. It's becoming a theme in what I'm starting to think will be a disastrously short friendship. Moving to the sofa, he slumps down and makes some vague gesture towards the TV. I can't think of anything to say, so I duck back through the hole and retrieve *Love, Simon* from the issue desk. I can feel Eric's eyes on me as I slip the disc into the slot then step back to perch on the far end of the couch. The film loads and I press *PLAY MOVIE*.

I don't honestly know how to describe what happens next. We've all seen the crap put out by British Protectorate Broadcasting: the nightly "Isn't everything great?" news; the lifestyle programmes that show you how to stretch your ration for the month; the weekly drama, pretty much always a crime story highlighting those fearless boys from

Protectorate Investigations outwitting some foreign mastermind. But this movie? This is like a window into a better, braver world.

We sit in silence, not understanding everything, feeling our way into the story. This schoolkid, Simon, is hiding the fact he's a degen from his friends and family. So far, so familiar. But his reasons for deception have nothing to do with Filth-Finders and Re-Pure camps. It's because he's nervous of change. But he's fallen in love with this other kid and he's just yearning to meet the guy in real life.

Simon and his friends: they eat in restaurants and own home computers and use "cell phones". It's all so gloriously mind-blowing. My dad just about remembers when people would chat to each other on mobile phones; now it's only Protectorate officers who use devices like that. And Simon has his own car! Albert's the only non-official I've ever seen driving a car – some rickety pre-Outrage model he fixed up with his dad. But here, in old-time movie world, cars are literally *everywhere*. And the houses are huge and neat and perfect, and the clothes are colourful and comfortable. And the food! Jesus! I've never seen so much food.

"This is incredible," I murmur. "Not just the film but... Do you think the US is still like this?"

I turn to Eric. He's slipped from his corner of the couch and is sitting right next to me. I don't think he's done it consciously because when he looks up he seems equally surprised. Edging away again, he starts to bite at a thumbnail.

"Don't." I reach out and take his wrist. "You'll make it bleed."

I place his palm gently on his knee.

"You mean everything they have?" He shakes his head. "I don't think so. But America? My dad says they tried it our way, for a while at least. Pioneered it, actually." He shakes his head. "But in the end they didn't have the stomach for it. Dad says they once had this great leader but the press tried to tear him down. The Protectorate learned from that. A free press sounds great, but really all it does is confuse people and make them unhappy."

"Not like now then?"

He turns, searching my face. "It was the same with that thing." He points to the screen where Simon is using his computer to communicate with the boy he likes. "The internet? It might still exist over there, I don't know, but we had to get rid of it. The press and opposition parties and the internet – there were just too many voices... Don't you think?"

There it is again: the Protectorate line, perfectly parroted. But also again: the pause, question, the doubt – the sense he's caught between something, that he's resisting, or at least beginning to. And there's the fact that he's still here.

We turn back to the film. Eventually we forget the differences between our world and Simon's and just get lost in the story.

"Do you think it's still legal over there?" Eric shakes his head, as if what he's saying is beyond crazy. "To be like Simon?"

I twist my body towards him and my knee bumps his. "I don't know. But I know it was legal here once, and that people like Simon could marry and adopt kids and—"

"I can't…" His eyes shine, as if full of tears. Or is it just the light? "It doesn't seem real," he says quietly. "It can't ever have been like that. Not for people like—"

People like…

The air catches in my throat.

Like us, Eric?

I can feel the goosebumps on the back of my arms. The tiny tremor in the pit of my stomach. Eric's attention remains fixed on the screen. Slowly, I turn my head and follow his gaze to where two boys roughly our own age are kissing. Kissing in public. It's preposterous. I keep expecting the people around them to start screaming and throwing things; I at least expect an official to appear and drag them away for questioning. None of that happens.

Although I've been kissed, I've never seen two degens kissing before. I've often wondered what it must look like from the outside. I guess it was always difficult to picture without the Protectorate filter of it being something warped and twisted.

There is *nothing* twisted about what I'm seeing right now.

From the corner of my eye, I notice Eric's hand lying right next to mine, palm up. His fingers tremble. I want to comfort him, to tell him that whatever he's feeling, it's okay. He shifts slightly and the knuckle of his thumb brushes my little finger.

"Eric…"

He swallows. Licks his lips. Turns to face me. Then, slowly, slowly, he reaches up, as if to touch my face. I can see the little hairs on the back of his hand stand to attention. He's like me. I know he is. My gaydar, or whatever Dad called it, is pinging off the scale. And Eric? He's sweet and beautiful and clever and…

Suddenly his eyes are huge. I've never seen fear like this, and believe me, I know fear. Every kid in the Protectorate does.

"I'm sorry. I'm sorry, I'm sorry." The words tumble out as he snatches his hand away. "I didn't mean to. I shouldn't have come here. Shouldn't have tried. I—"

He covers his mouth. And in the next second, he's up and tearing through the hole in the wall. I sit there, stunned. I can hear his feet pounding the stairs. My gaze drifts back to the TV where the credits are rolling. For some reason it takes a long time to get my shit together.

I give the cardboard box a glance as I race by the issue desk. If what I fear comes true then I'll never get to experience the rest of those films. The thought almost winds me and I have to clutch the bannister of the stairs. The main library is empty. Up ahead, way beyond the scorch mark, I can see the double doors swinging in the lobby.

"Eric. Eric, wait!"

By the time I'm out of the library and down the steps, my head is a hurricane. I hop awkwardly through the gap in the fence and straighten up, just in time to see Eric cycling out of the square.

I grab my bike, determined to catch him, but a sudden weariness overwhelms me. I catch him, then what? Do I drag him off his bike, grab him by the throat and make him promise he'll keep his mouth shut? I couldn't do that. And anyway, coming here was his idea. He found the library; he found the discs. He's as guilty as I am.

Surely he won't tell.

NOW

11

We crouch-walk below the level of the big windows, conscious of the moonlight streaming into Miss Calloway's classroom. At the desk where Albert was interrogated this afternoon – *my desk* – I pause. I'm still slightly stunned by Eric's revelation that Albert has a thing for me, but Eric is pretty perceptive in that way quiet people often are; it's blabbermouths like me who crash through life, never noticing anything. But Albert? Well…he's Albert.

And yet I had that dream about him, so maybe even my oblivious brain picked up on something. I don't know. It sort of feels like Eric's right, but that he's missing something too.

We move swiftly past other familiar desks. I picture Ben and Grace in the early days of their relationship, puppy-eyed and passing notes. That was around the same time that Pete Carney was told if he handed her the Valentine's card he was holding behind his back, June would devote her life to inventing a time machine so that she could travel into the past and ensure his parents never met, although she admitted keeping close cousins apart like that would be a challenge. I remember Liz rolling her eyes but being unable to suppress a small grin.

At the back of the room, Eric kneels in front of the busted air-con unit and I scoot in next to him.

"You're sure you want to do this?"

"Why not?" He shrugs. "How difficult can it be?"

"I'd say not difficult at all. But let's be realistic – you're not the most practical of people. Have you even handled a tool before?"

He pokes my cheek. "I handle you quite well, don't I?"

"Wow. I am both offended and aroused by that comment," I say. "But seriously, why don't I—"

He places his hand over mine. "For the last time, Gabe, we're in this together. I want to do my part."

"Fine," I sigh, admitting defeat. "Just, be quick."

Rummaging in my bag, I pass him the screwdriver. Then, to distract myself as the endless seconds stretch out, I go and rest my back against Albert's usual desk. From here, he has a clear view of his fellow Rebels: Ben and Grace and me and Eric, side by side, then June sitting right in front of Liz. Glances exchanged when we think it's safe, a whispered word – alone, he must see it all. Is the feeling

I get about him just that? A sense of Albert's loneliness; his isolation within a group of couples?

A deafening clang brings me back to the room. Eric looks up, teeth clenched, the unscrewed panel vibrating at his feet.

"Sorry," he says, wincing. I roll my eyes and make a hurrying gesture. Delving inside the unit, Eric scrabbles around in a decade's worth of dust before finally pulling out the silver jewel that started all this. Beaming like he's just overcome a challenge that might have defeated lesser mortals, he shuffles forward on his knees and hands me the disc. I use my sleeve to clear the grime and the title – *Love, Simon* – shines through.

"Hey," I whisper, as he turns back to reattach the panel. "D'you remember that kiss in the movie?"

"Don't remind me," he groans. "Did I ever say how sorry I was for taking off like that?"

"Now you mention it, you never did..." I sigh. "You know, that was the first time I ever felt that it was truly okay? Being who we are. Seeing those two kids kissing and it feeling completely normal."

"I know," he says, pausing for a moment. "Me too."

I run my thumb gently across the surface of the disc.

Once the panel is back in place, Eric stands and we move into a shadow between the windows. Sweat beads his forehead and I can feel a cold trickle skating between my own shoulders. Out of nowhere, my heart suddenly kicks up a gear. Mission almost complete, but we've still got to get out of here and stow the disc before we're totally safe. Eric drops the screwdriver into my bag and I'm about to slip the disc into a mesh side pocket when he trails his fingers along my arm.

"Gabe, there's something I want to say. Just quickly."

"Eric, we have to go."

"I know. But listen, what you said tonight, about representation…about seeing yourself reflected as a human being and how it can change minds? I believe that. You did that for *me*. Showed me who I am. And listen, I don't know how, but I know you're going to do the same for lots of other people one day. You're going to make those kinds of films."

He smiles. And I know now that I won't ever give up this smile. I am his and he is mine, and the Protectorate can't have either of us. Whatever it takes, we're going to stay together. Always.

I lean in and kiss him. A soft, sweet connection. Eric touches my hair, the side of my face, his lips pressing more firmly against mine, and I…

The lights go on.

Voices crash through the room.

And all around us the world begins to end.

12

I know it's too late. I know there's no hope for us now. I know that from the second that light went on we were dead men, because even if we survive what comes next, it will change us beyond recognition. But I'll fight just the same.

One of the men shouts something. I don't hear what. I'm thinking fast. We're at the far end of the room, shrouded in a band of shadow. Maybe there's a chance they haven't seen our faces. I pull Eric down with me into a crouch and a drop of sweat from my chin bursts against his knee. I don't dare a backward glance, my glasses might mark me out, but from the sounds I get the idea there are two, maybe three of them. Still crouching, I make a grab for the nearest chair.

"Get ready," I whisper.

My fingers tighten around the leg and I whirl upwards,

hurling the chair the length of the room. As I swing back around, head down, I hear a bright cry of pain and a muttered oath. Two. Only two of them. I take Eric's wrist and try to haul him to his feet but it's like lifting a dead weight.

"Get *up*."

I shake his arm. It feels limp, boneless. I need to wrench him out of his shock, so I press my hand flat against his chest. Against the scars beneath his shirt.

"Everyone will see," I tell him, hating myself for the words. "In the camps, they'll all get to see."

When I tug again, he scuttles to his feet.

Our classroom: hot in summer, freezing in winter. Thank God the Protectorate has never answered Mosley Grammar's repeated requests for doubling glazing and a few fixed air-conditioning units. I thrust my bag into Eric's arms.

"Keep your back to them," I say, "no matter what."

"Filthy degens!" Rough as sandpaper, I immediately recognize that voice. The caretaker whose name no one ever remembers; who's always half asleep during the day; who lives miles from school, but who's inexplicably here, in the middle of the night; who heard the panel slip and who will testify against us.

"There's no way out," the other man grunts. "And I swear, if you try anything, I'll smear your brains all over these walls. But if you come quietly, well maybe I can have a word with my colleagues in the Green Jackets. You're only kids. We can still set you straight."

Only kids? Go screw yourself. That's never saved anyone from a Re-Pure camp.

The Grey Jacket's boots clump down the row.

"Ready?" I ask Eric.

He nods, though he has no clue what I'm about to do.

In this moment, I thank my useless mother for that first swimming lesson, just as I thank my almost constant anger at this cruel, stupid, petty world. Come rain or shine, it's motivated me to swim myself ragged every morning, and so, physically at least, I'm strong.

Bent almost double, I take hold of the rust-encrusted hulk of the portable air-con unit. I'd briefly considered using a chair again, but I'll get one chance at this and the windows are thickly glazed. My right arm strains to cradle the unit while I use my left hand to grip the underside's razor-sharp edge. The machine groans as I push upwards and something pops in the small of my back. Pain cinches tight around my hips, but it all feels distant, like the idea of agony in a dream. Grunting, I heave the unit up to the level of my chest.

"Don't play silly buggers," the Grey Jacket roars. A desk scrapes back. "You've already got one degen crime to answer for."

"And assault with a fucking chair!" the caretaker calls after him.

But I can't hear them any more. Blood booms in my ears as I half stagger, half race towards the window, thrusting the unit higher as I go. With the base now at my breastbone, my arms are screaming. That keen bottom edge must have cut my shin as I lifted it because I can feel a flap of tattered trouser lapping at my calf and something warm and wet running into my shoe. It makes me think of Albert, not twelve hours ago, piss dribbling down his leg. A noble attempt to save an idiot. Shame it was all for nothing.

Unless.

Side on, my face appears in the window. I look ridiculous – glasses fogged, veins roping my neck, a gigantic metal box perched precariously on my shoulder. Eric's hand rests against my back, steadying me as best he can while beyond the window the moon glows, full and fat. Just one last push and–

The crash is mythic in the stillness. I know my own bellow is tiny against it. But inside my head I can still hear the rip of muscle in my shoulder, like the tearing of coarse, damp cloth. Now I feel pain and, for a second or two, I'm lost in it. Then I see the moon's rays, sharper and brighter, flooding through a frame of shattered glass. And now it's Eric taking the lead, snatching my hand, yanking me towards the opening.

There's no time to clear the glass. Together, we're up and over the sill, our palms glancing across jagged fragments. My right arm feels weirdly heavy as I tumble onto the concrete path outside, just missing the buckled corpse of the air-con unit. On my feet again, I'm turning towards Eric when I see the Grey Jacket's baton arc through the window. The nub swipes the side of his head and Eric staggers against me, not making a sound. I take his face in my hands and turn it this way and that. No blood that I can see.

"You okay?"

He nods, his eyes clear.

I look back at the window. Grey Jackets have leather gloves to go with their coats, but it's a warm night and I guess this loyal officer must have left his at home. Anyway, it seems he's reluctant to follow us over the splinters. Instead I hear running footsteps in the classroom. His nearest way out will be through the gym doors. We have a second or two.

"Show me your hands."

Eric holds out his palms. Scratches. Mine are the same.

"Your leg," he murmurs.

I glance down. My trousers are baggy with blood, though the adrenalin seems to be taking care of most of the pain. It does make me wonder what the hell I've done to my shoulder, though; that joint is pulsing like a bastard.

"We'll say I hurt myself swimming in the river," I tell him as we set off across the playing field. "You too. We've got the curfew passes from your dad so we can pretend we fancied a midnight swim. Didn't see the rocks in the dark cos we're idiots."

"But that's *our* classroom," Eric pants. "Won't they...?"

"Kids have been breaking into the school for food," I remind him. "No reason to suspect anyone in particular."

I dare a smile. Maybe I was wrong. Maybe the world isn't going to end tonight.

We're almost at the wall when the dark is snatched from us again. This time it isn't just a few bulbs in a classroom. This time the entire field turns to day. Stationed all along the pitch, the new Protectorate-funded floodlights crash down, robbing us of every shadow. I throw my arm over my face and tell Eric to do the same. Faster now, ignoring the agony coiled around my shoulder, I watch the dew-dappled grass roll beneath us like constellations.

Fresh voices are drowned out by a sudden gust of wind. There's rain on the air. The first real rain we've had in weeks. A dog barks; a whistle blows. Long shadows splash across the field, black heads bobbing against the wall where our own darkness leaps and shivers. Coming to a stop, I cradle my hands.

"Go."

Eric shakes his head. "I won't be able to pull you up."

He's right. I hate it, but he is. And so, with Eric boosting me, I make a grab for the top of the wall. On my second attempt, I manage to swing my arm over the ledge, but the momentum jars my injured shoulder and a sweet green nausea flushes through me, clenching my stomach, curling my toes. Choking back a mouthful of acid, I haul my legs onto the wall before turning and placing one damp palm flat against the brickwork. I reach down with my good arm and twitch my fingers. Eric looks up at me, the bag strap slung around his neck.

"C'mon, I've got you."

Hectic torchlight hits the wall.

Eric grips my hand.

And slips.

My palms are running with sweat.

"Again." I heave against the sickness. "Truh-ry."

"Gabe, you're hurt."

"*Try.*"

He jumps, snags my wrist, and my arm shunts up into the red-hot mess of nerves in my shoulder. This time I can't help it. This time I scream. Turning sideways, I hawk up a ball of phlegm, then shake my head and blink Eric back into focus. To my surprise I still have hold of him. My hand tightens around his forearm and I lift my eyes to the sky, spit fizzing between my teeth.

All at once the clouds break and I feel my heart hammer

with the rain. Eric's head is now almost level with the top of the wall. Already soaked, his shining face grimaces up at me. I take hold of the back of his shirt, ready to pull him the last couple of inches, when the strap snaps like a noose around his neck.

His eyes widen. His body lunges downwards, his chin striking the edge of the wall. There's a clack of teeth, bright as broken china, and blood flashes from the underside of his jaw. When he speaks, red bubbles foam between his lips.

"Go!"

I shake my head. Make a grab for him with my bad arm. Another huge tug from below.

"No," I shout down to them. "No!"

Eric's fingers are still fixed, bone-white against the ledge. I try to hold onto them but my hands are trembly and slick. Pitching forward, I catch hold of his sleeve and glimpse the upturned faces below. Their fury – huge, senseless – hits me like a fist between the eyes.

Another jerk and Eric flaps against the wall.

"Love me?" he asks.

I nod.

I love every atom of you, Eric Dufresne. I always will.

"Then go. *Go.*"

I watch as he falls, as they pull him down, as they throw him into the churning mud and let their dog lap the blood from his face. There's no fight left in him. He just lies there staring back at me, his eyes like lamps. And all I want to do is crawl down and lie there with him, huddled together under their fury.

THEN

OCTOBER – SIX MONTHS AGO

I pretend to pray, all the while wondering what it would feel like to spend a lazy Sunday morning lying in bed with Eric Dufresne. My gaze wanders across the church, over dozens of bent heads, and the now familiar dizziness hits me. Eric's long, nervous fingers are clasped around a hymn book and his messy hair hides his eyes.

I think back to those final moments in the library. How that invisible cage fell over him again. In the hours after he bolted, I remember coming home and just sitting on my bed, waiting for the knock at the door. Why I didn't tell my dad what had happened, I've no idea. The Green Jackets would've torn our house apart and inevitably discovered the banned books hidden under our floorboards. I guess I was just numb.

Next morning, I cycled the couple of miles back to Old Town. Only our footsteps marked the dust, and the box and its treasures were where I'd left them. Later at school, I tried to engage Eric with a joke. He flashed his gaze to the floor and said he needed to concentrate on his work. He's barely spoken to me since.

When Reverend Moran announces it's time for the traditional prayers for our beloved Lord Protector, everyone bristles to attention. Over in the corner I can see Miss Calloway and her friend from the school canteen sharing a prayer book. Near the front, Sergeant Huxley stands with a couple of Young Lions. I'm pretty sure Patrick Gilligan is developing muscles that don't exist anywhere else in nature. Further back, June is yawning alongside Albert and Liz, while Ben and Grace shoot each other longing looks across the aisle.

Okay, this is a bit reckless, even for me, but I've been thinking about sharing the librarian's movies with my friends. It's a small group and I trust them with my life. I have to. They all know about me. Liz and June are degens too, and Ben and Grace? Yeah, that was awkward at first. Ben has this cute hockey club buddy, and about a year ago I was helping clear up the changing rooms after a match when… Well, unlike with Liz's cousin Adam, this time someone walked in. Luckily for me it was Ben Dempsey.

We hadn't known each other super well back then, and honestly, I was scared shitless, but later Ben came to find me. He didn't say anything about what he'd seen, just reminded me that I'd once helped him with some trig homework, then out of the blue asked if I knew Grace Everard. She was new to Mosley and he was wondering, *if* he decided to ask her out, could I possibly play his wingman? We've been mates ever since.

Then there's Albert. He's a lot quieter than he used to be, but we've been talking books and playing old board games pretty much since primary school, and I know how much he'd love these films. I've now watched around half of them, and Jesus, they're phenomenal! One thing I know for sure is that whoever hid them away wanted their message to be shared: a message that difference is good and that defiance is essential.

Most of all, I need Eric to hear that message.

Every night since the library, I've pictured us together on the stairs, how his heart pounded against me, then in the hidden room when he reached for my face, a kind of pleading in those vast dark eyes. His words, spoken and unspoken, as we watched the film keep coming back: *It can't ever have been like that. Not for people like us...* Eric was trying to do something that day, trying to reach for some sort of truth about himself, I know it. I think of the hate he's been fed all his life, poisoning him against himself. Whatever happens between us, I want Eric to know that he's okay, just the way he is.

My dad's mumbling. I elbow him and he grunts awake,

interrupting Reverend Moran's parting words. The vicar gives us both the pulpit stink-eye. So Dad hasn't said anything more about me going to live with Mum and the Farmer, though I have to admit it's been playing on my mind. Maybe he's right about it being an opportunity for me to escape. I keep getting this image of a future-Gabe racing for some foreign border, a new life waiting up ahead.

People begin to stir in their seats. I help Dad along the row as someone brings his wheelchair from the back. Dad can usually manage a fair distance with his sticks but he has occasional days when his stiffness and pain become a bit much.

"So, shall I start the traditional ramming of ankles?" I ask.

Dad starts to quip back, but I'm not listening any more. This tall, hawk-faced man is stalking down the aisle, Eric beside him, trying to keep up. I don't know how I missed Chief Inspector Dufresne in the congregation.

Before I know what I'm doing, I've stepped into his path. "Hello. Mr Dufresne?" I hold out my hand. "My name's Gabe. Gabriel. I'm a friend of Eric's. From school."

We're like an island in the aisle, a river of people cutting and reforming around us.

"Gabriel Sawyer." Inspector Dufresne glances at his son. "Yes, I've heard all about you."

And I think I'm gonna puke. Maybe Eric has told his

father about the library and the box after all. The inspector grips my hand.

"Eric says you've gone out of your way to make him welcome at Mosley. He also claims you're quite the scholar. Quite the athlete, too." His eyes flick to my dad and he leans down to shake hands. "Mr Sawyer. Your son hasn't inherited your…weakness then?"

Dad smiles. "It was an accident that put me in this chair."

"Not a genetic abnormality." Dufresne gives an approving nod. "That's good."

"So, I was wondering," I say, screwing down my anger as best I can, "if Eric isn't doing anything for the rest of the day, maybe he'd like to hang out? Unless you have family plans?"

Dufresne makes a beckoning gesture and Sergeant Huxley comes forward. They exchange a few words and I think I hear the Farmer's name mentioned.

"You work in the design department at the Culture Protectorate, Mr Sawyer," the inspector says, as if reminding my dad of his job. "Putting out our message is a worthy contribution to the state… Very well then."

Hands planted on his son's shoulders, he steers Eric towards me. Eric shakes him off.

"I'm not eight years old," he mutters.

"No," his father agrees. "You're a boy with no friends."

With another nod to my dad, the chief Filth-Finder sweeps out of the church. Even Reverend Moran makes way for him. Meanwhile, Eric gives me a look I can't quite read and moves towards the door.

"You'll be okay getting home?" I ask Dad. "I think Mrs Lebbon could give you a push if you get tired. She pretends to be frail but I know for a fact she bench-presses three hundred."

He searches my face for a moment. "Be careful?"

I laugh. "Course." Then I rub the back of his hand. "Of course, Dad."

By the time I get outside, only Ben and June are still loitering in the churchyard. I give them a self-conscious wave as I weave between the gravestones, making my way towards Eric. June's head bolts up like a meerkat and they both shoot me slightly puzzled, slightly concerned glances. Honestly, I can't blame them. What am I *thinking*?

Eric waits by the gate. He doesn't look at me as we pass through and start down the hill, our feet scuffing the beaten earth. I guess this road must have been tarmacked once but, like most in Westwick, weeds tore it to pieces long ago.

"So, um, hey, are you okay?" I ask, nudging his shoulder with mine. "Because I'm sorry if I made things awkward with your dad back there. It's just, I'm sort of a nosy git and you were kind of blanking me at school, so I thought I'd take the risk and—"

"Yeah," he says, head down. "I've noticed that about you."

"That I'm a nosy git?"

"That you take risks."

"Oh." I bury my hands in my sleeves. "I'm sorry?"

Eric shrugs.

At the bottom of the hill we leave the road and turn into this narrow avenue that runs through the allotments. Old men straighten up from their potato patches and give us the evil eye as we pass. When everyone's hungry, allotments are guarded like bank vaults.

"So the weather's weird again," I say, blinking up at the sun. "My dad reckons there used to be proper seasons but that we only call them spring, summer, autumn and winter out of habit now. It doesn't really mean much any more. Which sort of…sucks? Sorry, am I babbling?"

"It's okay." He keeps his gaze fixed on the track, though the side of his mouth creases upwards. "I like how you babble."

And I can't help it, this huge grin spreads right across my face. So of course I immediately have to ruin everything.

"Well, I like how you're so moodily unnerving all the time. It keeps me on my toes."

His lips straighten out again and he presses his hands together.

Jesus, Gabe. Just…shut up!

150

We cross the park, its single rusted swing steady in the airless morning, and step under the shade of Hamilton Woods. There's a hush in the forest today. Drifts of yellow pine needles muffle our footsteps while sun-drunk birds glide listlessly from branch to branch. Suddenly I realize I'm walking alone. Glancing over my shoulder, I find Eric looking back at me.

"I didn't tell him," he says, his voice somehow shocking in the stillness. "I thought you should know. I wouldn't."

"Hey." I jog back and duck my head so that I can see under his bramble of hair. "I know. I know because your dad isn't currently using my balls as a set of decorative paperweights."

He bursts out laughing. In that moment, I decide that moodily unnerving Eric Dufresne is seriously gorgeous, but I like laughing Eric even better. His shoulders lose some of their tension and we wander further into the trees. Up ahead, a blue-green shimmer sparks between the trunks.

"Wow." I puff out my cheeks. "Is it really hot or is it just me?"

He stares at me. "It's pretty warm."

"Hot," I insist, nudging his shoulder again. "Really. Freaking. Hot."

It's child's play, making Eric blush, and I feel sort of terrible, but I just can't help it. I hop away, undoing the laces of my Sunday boots as I go, and throwing them towards the bank.

By the time I reach the river I have my socks off and I'm making a start on my shirt. I force myself not to look back. If I startle him, he might bolt again. I strip to my pants and dive into the achingly cool water. I know I need to back off, that I can't push my luck, keep taking risks like this. But I feel like something has to give…or else we'll always be stuck in this moment. Powering down, combing my fingers through inky reeds, I wonder if I really am crazy.

When I resurface, Eric is nowhere to be seen. I jerk all the way around, scanning the bank.

"Hello," says a small voice.

He's right there, under the mid-morning shadow of a willow tree.

"Oh." I grin. "Hello."

He hugs his knees to his chin.

"Fancy coming in?" I ask. "The water's amazing."

"Oh. Sorry, no." His chin drops to his chest and he plucks self-consciously at his shirt front. "I have eczema. It's kinda disgusting."

I duck my head under for a second and knuckle my forehead. "*I'm* sorry," I say, rising again. "I shouldn't have just assumed you'd want to go swimming. Do you want to do something else?"

"No. No, I'm cool watching. *And talking*," he adds quickly.

The blush is back, a delicious supernova. "If that's okay?"

That's very definitely okay. And so I float onto my back and let the sun glint off my chest. Yes, I know exhibitionism is all kinds of cringey, but I can't help it. Anyway, I'm thinking about Eric's confession: I couldn't care less if he has eczema. All I want to do right now is kiss his bloody face off, but this blemish clearly bothers him. Trouble is, for a blabbermouth I can't think of the right words to reassure him, so I do what I always do when I'm frustrated. I start ploughing the water.

"Whoa," he says when I come up for air. "You're a really good swimmer."

"My mum got me into it when I was little," I explain. "I like the repetitiveness. After a while your mind goes blank and you can go anywhere you want."

He grips his ankles. "You don't want to be here?"

"Here, as in here-here, right now? Absolutely. But here?" I flick a finger at the ripples. "I don't think so. Do you?"

It takes him a long time to answer. Finally, and very quietly, he says: "The Protectorate's our family. It's always there, looking out for us, keeping us safe, and we have to keep it safe in return..." He shakes his head. "My dad would watch his whole world burn for the Protectorate."

I'm opening my mouth to say something, I'm not sure what, when I notice his fingers. Something small and pale

153

is dancing between them. I swim over and belly-flop onto the bank, planting my chin on my palms. Eric's pretty close to the water, so I'm practically dripping onto his shoes. He looks up from his game and I see this tiny spider running and tumbling over his palms.

"*Anyphaena accentuata.*"

"That's a very cool magic word." I smile.

"It is magic," he grins back. The creamy arachnid scurries an orbit around his thumb. "Did you know only about half of spiders spin webs to catch their prey? This little guy, the buzzing spider, he's a no-thrills hunter."

"Does he buzz his victims to death?"

Eric frowns. "No. His name comes from how he vibrates his body to attract mates."

"That's hilarious. Who knew spiders and humans had so much in common?" I prod his shin with my finger. "Do you like to dance, Eric?"

He shuffles sideways and places the spider delicately on the bark of the willow. Turning back to me, he allows himself a half smile.

"I like this," he says. "Spiders, insects, trees. I like how it all fits together, like this perfect clockwork. And it's for ever, you know? Eternity in a hatchling and a cocoon." There's no pause, no stutter. It's just that rising, falling voice, holding me, drawing me in. "So many species are gone now," he murmurs. "My dad says the Protectorate tried to save them

154

but it was too late. The damage had been done."

I say nothing. According to my dad the planet was pretty screwed even before the Protectorate (or the Public Good Party, as it was known back then) came to power. But still they gave their business allies free reign to use up whatever resources were left. Now the well's dry and those old vampires are extinct too.

I climb onto the bank and collapse beside him. A feeble breeze crackles in the forest canopy; little waves ruffle the river. Eric nudges his knee against mine.

"Have you been back?" he murmurs. "To the library?"

"I have." I pick up a stone and pitch it into the water. Apple-green circles spread back towards us. "Eric, do you want to—?"

"No." He gives a determined shake of the head. "No, it's wrong. I won't tell my dad about the films, but I can't betray him. He's given me a new life here. A new chance…"

I take a breath. "Why did you need a new chance, Eric? What happened back in London?" When he turns away, hiding his face, I try a different tack. "That day in the library, it felt like you were trying to do something. To push back against something." This feels important, like a tipping point we won't be able to retreat from, like a door that won't ever close again. "Eric, what did you want to try?"

I move around so that I can see him. And there it is again – fear in his eyes, just like in the library.

"I'm sorry," I say quickly. "Hey, I'm really sorry. I didn't mean—"

He moves as if to go and I catch hold of his sleeve. The button snaps and suddenly a long bone-white scar is glinting in the sunlight. It runs from just above the crease of his wrist and disappears into his shirt. Eric spins around, wrenching back his wrist and masking the scar with his hand.

"It's not him," he blurts. "It isn't. I do it, it's me."

He presses his wrist to his chest. When I reach for him again, he shoves me away.

"But Eric, *why*?" I ask. "You know how dangerous this could be? If you ever got an infection…"

"It's dangerous, yes. And that…" He shakes his head. "That's exactly why."

NOW

13

I need to go back to the school. No matter what he said, I need to go back.

I sit under the willow tree where the river runs by, black and rain-lashed. Nothing like that Indian-summer day in October when a pale spider played through his fingers. Lightning carves the sky, and in the spaces between flashes I imagine a tall man on the far bank, catching two boys unawares. The shorter boy folds in on himself while the inspector's son stands defiant. As the vision fades, I wonder: did Dufresne know then, way back in November, that we were lying to him? Not just about Totes, but about who we were and what we meant to each other? I'm so sick with pain it's hard to think.

All I know is that I won't let Eric face this alone. So I'll go back, but first I need to warn Albert.

Cradling my shoulder, I stagger upright and start

stumbling through the trees. It's weird, but I really don't mind the storm. After all, it might be a long time before I feel the wind on my face again.

At the base of Chapel Hill there's an old-fashioned phone box. Another piece of easily monitored nostalgia. But they don't have the manpower to listen in on every line, and anyway I have to risk it. The booth's heavy door grumbles behind me as I pluck the phone from its cradle and press a shaking finger into the dialler. I picture my dad reaching for his canes, swinging himself up from the kitchen table. Maybe he thinks my mum is feeling sentimental. She does this to him sometimes, drunk-calling in the early hours, jabbering nonsense down the line, and he lets her.

"Yes?" he answers, his voice sharp. "Who's this?"

I wonder now how long I've spent in the woods. The phone lines are reconnected at five a.m., so...

"Gabe? Is that you?"

How does he know? Has he checked my room? Or are the Filth-Finders there already?

"Yeah, Dad. S'me."

"Where are you?"

"Dad, something's happened." I thumb the rain from my eyes. "Something bad. You need to get hold of Albert. Tell him they've got his tools." Strangely, this strikes me as funny; I can feel blades of hysteria sawing under my skin.

"It's important. He has to tell them I bullied him. Made him give them to me."

"Albert's here," my dad says.

For a second I rest my head against the back of the phone, trying to understand. "What?"

"He's been here for a while."

"But that doesn't make any—"

"Gabe, listen," my dad breaks in, "you need to tell me where you are. There might still be time."

"Time for what?" I laugh. "Dad, you don't understand. They've got Eric. They caught us at the school and it's all over and...*they've got Eric.*"

That's the first time I've admitted it out loud, and the truth almost takes my legs from under me. All at once, the old nightmares come back, howling with the gale: the blank walls of the Re-Pure camp, the constant hum of the electric-shock machines, the screams from the aversion therapy cells, hollow-eyed people shuffling out of chemical castration units, and the shadow of the gallows always waiting, if we sin again. I push the images away.

"You need to tell Albert he's in danger," I say. "He needs..."

What does he need? What can he do? Where can he go? He's as condemned now as me and Eric, and it's all my fault.

"Gabe, tell me where you are."

So I tell him. And then I slide down the wall of the booth and curl up into a ball. Lying there, I see I'm not the only one taking refuge from the storm. A black and white butterfly trembles on the glass.

"Are you a white admiral?" I reach out to touch it. "If I catch you, will they believe we were hunting butterflies tonight?"

The dark throbs around the little insect. Its wings seem to shudder with the lightning strikes. I watch as my reaching fingers drift towards its soft black fur.

"I'm telling you, this daft mutt is unteachable."

Eric shoots me the stink-eye. He scoops Totes into his lap and places his hands over the puppy's adoring eyes. Utterly baffled, Totes starts licking Eric's fingers while I'm instructed to hide the ball one last time. I sigh and get up from the lush March grass. When Totes is released he scampers around, examining every inch of riverbank, missing only the large round red rubber thing right at the water's edge.

"Hopeless," I say, falling down beside my boyfriend.

This earns me a prod in the cheek. "Hey. He's still learning."

"He's been learning for five months. I think it's time we admit, as realistic but loving parents, that our boy is going to have to get by on his looks."

Totes runs back, empty-mouthed, and launches himself into our laps. I scruff behind his ears and he immediately demands the same treatment bellywise.

"You could be right," Eric sighs. "And anyway, they'll be

putting him to sleep in a few hours. Won't they, boy? Yes, they will! They'll be putting you to sleep, you silly old sausage!"

I stare at him, and Eric stares right back.

"You know it's true," he says, shrugging. "I told you what my dad would do way back in November, so don't look all shocked and horrified. Anyway, it won't be so bad. Just a little pain and then no more Totes Sawyer-Dufresne, or is it Dufresne-Sawyer? Did we ever decide? Anyway, he's lucky really. There's no Re-Purification camp for doggies, is there? No there isn't. It'll be a bolt gun to the brain for you, boy. Uncle Marty doesn't like wasting bullets, does he?"

As I continue to stare at him, a bright red flower begins to bloom against the white of Eric's T-shirt.

"Monkey…" he murmurs, and glancing down at the bloodstain, plucks at the fabric.

Suddenly Totes is gone, and the sun has vanished, and a black and white butterfly is fluttering against the stain. When I reach out, a hand with red-painted nails smacks my hand aside.

It isn't Eric sitting beside me any more. It's Lana Heck.

"I told you," she laughs, "but you wouldn't listen. Now he's going to die for your hopes, Gabe. You're both going to die."

I gasp as my dad shakes me awake. Pushing past him, I stumble out of the booth and into the lane. Out across the rooftops, the first rush of dawn is lighting on fallen branches and broken tiles.

"They saw us," I say, turning back to my dad, shouting over the gale. "Did I tell you that? The caretaker and some Grey Jacket. I tried to pull him up onto the wall with me but my shoulder..." I go to grip the joint and hot wires of pain reignite, almost bringing me to my knees. "I told Eric that they'd never find out about us. Dad, I made him that promise."

My dad swings towards me on his canes. "Gabe."

"Did you warn Albert?" I say. "They'll link him to the tools, unless—"

"It's okay," says a voice from behind us. "That doesn't matter any more."

I turn to find a rain-slick Albert blinking up at me. His poor eye is still flamed red from the injury Patrick Gilligan inflicted. My dad looks between us.

"You have to go," he says. "Both of you. Now."

"Go where?" I give this bright, shivery laugh. "And Albert? Why does he even need to?"

Albert steps towards me. "Like you said, the bag. My tools."

"Say I stole them," I tell him. "Say I forced you to give them to me."

He shakes his head. "No, Gabe. I *need* to go. I have to."

"But why?"

He looks away. "My reasons don't matter."

"Albert, if this is because you want to help me, I'm

grateful. But the risk of running away? The trouble you'll be in if you're caught? It just isn't worth it."

"Not everything is about you, Gabe." There's no meanness in his words, just a heavy kind of exhaustion. "Why I'm coming with you isn't your business."

"But how do you even know what happened tonight? Why are you here, Albert?"

"I heard through our neighbour," he says. "He's a Grey Jacket. A real piece of shit, so of course him and my dad get on like a house on fire. He knocked on our door about an hour ago. Straight away Dad started bitching about being woken up at the crack of dawn, but our neighbour had big news. He'd been called in early. Two degens discovered breaking into the school, and the best part? One of them's Inspector Dufresne's son.

"Gabe, I'm so sorry about Eric." Albert digs into his pocket and brings out two official-looking scraps of paper. He pushes one of the papers into my hand. "Travel passes. I made one for all the Rebels."

I stare at him. "How?"

"My dad's a Protectorate administrator, and he's a spectacular idiot. Wasn't hard to steal a few slips."

Dad takes mine and examines it. "It's a pretty decent forgery."

"Genuine pass, forged stamp," Albert says. "The stamps aren't difficult to make. Look, I knew it was always possible that one of us might be suspected. I just wanted to help."

One of us. Is Albert talking about the Rebels generally? After all, associating with a degen is a crime that can get norms like Ben and Grace sent to a Re-Education Camp. Or is Albert saying he's gay? *Why I'm coming with you isn't your business.* Maybe I just need to respect that.

"But where are you suggesting we go?" I ask, turning to my dad.

"Ireland, to begin with," he says. "Then wherever you like. There are no anti-degen laws over there, no Re-Pure camps. You can be who you are."

"Jesus!" I take a few steps down the rain-hammered road, trying to process the idea. "I've never been out of this stupid town. How do we even begin to get to Ireland?"

"I have a plan."

"*You* have a plan?" My dad, who draws pictures and reads books all day, has a plan? I hold up my hands. "Okay, but before we hear this plan, I want to know, how do we get to Eric? Because there's no way I'm leaving without him."

"He'll be bailed," my dad says. "Or released without charge. He's the son of the chief inspector, Gabe. These people look after their own. I can talk to Eric later, send him on after you, but here's the thing: if they let him go then they'll need another scalp, and believe me, Dufresne will make it his personal mission to take yours."

"But why? I haven't done anything worse than Eric."

"Come on," my dad says, "you're not stupid. You know that's not how the world works."

"Here," Albert says, taking back the forged pass. "You're soaked through. I'll keep them safe for now."

Dad looks at him and asks, "Albert, can you give us a minute?"

Albert nods and heads off to find shelter across the street. All along that brightening road, houses groan in the gale as if they're about to be picked up and launched into the air.

I turn back towards the hill. Despite Dad's reassurances about the Protectorate looking after their own, I'm suddenly imagining Eric at the mercy of his father. Would the inspector really spare his son? Honestly, I've no idea. All I can think about are those words Eric said on the riverbank: *He'd watch his whole world burn for the Protectorate.*

"...I should have told you a long time ago," my dad says. "But you have to understand, Gabe, lives were at stake."

I've no idea what he's talking about. I haven't been listening.

"No," I say abruptly. "No, I can't do this. Dad, I can't."

"Gabe?"

"I can't leave him. No."

I start towards the church, no idea where I'm headed.

"Son, listen," Dad calls after me. "You can't save Eric. No one can."

I turn on him, my eyes stinging. "So that stuff you said about him being released, do you really believe that? Or was it just a lie to convince me to go? Be honest, Dad! Please."

He looks away. "I don't know what's going to happen. I don't think it's likely that they'll prosecute him – Dufresne's bosses won't want that kind of embarrassment – but as I told you, a head must roll." Propped on a single stick, he tries a smile. It doesn't take. "I don't want it to be your stubborn head, that's all."

"Dad." I rake trembling hands through my hair. "I can't just leave him. I can't."

"Son—"

"GABE!"

An engine roars across the hillside, an uncommon enough sound in Westwick to bring practically everyone to their door. Just where the lane turns, a motorbike and rider appear, dodging the storm-tossed debris that litters the road, making straight for the church. For us. I think about running, but to what and to where? It's too late anyway, and so I wave Albert back into the shadows.

The rider dismounts at the foot of the hill. Rain streaks his tinted visor and his flapping green jacket gleams, slick as sealskin in the morning light. The first thing I see when he removes his helmet is the smile.

"Gabriel Garcia Sawyer," Rakes shouts up to us. "You're under arrest."

166

14

I turn to my dad.

"The books. You need to get home—"

He shakes his head. "It's in hand. Don't worry."

"And Totes, he's still in the cabin. We were thinking Mrs Lebbon could take him."

Yes, we were thinking Mrs Lebbon could take our dog. Next year, when we graduated and had to say our final goodbyes. Funny how that seemed like the worst thing that could ever happen to us.

"I'll see to it," my dad says.

I want to tell him about the films, but I sense Rakes closing in. Even now I don't understand why I've kept this from him. Growing up, my dad and I have shared so many secrets – the banned books under our floorboards, our late-night conversations about what the world was like before the Outrage, my coming out to him when I was thirteen.

I don't know. I suppose the cardboard box wasn't only my secret. It belonged to all the Rebels.

Anyway, it's too late now.

Gloved hands pull my wrists behind my back. A second later, I hear the snap of handcuffs.

"There," the constable says, as if he's tucking me up in bed. "Nice and snug."

He spins me around and starts to march me down the hill. Forty or more people have come out to brave the dregs of the storm. One or two give me limp-wristed waves and wolf-whistles; a few spit on their own doorstep, which strikes me as a bit self-defeating.

"Hey!" my dad calls after us. "Just wait a minute."

Rakes doesn't wait. We pass his motorbike and stop at the kerb, as if we're standing for the bus. The constable still has hold of my wrists and, bringing me to a halt, jolts them upwards. My fingertips brush my shoulder blades and pain explodes along my spine. I scream, and there's something about the rawness of my voice; even the people mocking me cease their catcalls.

Dad hobbles around to face us. "Gabe? Gabe, are you okay?" I nod, panting through my teeth. "There's no need for that," he says to Rakes. "My son didn't try to resist."

Rakes's smile spreads like butter. "Oh yes, Mr Sawyer, he's very obliging, your son. Likes to please, doesn't he? The problem is *who* he's been pleasing."

"That's an allegation. I'd love to see your evidence."

Rakes checks his watch. "We have eyewitness testimony. That's enough to be going on with."

"And what's the charge? Under Section 17 of the Declaration of the Public Good, no minor can be arrested without a proper charge."

"That's right," the constable agrees. One hand still gripping my wrists, he takes out his baton and taps my dad very gently on the chest. "I heard you're a know-it-all little crip. Must run in the family. This boy of yours was giving me some lip only yesterday, and just look where it's landed him. You know," he turns to me, his mouth a hair's breadth from my ear, "I'm going to enjoy what comes next. Me and my oh-so-entertaining moustache."

"Whatever your history is with my son, none of that matters," Dad insists. "The Protectorate oaths and regulations clearly state—"

Rakes lets go of my cuffs and draws the baton over his shoulder.

"Dad, stop!" I shout. "The constable's right. He's got enough evidence to be suspicious and we need to respect that."

The words pour from my lips like poison. Rakes gives my dad a wink.

"What a clever little faggot you've raised."

Another rare sight for the neighbourhood: a shamrock-green Pansy Wagon rolling under the shadow of the church. The belching van pulls up in front of us and Sergeant Huxley flops out of the driver's side. Yawning into his fist, he helps the constable load me into the back of the transport. His boredom with the whole thing is almost as chilling as Rakes's delight.

"He needs a doctor," my dad says, as Rakes climbs up and takes the bench opposite me. "He's hurt."

"Your son will receive all the attention he deserves," Rakes assures him. "And you, Mr Sawyer, we've already instituted a Section 28 visit at your property. You can expect my colleagues to be waiting for you when you get home."

My dad stumbles forward. He can't reach my hands, so grips my ankle instead.

"It's going to be okay. I'll speak to your mother. There might be something he can do."

For once Rakes's smile falters. He pushes my dad away and slams the doors. Then he bangs his fist on the partition and Huxley starts the van.

"I wouldn't pin your hopes on that stepfather of yours," he says, swaying as the Pansy Wagon lumbers uphill. "The Deputy Protector for Agriculture won't want to dirty his hands when we have so much evidence. Bad luck for you the headmaster told that rancid old caretaker he had to stay over at the school last night in case of storm damage.

You know," he says, leaning forward, "some people believe storms are a punishment from God for sodomous behaviour. What do you think?"

"I think 'sodomous' isn't a word," I retort. "I also think cooling air, condensation and latent heat might explain storms better – but hey, I'm not a scientist."

Rakes chortles. "Still the smart-arse, though, even when it looks like you're about to pass out from that shoulder." The nub of his baton taps my torn muscle and I have to blink hard to stop the tears. "This is what I keep telling Huxley and the other boys – just because they're pansies, we shouldn't make the mistake of thinking they're feeble. In the end, that's what's so dangerous about degens. Not the threat that they'll contaminate our kids or the plain fact that what you do is the most disgusting filth imaginable. No, it's that you *persist*, like some virus growing in the dark."

I try not to bite. Instead I ask the only question worth asking.

"Is Eric okay?"

Rakes leans back in his seat and starts humming the Protectorate anthem. He's run through the tune eight times before the van comes to a halt. Huxley swings open the doors.

"Home sweet home," says Rakes.

The storm has passed and I'm thrown into a monochrome

world. Watery clouds hang in the washed-out pre-dawn sky while the cobbled stones of the yard shine almost black. I've never seen the Filth-Finders' headquarters before. It's a dumpy Victorian building, crenellated like a castle. A couple of motorbikes and a few clapped-out cars stand idle in the yard. I'm taken through a side door and shoved along a narrow corridor, down a spiral stairway and into an icebox of a shower room.

"Get undressed," Huxley grunts.

He unlocks my cuffs and a little warmth creeps back into my hands. I glance between the constable and the sergeant.

"Why so shy?" asks Rakes. "I thought you'd enjoy two burly blokes watching you shower." He turns to Huxley for an approving grin but receives only a yawn.

I massage my wrists and start unlacing my boots, every movement twisting the invisible knife in my shoulder. There's no hook or bench in the room. Huxley comes forward with a plastic bag and I drop my clothes into it. Naked, my feet slap against the dead chill of the stone floor. There's no curtain, no screen. I have this weird flash of me in the river, Eric watching as I show off my body under the ferocious sun. Now all I want to do is hide.

I turn a tap on the wall. A blaze of freezing water shrieks against my skin and I gasp as blood from my injured leg pinks the tiles.

"I think the doc's somewhere upstairs," says Huxley. "Probably oughta take a look at him."

My back turned, I hear Rakes march away. I lift my knee and clean the dirt out of the cut as best I can. Suddenly the water stops and a rough towel lands on my good shoulder. I dry off and cinch the towel around my waist.

"Take it off," Huxley orders.

Naked again, I'm told to close my eyes. An odourless powder sprays against my body and I'm instructed to turn around. I know what's happening. It's the same as that scene from *The Shawshank Redemption* – one of the librarian's movies – in which the imprisoned hero is doused with insecticide powder. I remember us laughing because the main character shared Eric's surname.

"If only I'd seen this film before I met you, I might have known how to spell Dufresne."

"Silly Monkey."

Other films flip through my head as I dress in the grey overalls Huxley hands me. *X-Men*: a story about superheroes who are persecuted and outlawed for their difference. *Cool Hand Luke*: the tale of a defiant prisoner brutalized by his jailors. Most of all, I think about *Love, Simon*. The first of the films, set in that impossible world in which a boy loved a boy and that love could be celebrated.

Guided by Huxley, I drag myself back up the staircase. Although we don't pass anyone, there's a kind of weight to the silence of this building, as if a hundred hearts have been stilled. Up another two flights, past a dozen iron doors, my bare feet sticking to the filth that coats the slabbed floor, and we arrive at number seventy-three. My cell.

Rakes is waiting inside with this bald guy in a white coat. I'm told to undress again.

"What a bloody waste," the doctor says after his examination. "Good breeding stock if he weren't a perv. Anyway, you can't interview him yet."

Back in my overalls, I sit on the edge of a thin, hard mattress.

"He's suffering from exhaustion and exposure. He'll need antibiotics for the knee and pain relief for the shoulder."

"No pain relief," Rakes mutters. "Orders from the boss."

The doctor shrugs and rifles through his bag. It's weird, but suddenly everything feels very distant, like I'm watching a movie version of my own life. I can understand my pain but I don't really feel it. When a needle enters my arm I don't even blink.

The doctor gives me a long look. "Might be a day or two before you can go to work on him. He's clearly in a state of shock."

Rakes crouches down so that he's eye level with me.

"Doesn't matter. The chief is still trying to get his faggot son to talk."

The constable slides my glasses off my nose, folds the arms and places them in the top pocket of his tunic. My cell all but disappears. Only Rakes's smile persists.

"Once we've got Eric's story? Well, let's just say the shocks have only just begun."

15

It was dark and I didn't have my glasses, so I couldn't see the names scratched into the walls. But I could feel them. My fingertips spelled out *Micah* and *Sam*, *Davey* and *George*, *Christine* and *Lola*, maybe a hundred more. Sometimes there were words like *for ever* and *remember*, sometimes just simple, jagged hearts.

I covered my face with my hands and laid back on my prison cot. It was as if someone has torn a library of love stories to pieces and arranged random fragments on the wall. Who were these people? Where are they now?

There are only two answers to that question: they're either rotting in the ground or else they're wearing the pink cross. Either way, they're dead.

When I first found the names, I started to blunder around the cell, looking for something I could use as a tool. The idea of scratching *Eric* and *Gabe* into the wall seemed like the most important thing in the world. I investigated the stone room inch by inch, and when I finally had to admit there wasn't anything I could use, I huddled myself into a corner and cried like a little kid. It was only hours later the thought hit me: what persistence and ingenuity went into carving those names. What love. Hugging my knees to my chin, I wiped my eyes and smiled.

Time passes. Sometimes I hear other prisoners whispering to each other, sometimes even singing. At first a few of them try to talk to me. They tap on my wall and murmur through the air vents.

"Hey, Number Seventy-three, how's it going?"

"You awake, Seventy-three? What's your name? Look, I know how you must be feeling, but sometimes it helps to talk."

I don't answer them. I don't know why.

Food is slopped through a hatch at the bottom of the door. I crawl over to it. I try to eat. Can't. The stuff looks grey, rancid, and I'm glad I can't see it properly. But after a while, my stomach howls and I have to choke down a little. It doesn't taste bad exactly. It doesn't taste of anything at all.

Thoughts come and go. Some linger and circle back around, others stab out of the dark and vanish in a moment. Will Mum convince the Farmer to help me, or is Rakes right about the useless bastard not wanting to get his hands dirty? I'd put my chances at a slim one per cent.

I wonder about my dad. About how he stood up to Rakes. I've never seen that side of him before. It makes me curious about the plan he had to get me and Albert to Ireland. Curled up on my cot, I can't help but laugh. Knowing Dad, it would have been some crazy romantic scheme right out of Shakespeare or Alexandre Dumas. I hope my dad's okay. I hope they didn't find his books. I hope he rescued Totes from the cabin.

I hope.

I wonder about Albert. Those long-ago nights when he'd sleep over – best friends lying top to tail, waggling each other's feet and telling spooky stories in the dark – they seem somehow more vivid now, more precious anyway. Something has shifted – or is shifting – in how I see Albert, but I suppose I'll never get to find out what was really going on with him. I just hope he made it out of Westwick.

I hope.

I wonder about them all. Ben and Grace and June and Liz. I hate the idea that we might have contaminated them by association; that maybe even Miss Calloway could be dragged into this because she taught me and Eric. Lying here, there doesn't seem any end to the shock waves of our discovery.

Most of all I wonder about Eric. You were right, Scarecrow. Right about my big mouth and my risk-taking. I did this to us. Now all I want is for you to be okay. I want you to survive this. And I want you to forget me. Maybe that's the only way you *will* survive. But before you forget, please know that I'm sorry. Not just about the disc, but for how I put you on the spot that first day in the library. The world changed for us then and now it's changing again. I hope you'll still be standing when the change is through, and that those days of hurting yourself won't ever come back.

I hope.

I trace names on the wall. I heal. The antibiotic the doctor gave me seems to be working, which is pretty much a miracle. The skin on my leg is knitting together and my shoulder feels better too. During all this, I have no idea how much time passes. In the windowless cell, my internal clock is busted. A world without sight and time can be scary at first, but it's amazing what you can get used to, and in prison you're never completely alone. You have your thoughts and your fears, and then there are the visitors.

Insects pootle across my thin blanket. Knowing what Eric might say, I resist the urge to swat them. Instead I cup them carefully into my palm and usher them under the door. Sometimes they escape, sometimes I hear a guard's boot crack against their carapace. At first this almost overwhelms me, then I figure that at least I gave them a little more time, and maybe that's the best any of us can hope for – a moment to breathe freely before we're crushed.

Eventually it gets to the stage where I think they've forgotten me. Perhaps that's how I'll be dealt with, like *The Man in the Iron Mask* or Edmond Dantès in *The Count of Monte Cristo*: a prisoner that's never tried, an embarrassment who's simply left to rot.

I'm picking out the names on the wall one day when the door opens and hands grapple me to my feet.

"Rise and shine, Gabriel!"

Rakes's moustache bristles against my cheek. It's the first time I've seen him since the morning of the storm.

"Eric," I croak. "Is he okay?"

"Still singing that old tune?" he grunts. "You'll find out soon enough."

I'm thrown through the door and into the corridor. As I pass other cells, a couple of starved faces appear at their food hatches. The prisoners who tried to comfort me when I first arrived here.

"Good luck, son," one calls. "You stay strong now."

Boots lash out at them. Then we're plunging down the stairs. Here I'm virtually held up, my laceless prison shoes skimming the steps. We seem to be heading into the bowels of the building, below even the shower stall where I was first taken. Finally we arrive at a room that feels not much larger than my cell and I'm dumped into a chair behind a desk.

Rakes looms over me. "Get your fucking hands out of your sleeves."

Two figures sit opposite: Rakes and a taller, thinner Green Jacket. Definitely not Huxley. The door to the interrogation chamber slams shut. I squint, hear the shuffling of papers. Rakes clears his throat.

"Before we begin, Mr Sawyer, I'm just curious – why have you never had a girlfriend?"

The question seems so ridiculous I laugh.

"Oh, is that funny?" Rakes asks. "Because, you see, we've been conducting some pretty thorough interviews while you've been recuperating, and it seems that you're quite the fantasy pin-up among the girls at Mosley Grammar. I can understand that. You're a good-looking boy. Yet not a single snog behind the bike sheds. Would you care to explain?"

I lay my hands flat on the desk to stop them shaking. "I just never—"

"Speak up!"

I swallow. "No one ever asked me."

"But I have three testimonies here from young ladies who say that you rejected them."

"It...it wasn't like that."

"So you're saying these girls are lying? Very well. I can easily send the Grey Jackets round to interrogate them more thoroughly, if you catch my meaning?"

"I wasn't ready," I say. "My studies. I wanted to concentrate."

"Oh, Gabriel, I think we all know what you wanted to concentrate on."

Rakes stands up and a moment later a collection of metal clatters across the desk.

"Mr Heck's tools. Where is Albert Heck?"

I grip the underside of the desk. Albert got away. He got away! I fight to suppress a smile.

"I don't know how you expect me to answer that," I say. "I've been here for days. Albert hasn't exactly been popping round for tea and cake every afternoon."

The constable lunges across the desk, but something stops him. Anyway, I'm not thinking about Rakes any more. I've suddenly realized that the tools are old evidence. The Green Jackets wouldn't lead with them if they had something better, which means Eric hasn't told them about the librarian's movies.

I'm vaguely aware of the tools being collected up and swept into a bag. Then the other officer mutters something and Rakes stands and turns sharply out of the room. The door clangs behind him, the reverberation echoing into stillness. I fold my hands under my armpits and wait. Somewhere a tap drips. Somewhere a man cries. My heart drums out the seconds.

And then the figure sitting opposite me moves. I jolt back in my chair. I'd almost forgotten he was there. He reaches out and this fuzzy shape is pushed across the desk towards me. I bend my head and, seeing what it is, almost sob. Slowly, reverently, like I'm handling a sacred object, I pick up my glasses and hook them over my ears. In the dark of my cell, I often wondered whether I'd ever see properly again.

The sudden sharpness of the single electric bulb is like a thousand suns. My eyes dazzle and the room comes to me in snatches: Uncle Marty's smile glimmering behind a frame on the wall; a bluebottle droning around the gap under the door; a slim folder on the table next to the little black book of *Protectorate Oaths and Regulations*.

Finally my gaze settles on the thin, hawk-nosed man.

"Hello, Gabriel," says Inspector Dufresne.

I wet my lips, take a breath. "Is Eric—?"

The chief of the Green Jackets sits perfectly still. "My son is very well, thank you."

I nod. "Sir, you have to understand—"

"Eric has come to his senses," the inspector says. "Now it's time for you to come to yours."

He slides the folder across the desk and opens the cover. At first, the pure white of the paper is too bright. I can't read the closely-typed words.

"I'm sorry," I say. "My eyes."

"Of course," he replies. "Stupid of me."

He rounds the desk and, leaning over me, places a gloved hand on my shoulder. The leather creaks as he grips.

"This is a legal document that requires your signature."

"What does it say?"

"The truth."

"What truth?"

"About what happened between you and Eric. About what you did to him."

"What I did to him? I'm sorry, I don't understand."

"It's very simple. You see, we have the eyewitness testimony of Mr Harold Pinborough, the school caretaker, and of Constable Arthur Hutchison of the Grey Jackets. We also have the testimonies of several teachers and students saying that, from his very first day, you took an unnatural interest in Eric. That you pestered and stalked him. Now, I would prefer that this case does not come to trial; that you take responsibility for your degenerate crime and confess so that Eric isn't made to testify in open court. I think you owe him that. It might also be a blessing for your poor father."

A shaft of light in this growing darkness. *My poor father.* That means they found nothing during the Section 28 visit. Dad's in the clear.

"And if you could help us in our hunt for Albert Heck—"

"Albert didn't do anything," I cut in. "I bullied him, made him give me the tools."

"Oh, Gabriel, it's a noble effort, but we've done our

homework. We know you've been close friends for years; you would never harm Albert Heck. The fact he's disappeared is also indicative of his guilt in aiding and abetting a known degenerate. But, as I say, if you help us locate him, then I might put in a good word for you with the warden of whichever Re-Pure camp you end up in. I think that's more than fair, don't you? Under the circumstances."

"What circumstances?" I shake my head. "Please, I don't understand. What am I being charged with?"

His grip tightens and I feel the ghost of the old pain in my shoulder.

"Come on now, you know exactly what you did. Eric's told us the whole story."

"I didn't do *anything*. Mr Dufresne, I care about Eric. Very much. I'm his friend."

"No. A friend doesn't do what you did to my boy."

Dufresne releases my arm and moves to the door. A moment later, it's opened and Rakes and three other men crowd in behind him.

"It's all in the folder," Dufresne says. "Eric's sworn testimony. And before this day is out, you *will* sign a confession to the crime you committed."

"What crime?" I begin to stand. "That we're degens?"

"My son *isn't* a degen," Dufresne barks. "That wasn't what the witnesses saw. It isn't what Eric testifies."

"Then what's he said?"

The inspector gives me a final lingering look.

"That you forced yourself on him that night in the school. Now, gentlemen," he turns to the other officers, "get me my confession."

THEN

OCTOBER - SIX MONTHS AGO

There's been a bomb scare, so we're all out on the football pitch, soaking up some Halloween rays. No one's particularly spooked, either by the day itself or by the threat that we might theoretically be blown to bits. First, I guess because when it's twenty degrees in the shade it's difficult to feel much of a creepy chill; and second? Well, the Protectorate invent a bomb scare every couple of months, just to keep everyone terrified of the Resistance, so after a while they lose their edge.

I'm standing in this loose circle with June and Liz and the rest of the guys. They've been pestering me for the past fortnight about what happened after I went off with Eric that Sunday. I've been maintaining an air of mystery, mainly to annoy June, but also because I'm not really sure how to answer their questions. What *is* going on with me and Eric?

I look over to the penalty line. He's standing there by himself, biting his fingernails. Catching my eye, he pulls his hand away and shoots me this quick, fluttery smile. I smile back, and my eyes go to his sleeve. The hiding place for that bright white scar.

Eric and I have been hanging out together after school almost every day. Sometimes we talk – about his love of nature, about my swimming, anything and everything, really – but mostly we just take these long walks, comfortable as we can be in our silences. One thing he won't talk about is why he hurts himself, though I continue to wonder. He's a degen, like me, but he's also his father's son, fed on all the lies about what he is – about what *we* are. It isn't hard to make the connection with his scars, but something tells me the reason runs deeper than self-hatred. Whatever it is, I want to help him. I've wanted to help him ever since that afternoon in the library when I realized we were the same. Anyway, I made him promise that, if he ever feels like doing it again, he'll tell me.

I go on at him about dangers of infection, as if he's a three year old who's never had the talk: infection kills! Report all injuries! For once, this isn't propaganda bullshit designed to terrify us. Way back before the Outrage, the big pharmaceutical companies stopped developing new antibiotics, because there wasn't any money in it. Result: we now live in a world where a simple scratch can kill you in hours. Anyway, Eric doesn't seem to care. As he said at the riverbank, it's *because* it's dangerous that he does it.

I'm pretty sure the library would once have held at least some of the answers to what's going on with him, but now subjects like this are taboo and no one talks about them. Those with mental illness are seen as a weak link in the Protectorate and are quietly sent away to Wellbeing camps. Some come back "cured", or they don't come back at all, just like the "incurable" degens sent to Re-Pure. But in the end, the library reveals a kind of answer. I'm browsing through the cardboard box one evening (alone, because Eric's still refusing to come back here) when a title catches my eye: *Girl, Interrupted*.

It's a film about a young woman who suffers a mental breakdown. She's taken to a psychiatric hospital where she makes friends with some of the other patients. It's a sad, thoughtful movie, and a huge eye-opener. A character in the film called Daisy cuts herself, and it's revealed that the reason is all tied up with the abuse she suffered at the hands of her father. My stomach twists during these scenes. Could something similar have happened to Eric?

Finally the headmaster announces the bomb scare is a false alarm (No, really?) and, as it's the end of the day, he decides to dismiss us. I turn back to the circle. Ben is leaning on his hockey stick, reliving last night's victorious match against Givesby Grammar. June tries to stifle a yawn while Liz, Grace and Albert listen politely. At the sound of the bell, Ben starts pulling people into hugs.

"What have I told you, Dempsey?" June says. "You are rationed to one Juniper hug per week."

"But I won't see any of you until Monday," Ben pouts. "So?"

June rolls her eyes and holds out her arms. "Fine."

I stand back and watch them. I haven't pursued my idea of forming a film club yet. I suppose I don't want to involve other people if Eric can't be a part of it, which makes me a selfish git, I know.

They all start trailing off until only June remains. "Okay," she sighs, heading over to me. "So I guess we're doing this. What's going on with you?"

"Huh?"

"Don't play dumb. I'm worried about you. I know that look."

"What look?"

"That 'idiot-in-lust' look. You tend to drool."

"I do not drool."

"It's an unconscious thing. But seriously, what's going on with you and Dufresne?"

"Nothing..." June gives me a very June look, and I instantly cave. "Okay, we've talked. And yes, he's cute and funny and infuriating and messed up, and I'm pretty sure he's on our team."

She holds up her hand for a sarcastic high five. "Go team!"

"But we haven't…"

"Oh dear Lord." She takes my head in her hands and waggles it left and right. "You're so adorable it would make a Botticelli cherub puke. Okay, so I'm not going to ask you to submit to the benign dictatorship of Juniper, and you know I could do that if I wanted."

I nod. This isn't even a joke. June has the power.

"So you may continue this ridiculous infatuation. But, Gabe, never forget who he is, okay?" Her incredible green eyes cut across to the penalty line. "Cute can be dangerous."

She flicks the end of my nose and joins the herd swarming out of the gate. Really, I don't need my oldest friend to tell me what I'm risking with this whole Eric thing… Except maybe I do.

Picking up my bag, I head on over. "Hey."

"Hey," he says, smiling.

Apart from the caretaker, Mr Pinborough, lurking impatiently with his ring of jailhouse keys, we're pretty much the only ones left on the field. Pinborough hacks out a cough and watches us from under crusty lids as we pass.

"So I've got a surprise for you," I tell him.

Eric side-eyes me with this weird mixture of happiness and apprehension.

"Okay, it's nothing…" I try out half a dozen conclusions

to that sentence: *Sexual? Degenerate? Mind-blowingly illegal?*
In the end I settle for: "We're just mates, right?"

Mates, sure. Mates who hug each other on riverbanks.

He nods.

"Only, do you need to be home for tea or anything?"
I ask.

"Nope. My dad's staying late at the Oxford HQ."

"Good. Good," I stumble on, "to be busy, I mean. Busy is
good."

"You looked busy yourself today," he says, and there's
this strange half smile on his lips. "Chatting to Evie Glover?
Is it true that she's asked you to the Christmas dance?"

"She has."

"And?"

I arch an eyebrow. "Why, Eric Dufresne, anyone would
think you're jealous." A blush of stellar intensity erupts
across his cheeks. "Anyway, I told her that I have too much
homework, but that I was very flattered."

"Good." He smiles again, and his blush is a keeper.

En route to Hamilton Woods, we swing by Godfrey's and
pick up a couple of sausage rolls. Then we hit the forest. This
time we cross the river by the yellow stepping stones and trek
up towards the hill that overlooks Westwick. The countryside
round here is wild and overgrown. With most of the big
agricultural machinery broken down or commandeered by
the government, no one's farmed it in decades.

Hacking our way through the undergrowth, we're quiet for a while. Then suddenly Eric touches my elbow.

"I'm sorry," he says. "All this time, I don't think I ever apologized."

I turn to him. "For what?"

"For what my dad said to your dad in church that day. About his disability. How he said it was just..."

"Okay." I reach out and pick a bit of stray bramble from his shirt. "But isn't that just how people talk to disabled people?"

"It is, yes. But it shouldn't be."

I grin. It's a tiny admission that feels like a crack in the cage: Eric beginning to question the norms of the Protectorate, a little of the boldness of that first day in the library coming back, maybe?

"So what actually happened to your dad?" he asks. "Unless you don't want to talk about it?"

"It's cool. It happened when he was little. He fell off a platform at a train station and shattered both his legs. He was lucky, though. No infection."

The "i" word. Eric nods and looks away. "That's awful. I'm sorry."

"You're very apologetic today," I say, bumping his shoulder.

"Am I? My dad says apologies should only be offered if there's some advantage to be gained from them."

I puff out my cheeks. "But here's the thing, Eric – your dad can be a *bit* of a dick."

He blinks at me, then bursts out laughing.

We walk on, higher and higher, until the town spreads out like a model village below – the bilging smokestacks of the factories, threads of broken roads, and over in the east, the blackened smudge of the Old Town square where the library and its secrets lie hidden. I steal a glance at Eric and see he's looking in the same direction. I don't say anything and we move on, a hand brushing a hand as the path forces us closer together. At first we flinch at the contact, and then we don't.

"Tell me something new you thought today," I ask him.

"Pardon?"

I keep my eyes on the bracken. "I've decided this is my new obsession – Eric Dufresne's Thought for the Day. It doesn't have to be deep or meaningful, just something you've never thought before. Like, I think I prefer coffee to tea, or, why are Mr Joyce's suits always that absolutely perfect shade of turd brown?"

"Gabe, you are very weird."

"It's been said."

Insects drone around us, dipping to the dandelions that now bloom into late October.

"I'm happy," Eric says at last.

On impulse, I take his hand and swing him in a wide circle. He doesn't pull away.

"Happy can't be your original thought," I laugh. "You must have been happy before."

"No." He pulls me to a stop. "Not for a long time anyway."

I sense it: this moment is as fragile as the rain-starved grass under our feet. If I bend it too much it will break, just like it did in the library. Still holding his hand, I pull him to the lip of the hill. Here the ground gives way sharply, plunging down to the valley below. In the hazy distance, the wavering finger of a church steeple points to the horizon.

"Come on."

Behind us an immense tree clings to the hillside. This should really be the other way around, Eric being a head taller, but I swing myself up onto the lowest branch of the oak and reach down for him. His face takes my breath away. Upturned and laughing and heart-shaped and perfect. I grip his forearms and hoist him onto the bough. Then we're climbing again, scaling the tree, branch to branch, until we find ourselves impossibly high.

Drifting above the valley, I hug the trunk and loop my arm around him.

"Your treat," I announce. "Not bad, eh?"

I can feel the thud of his heart. He goes to speak and stops. Then he turns to me and very slowly places his hand against mine.

"It's beautiful, Monkey."

"Monkey?"

He shrugs. "You're a pretty good climber."

Everything's still for a while, just the shush of the wind and the creak of our tree. Then, in a single burst, a flock of birds cannon out of the canopy below us – a brilliant green fusillade that passes within touching distance. I gasp and Eric's head snaps up. He's hooting as his hands grip my waist.

"We should stay up here for ever," I say excitedly. "Build a treehouse, just you and me."

He smiles broadly. "But I suppose we'd have to go down eventually."

"Yeah? To do what?"

"Everything. One day we'd have to get jobs so we could pay our treehouse rent to our squirrel landlords. And anyway, when we get married and have our own families, then we'd have to get our own individual treehouses. But we'd stay neighbours, right?"

He sees my face and his smile falls.

"You want those things?" I ask.

"Don't you?" He dips his head. "Traditions have meaning, Gabe. They give us security. If you don't... Well, what do you want?"

The answer spills out of me before I give it any thought. "I think I want to make films." We sit in silence for a while. Eventually I nudge his shoulder. "We better go down before it gets too dark."

There's this dull ache in my stomach as we descend. I know why it's there but knowing doesn't help. By the time we reach the ground, twilight has crept in and deepened the creases of the valley. Near the foot of the hill, a forgotten scarecrow nods in the breeze.

I'm starting back down the track when Eric calls out to me.

"Gabe? Will you please wait a minute? I need…I just need you to—"

"Eric," I begin, "I want to go home."

"Please. I need you to see."

So I turn, and in the darkness, I see Eric Dufresne. Really *see* him.

And I can barely speak.

He has unbuttoned his shirt and pulled it away from his chest. His torso quivers, a mesh of white streaks stark in the dying light. He keeps eye contact for as long as he can. Then, all at once, he doubles over and clutches the jags and spirals that mark his skin. I run to him, hold him tight, tell him it'll be okay, that I'm here, that I'll help him. His body shudders against me.

"Eric, why?"

He pulls free and starts to rebutton his shirt. Once he's covered again, he reaches for my hand and guides me back to the edge of the hill.

"I'm like him," he says, nodding to the scarecrow far

below. "Stitched together from a hundred broken bits."

I speak his name and wait until he looks at me. "Eric, don't you know? We're all broken here."

And then I kiss him.

He hesitates at first, closes his eyes, and kisses me back. But I keep my eyes open. Because I want to see him. I want to see him, always.

NOW

16

He told them I forced myself on him.

As soon as I hear it, I bend double and bunch my fists into my stomach. I try to breathe, but the stale air of the interrogation room keeps catching in my throat. It feels as if I'm standing on a frozen lake and the ice is cracking all around me. Part of me doesn't mind. Part of me wants it to break so I can drown in the numbing blackness below.

I'm distantly aware of Inspector Dufresne leaving the cell while Rakes and the other Filth-Finders pile in. The constable takes the seat opposite, the others block the door. Rakes is speaking but his words are a blur.

Piece by piece, I begin to drag myself out of the dark: *He was scared. Confused. Brainwashed. That's why you've been locked up all this time. Not because they wanted you fit for interrogation but because they needed time to work on him.*

My imagination goes to places I don't want to follow. Eric in his father's study, abandoned and alone. What threats were made? What promises? *Say it, Eric, just say it and we'll do what we can for Gabriel Sawyer*. It's not like this is anything new. The accusation has been a get-out-of-jail-free card for degens before. As long as you're the first to use it then a Re-Pure camp isn't inevitable. Of course you'll always be treated with suspicion in the future, but hey, at least you get to keep two fully functioning testicles.

I take a breath. I wanted Eric to survive. Maybe this was the only way.

Except you would never have accused him, would you?

It's a mean, ugly voice and I try to ignore it.

"Well, now." Rakes grins. "Are we back in the room, Mr Sawyer?"

The others laugh.

"Excellent." He snaps his fingers and one of the guards comes forward with a small black pouch. "Now, one thing about this case still puzzles us. It's a pretty small detail next to the charge you're facing, but I don't like loose ends. So, I wonder, can you please explain this?"

He unzips the pouch and takes out a silver disc, spearing his finger through the hole.

"*Love, Simon*," he sniffs. "It was found in the bag Eric was carrying. *Your* bag. We've dug out some old tech and managed to play it. A revolting degen film from before the

Outrage. So tell me, where did this come from and what is its relevance to the case?"

I shrug. "Ask Eric."

"Eric, Eric, Eric." Rakes spins the disc on his finger. "Such a one-track mind. Eric won't tell us. But I'll let *you* in on a little secret." He leans over the desk, that pathetic moustache pearled with sweat. "I heard he was a pretty tough nut to crack, your sweetheart, and that when he did it was only for a couple of seconds. Enough to get his signature on that confession you're about to sign, then he shut right up again.

"So fair's fair, Gabe, tell me about the disc."

I lay my hands flat on the desk and stare right back at him. They've been interrogating Eric for days and that one devastating lie is the only thing he's given them. That's something, right?

"Okay," Rakes sighs, replacing the film in the pouch, "we'll return to this matter later. Right now, we have bigger fish to fry." He stretches back in his chair and removes the baton from his belt. He taps the weapon against my unsigned confession and the table begins to vibrate. "Look, we all know what's really going on here – the chief's son accused you to save his own skin. He's a bloody pansy. I know it, the boys here know it, even the chief knows it, deep down. That's why Eric never joined the Young Lions, right? But here's the thing – Dufresne still needs this signature, and believe me, he's going to get it."

Oh, I know he is, constable. Don't worry, I'm going to sign. If I refuse then there'll be a trial and Eric will be dragged through the court and made to testify. I know what that would do to him. So, yes, I'll play the monster; I'll claim he was my victim and I'll save him, both from the Re-Pure camps and from any fresh scars. But even if it's just for a few sweet moments, I'm not going to make this easy for you.

"If you sign," says Rakes, "you'll be sent straight to an enforcement court for sentencing, then on to one of the camps. If by the end of your treatment there the doctors agree you're cured, well then, you can come back to that shack you call a home. Under lifetime supervision, of course. And you'll have to wear the pink cross. And be spat at and humiliated every single day of your life. But believe me, it beats the alternative."

"You mean a noose and a pit?"

"Now, now," his forever smile broadens. "No one's ever proved those rumours. If you're not cured, it's imprisonment for life."

"Mr Rakes?" I say.

His smile is hideous. "Gabriel?"

I pick up the pen and twirl it through my fingers.

"I want you to know one thing before I sign this fairy-tale bullshit – there is absolutely *nothing* wrong in what me and Eric did. *Nothing* wrong in what the caretaker and the

Grey Jacket saw. I was holding the boy I love and I was kissing him, that's all. I would *never* hurt him, not ever. Because I *love* him—"

The table cracks into my ribs, punching the air out of my lungs. A second later I see the oil-black shimmer of Rakes's baton descend, and a pain too huge to understand shrieks inside my skull. Then, for a long while, I don't see or hear or feel anything. Except that's not quite right. There's this acid-green glare spreading across my mind and a chainsaw buzz in my ears. When my vision clears, all I can see is the space where floor meets wall.

"You dirty...*dirty*..." Rakes pants.

One eye is blurry, the other clear. I straighten my glasses and rise shakily to my feet. My jaw clicks when I speak.

"Go easy," I wheeze, "or I won't be able to sign anything."

I drag myself back into the chair and see that Rakes has lost his grin.

"If you don't say you attacked him, he'll wind up in a camp too." The constable uncurls his fingers from the baton and I notice a few flecks of red on the shaft. "You'll ruin him, and after what happened with his mother and *her* crime? The Dufresnes survived that shame by the skin of their teeth. A Green Jacket chief who couldn't even control his own wife? But the Protectorate gave him this second chance, and what d'you know? His own son turns out to be a disgusting little degen."

I pick up the pen again. My hand shakes so badly I have to grip my wrist to steady it. I look up. Rakes is wetting his lips. The others stand watch.

I love you, Eric. And I think you love me, though you never once said it back. Now you'll never get the chance.

"Green Jackets of the Protectorate Investigations," I laugh and curl my lip. "You protect *nothing*." I flick the point of the pen towards the framed photograph of Uncle Marty on the wall. "Have any of you ever even seen him? Our great Lord Protector? No, but you still lap up his lies. Stale, stupid ideas that were old and useless even before the Outrage. And where have they led us? To kids my age who are worked until they look like old men. To little kids running around, spitting hate at each other. To people like Eric Dufresne, who are taught to despise all the beautiful things that make them who they are. That's the evil you protect. So..."

I scratch out my name on the page.

"Fuck you."

Rakes grabs the paper and starts to get up. The others draw their batons.

"Oh yeah," I say, looking at each of them in turn, "and one more thing. I'm *not* a degen. I am GAY."

17

After a few days, they fit the metal mask.

It's hot and heavy and has slits for my eyes and a gag mechanism that holds my mouth shut. At first, I can barely breathe inside it, but it's amazing what you can get used to. After a week or so, I can even sleep in it. One thing's hard to bear, though: the mask has taken away a tiny bit of solace that I'd only just discovered. When they first dragged me back, broken and bleeding, from the interrogation cell, I crawled into a corner and, in the dark, examined each of my injuries. I knew that any of these could kill me, and the idea made me laugh, though I can't remember why. That was when I heard the voices calling to me through the vents.

"Hey kid, you all right?"

"Jesus, Harry, what are you even saying? Obviously he's not all right."

"Okay, Seb. I was only asking."

"Why don't you both shut up...? Son, can you hear me?"

I laid my head down by the vent and made some kind of harsh animal sound.

"*Shhh*," said the man, "*shhh*. Just lie still and try to count your heartbeats. See, they're steadying already, aren't they? That's it. That's it. You're going to be all right. We're all going off to their shitty camp together, and we'll all look out for each other once we're there, won't we?"

Seb and Harry agreed:

"That's right."

"We will."

"We'll get through it all, together," the man insisted. "Now, you just lie still and close your eyes."

I didn't have the energy to pull myself onto my cot and so, tucking my knees up to my chin, I listened as the man in the next cell started to sing. It was a hymn, one I'd heard in church many times. I've never believed in God, I still don't, but right then? I don't know. Maybe it was just the soul in that sweet voice that comforted me.

"*Abide with me, fast falls the eventide*
the darkness deepens, Lord with me abide
When other helpers fail and comforts flee
Help of the helpless, O abide with me."

This has been the hardest change – in those days when I was healing, I began to speak with my brothers through the vents. That's how I think of them: brothers. Of course I've always felt especially close to June and Liz because of who we are, but when you're being tortured for that identity and there are others being tortured with you, the bond between you grows fast and strong. I heard all their stories and I told them mine.

Maybe that's why the Green Jackets brought the mask. Because they started to suspect I had this one scrap of comfort. Well, they've taken it from me now. When I listen to Mark singing his hymns and the others whispering through the vents, I can't talk back any more.

Days pass like sand through my fingers. I lie on my cot, I heal, and I replay the librarian's movies in my mind, projecting images on the damp, dripping walls. The world they once opened up to me feels further away than ever, a fantasy land that can't possibly have ever been real. I picture Eric in those last moments before we were discovered, telling me that, by showing him who he was, I'd saved him, and how one day I would make films that would help others in the same way.

Childish dreams. I won't even get to watch another film, let alone make my own. Except, no, that isn't quite right. If the rumours are true, I'll soon see lots of movies – in the camps, horrific films are used alongside electrical torture as part of the aversion therapy.

I try not to dwell on the future. Mostly I just think of Eric. Does he think of me? Is he sorry for what he said? I don't want him to be. If it meant saving himself, I'm glad he said it. But part of me is starting to wonder what my life would've been like if I'd never met Eric Dufresne. If maybe I'd accepted my mum's offer and gone to live with her and the Farmer.

But it was worth it, wasn't it? To have someone like that to hold, even for a little time?

It was. I know it was. Because even here, even now, when all I want to do is forget him so that at least my heart will stop hurting, I can't. In whatever darkness comes next, I'll carry Eric with me.

And then one day the cell door opens wide.

"On your feet."

I've no idea of the time. No idea how long I've been here. Supporting my metal head in my hands, because the edges cut into my neck, I stagger upright. Through the mask-slits, I see Rakes and Huxley standing in the doorway. Rakes is grinning, naturally.

"Today's the day, little homo gay boy."

Ever since I insisted on the word, he's tried to claim it for himself. I won't let him. I tap the side of the mask and he steps forward to release the mechanism that frees my gag.

"'Homo gay boy' is a tautology." Dirt-dry, my voice rasps inside the mask. "Honestly, is there a test you have to take to get into the Green Jackets? Whoa, you can tie your own shoelaces? Sorry, you're overqualified for us morons."

Rakes reaches for his baton and Huxley grabs his wrist. "Judge'll want him presentable."

"What do you mean?" I ask.

Rakes reapplies the gag. "You've got a date with the enforcement court, sweetheart. We're taking you for sentencing."

I take one last look as I'm bundled into the corridor. My glasses have fogged behind the mask slits but I know my cell so well it hardly matters. My fingers flinch, as if tracing the walls one last time. Those carved names weren't my only comfort, though. My brothers call out from their food hatches as I pass, wishing me luck, hoping we'll see each other again in the camp.

"Gabe? You there?"

Mark's filthy hand emerges from the bottom of his door and, jerking free of Rakes, I drop to my knees. The mask clangs as I plant my head sideways on the flagstones. Mark's voice is sweet, even when he isn't singing, and despite the dirt and grime, the face that appears in the gap mirrors that voice. He grips my hand.

"Stay strong," he says.

I'm dragged back to my feet and thrown halfway along

the corridor. I bounce off the wall and Huxley mutters for Rakes to go easy. Then we're spiralling down the staircase and out into the yard.

The morning sun blinds me. It's the first time I've been outside in weeks. I breathe in the sweet spring air – not a hint of blood or sweat or filth. Stumbling over the last steps to the yard, I suddenly notice the crowd.

"Keep 'em back," Huxley barks. "We don't want any trouble."

"Just a little welcoming committee I've organized," Rakes purrs in my ear. "Quite a job, getting them all here at the crack of dawn, but I thought you'd appreciate the effort."

I see a few familiar faces from Westwick, each dripping with disgust. They're being held back by a cordon of Grey Jackets, with a narrow avenue between them leading to a Pansy Wagon. We're about halfway to the van when spit *chings* against my mask. The cordon breaks and Patrick Gilligan and Lana Heck step out to block our path. No one tries to stop them, maybe because Patrick's wearing his Young Lions uniform and Rakes is his commanding officer.

"Hello, fag," Patrick says, jutting his chin at me. "Just wanted to say, I always knew there was something off about you. All that time you used to spend at the swimming pool, surrounded by half-naked guys. I bet you even copped a few looks at me, didn't you?"

I shake my head.

"No?" Patrick spreads his arms. "Wow, I feel left out. Why not?"

I can't speak so I point at his groin, then hold up my thumb and index finger, so close they're almost touching.

"Dude!" someone shouts at Patrick. "How does he *know?*"

Laughter breaks out and the Young Lion comes at me. He pulls back his fist, then realizes that hitting me in the face right now might not be the wisest move, so starts to correct mid-swing. This gives me time to step forward and nut him square in the nose. Metal shunts bone and Patrick drops like a puppet whose strings have been cut.

"Beaten by a bloody degen," Rakes sneers as Gilligan whimpers on the ground. "Get the hell up or I'll beat you myself."

During all this Lana's unsettling grey eyes, so like Albert's, snap between me and her mewling boyfriend.

"Where's my brother?" she demands, stepping over Patrick. "No one's seen him since the morning they arrested you. He needs to be found and made to pay for the shame he's brought on our family. What is it with you people anyway?"

She marches up to me and stabs a finger into my chest.

"Why can't you just choose to be *normal*? Why is that so fucking hard?"

Rakes turns to her as Patrick rises sloppily to his feet. "Oh, he'll get the chance to choose correctly, young lady. And when we find your brother? He'll choose too."

Rakes shoulders Patrick aside and I'm pushed into the back of the van. Before I can turn around, the doors slam shut and I'm in darkness. Seconds later, the engine chunters into life and I grope my way to the slim wooden bench. I've no idea how far it is to the nearest enforcement court. No idea how long the sentencing will take. All I know is how good it felt to break Patrick Gilligan's nose. It's the closest I've come in weeks to that safety valve that swimming once offered me. For the past eight months, loving Eric was an even better way to deal with my anger, but Eric's gone now.

We drive for what seems like hours, the van jolting, turning sharply down different roads, finding every pothole. Maybe Rakes is doing it on purpose, knowing how the mask's collar will slice into my shoulders. But honestly, I barely feel the pain. I'm thinking about Albert. Albert who got away. Lana's rage back there seemed disproportionate, even next to the fury of the crowd. It makes me wonder—

A muffled explosion throws me to the opposite wall, where my head smacks against metal. Pain lances across my skull and, landing on my knees, I instinctively grab hold of the bench.

I struggle to catch my breath. At first, I think the crack to my head has affected my vision; then I realize that the impact has punched one of the lenses out of my glasses and that the other has cracked. This accounts for my hazy, shattered view of the van. Underneath me, tyres shriek as shouts erupt from behind the partition. Then another explosion sends the van fishtailing.

At last we judder to a stop. Voices bark commands from outside and Rakes shouts back. A door opens and there's a brief, mumbled conversation followed by a startled cry and the sound of a body hitting the ground. I let go of the bench and rise, half crouching, to my feet. A mad idea keeps running through my head: it's Patrick Gilligan and Lana Heck. They've ambushed the van. A Re-Pure camp isn't good enough for these sadists, they want me executed on the side of the road. Okay, so half of me knows this is nonsense even as the other half is convinced that it's true. I ready myself anyway.

The back doors open. A flood of daylight, shadows looming against the glare. I launch myself at them.

I land a couple of good punches before someone approaches from behind and pins my arms to my sides. I try to wrestle against them but this guy is strong, and anyway someone else has kicked my legs from under me.

I grunt onto my knees and a voice says, "Oh Jesus". It sounds weirdly familiar.

I try to snap my head around but it's being held in place and sweat is pouring into my eyes.

"Stay still," the voice instructs.

And then the clasps come undone and the metal mask is pulled off and thrown aside. I'm gasping, choking, pulling strands of phlegm out of my mouth. The arms that have been locked around me soften into a hug, and Ben Dempsey whispers into my ear.

"You're all right, mate. We've got you."

He kisses the top of my head. Other hands help me to my feet. Liz. Grace. June. I see them all through the broken lens of my glasses, and at first it feels like a dream.

Please don't let this be a dream.

But how can it not be? Because here's my dad, standing over an unconscious Rakes and shaking Sergeant Huxley by the hand.

"Gabe, are you okay?" June asks.

"No," I tell her.

And she laughs and rubs her eyes, and Liz squeezes my arm. Someone hands my dad a bottle of water, which he passes to me. His eyes are wet and angry behind his glasses.

"Gabe," he says when I stop drinking. "Gabe."

I drop the bottle, sit back on the step of the van, and hold my head in my hands. It's strange, I've worn that mask for so long it was like it was becoming part of me. Now my skin feels too soft for the world, too fragile. Hands crowd my shoulders and I look up.

"You're here." I beam at them with cracked lips. Then I stand up, scanning the cornfield into which the van has crashed. "All of you?"

I notice the van's two blown-out tyres and Huxley standing guard over Rakes. That's an image I can't make any sense of right now – Jesus, I can't make sense of any of it – but who cares, because there's Albert, standing to one side, as always. I shout his name and start running to him. Albert puts his arms around me and I pull back.

"What are you doing here? I thought you'd escaped." He shakes his head, those compelling grey eyes cutting away. "And Eric?"

I turn, sweeping the swaying corn. The smile on my lips begins to falter.

"Where's Eric?"

My dad rests his hand on my arm.

"Gabe," he says, "we need to talk."

18

"We haven't seen Eric since the day you were arrested. I'm sorry, Gabe, he isn't part of this."

My dad hands me the spare glasses I keep in my bedside table. Hooking them over my ears, I look around properly for the first time. There's the crashed Pansy Wagon with its shot-out tyres on the edge of the road, the Rebels all clustered to one side. Across the road another van is parked up, shadows moving behind tinted windows.

It's all so confusing, but the only thing I can concentrate on is the person who isn't here. In a way, I suppose nothing's changed. I'd already made peace with Eric's accusation, hadn't I? I signed the confession to save him, so why should I now feel distraught he hasn't tried to save *me*?

Huxley steps over.

"Take your time," he says to my dad. "We've got a few hours before they realize the van hasn't arrived."

The sergeant gives a nod and walks back to stand over the unconscious Rakes.

"Dad, what's happening?" I ask. My gaze returns to the second van and a memory, half buried, stirs in the back of my mind. "The morning they took me…you said something about lives being at stake, about something you should have told me. What did you mean?"

"Well," he smiles his sad smile, "the reality is, you don't read as many banned books as I do and not want to fight against all this."

It's hard to describe, that moment when the person you've known all your life asks for you to look at them in a totally different way. I guess it's a bit like when you realize your infallible parents are only human beings after all. This feels like that, only in reverse.

"Dad." I stare at him. "Are you involved with the Resistance?"

He shrugs. "Honestly, it's not that impressive."

But it is. My softly spoken father is in the freaking Resistance! Okay, so in peaceful old Westwick we don't hear much about the "terrorist scum" (as the Yellow Jackets call them), but their bombing of railway lines and robbing of Protectorate assets has made these freedom fighters into legends, to people like me anyway.

And now a lot of things begin to make sense: my dad taking a job with access to printing materials, a job that allows him a home phone line, and then there's his plan to get me and Albert to Ireland. I thought it was some crazy romantic scheme. Maybe not.

"And I called *us* the Rebels," I murmur, glancing over at the guys.

"Oh, you mean your movie club?"

"Wait. You know about that?"

"I have my sources."

"Seriously, Dad, are you like…" I hesitate because it still sounds insane. "Are you a Resistance mastermind or something?"

He laughs out loud and shakes his head in the direction of the second van. "I'm very glad my colleagues didn't hear you say that. No, Gabe. Thankfully I'm just an incredibly small cog in a very large machine."

"But how long have you been involved?"

He whistles through his teeth. "Since I was about your age, I guess."

"Seriously?" And then the obvious strikes me and I look down at his legs. "So that story about the railway line?"

"A railway was involved…" He pauses. "I made a bad mistake and here we are. It's also the reason I'm now tucked away in Westwick." He rakes his fingers through his thinning hair. "Imagine – I was a young man with a child on the way, and the last thing I wanted was for him to grow up in a world like this. You know," he prods me gently with his stick, "I think you'd be surprised how much I was like you back then. Sensitive, reckless and just a bit too hot-headed for my own good. But what I came to realize was that my temper would probably end up getting me killed, and so your mum and I decided to leave London."

"Mum?" I stare at him. "Mum knew?"

He looks deep into the rows of drifting corn. "Your generation isn't like ours, Gabe. The Protectorate is all you've ever known. But when we were very young, we had a glimpse of what the world used to be, before the Outrage. There's a beauty in freedom, you know. I actually think it's the most perfect beauty there is, to be able to think freely and to be who you are. But it's a beauty that can demand a very high sacrifice."

I nod. If the librarian's films have taught me anything, it's this.

Dad takes a breath. "Your mother was always one of us. That's how we met, at a Resistance meeting. I wish you could've seen her back then. She had my anger, but she was clever enough not to let it control her. My Mags. She was so focused on the idea of ending the Protectorate, I was surprised she agreed to come with me to Westwick. But by then, she'd found something she loved even more than the fight."

"You." I grin.

"No, Gabriel. *You.*"

For a few seconds, I find it difficult to speak. "But, Dad. She never once... She was always so—"

"I know," he says. "I know. Your mother had been through a lot in her life, and being part of the Resistance hardened her too. But believe me, she did love you. She *does*. Very much."

I shake my head. All I can think of is the woman I know – stern, unsentimental, never there. Tears prickle and I blink them away. "Dad, she left us."

He swings his cane, thrashing at the corn stalks. "Your mother left because she was asked to."

"By the Farmer."

He shakes his head. "Don't you remember how it happened? The Farmer came to Westwick to inspect the agricultural storehouses. Your mother was working a late shift and, as head of inventory, she took him on a tour. He became infatuated with her, started sending gifts to her work, love letters. Word got back to the Resistance. They reached out to organize a meeting."

"You mean *they* asked her?" I feel sick. "So that she could spy on him. And Mum *agreed*?"

I remember the night my mother left, the antique Bentley waiting outside our bungalow, uniformed men carrying her cases out the door. Dad sitting quietly at the kitchen table while I screamed and shouted at him: "*Talk to her! Make her stay!*" And that anguished look he gave me, as if he wanted to tell me something. My hand on her arm, trying to drag her back from the kerb. *Mum, please, don't.*

This is my choice, Gabe. I want this. Her eyes cutting to the bloated figure in the backseat. The man she'd only known a couple of weeks, waiting for her, entitled and silent. *You're better off with your father. He understands you. Like two peas in a pod, my boys...*

"She fed us intelligence for over a year," my dad says. "Vital information that saved lives. But in the end, her unhappiness became too much."

"The drinking," I say. "The pills."

He casts me a desolate look. "And now she's trapped playing her role. She plays it well."

A lot of things suddenly make sense: my dad's generosity to the wife that cheated on him, his willingness to forgive her. Because, of course, he had nothing to forgive.

"You could've told me," I say.

"Gabe, you were so young."

"So you let me hate her instead?"

It's too much. With everything else that's happened today, I can't think about what this new idea of my mother means to me. I have to change the subject.

"Those guys in the van? They're Resistance?"

Dad nods. "After what your mum gave up for them, I thought they owed us." He looks at me for a moment and whatever he sees – the fear, the pain, the anxiety of the past few weeks – it drains the blood from his face. "We would've come for you sooner, Gabe, but the Green Jackets' headquarters are impenetrable. This was our first opportunity."

My dad turns and calls Huxley over. The sergeant's gaze is alert and intense, nothing like the lazy bulldog stare I've seen before.

"So you're Resistance?" I ask as he reaches us.

"Undercover for the past fifteen years." He holds out his hand, but even now I'm reluctant to shake it. "I understand," he responds. "Difficult to change your mind about someone in a single morning."

"That's an understatement."

"Well, I'm sorry I couldn't do more for you. If I objected to your treatment it would've looked suspicious. It's just unfortunate that little sicko came along when he did." He casts Rakes a bitter glance. "I've spent years sapping the energy out of the local Jackets, dragging my heels on investigations, letting evidence get misplaced, then Rakes and Dufresne show up. You know," he strokes his chin, "it's a lot of work being this lazy."

I reach out to shake his hand. "Thanks."

He nods, and we shake. "Pity I didn't know about the disc. Pity all round really."

The sergeant wanders off again and Dad taps my foot with his stick.

"I'm sorry, Gabe. It's time we move things along."

Still reeling, I follow him back towards the Rebels.

"When the transport fails to arrive at the enforcement court, they'll send out a tracking team. They'll find Rakes and Huxley tied up on the roadside. This gives you and Albert a three-hour head start. The Resistance won't..." he catches himself, "can't offer you transportation. Vehicles are precious and they feel they've already repaid their debt."

"So rescuing me makes up for everything Mum sacrificed?" I shake my head, wondering for the first time about these people I'd always revered. "In what world can that be right?"

"War brutalizes us all, Gabe," my dad says quietly. "Even heroes."

It's a crappy answer and I can see by his expression he thinks so too. I can also tell that it's the only answer he can give me, so I try my best to stamp down my anger.

"So the guys know all about this?" I say, nodding ahead.

He chuckles. "I risked telling them. I knew they'd want to say goodbye."

"Okay, but why is Albert still here? Why didn't he leave the day they caught me?"

"Well, after you were taken, I did start making plans for him to escape to Ireland, but there was one difficulty I hadn't counted on."

"What difficulty?"

"His affection for you."

I glance over at the group: Ben and Grace holding hands, their backs against the Pansy Wagon; June and Liz with arms around each other; and Albert, always a little to one side, always separated.

"He wouldn't leave without you," my dad goes on. "He tried to make it sound more practical than noble. Said you were stronger than him and that he'd need your help along the way."

When we join the others, I notice that Albert's eye still hasn't completely healed from Patrick's attack outside the swimming pool. The faintest pink haze remains. He smiles at me, his pale lashes practically transparent in the daylight.

"Hey, Gabe."

I don't say anything. I just pull him into the biggest hug. And then everyone's piling in and my dad's laughing.

"Are you guys okay?" I ask. "They didn't come for you?"

"We were questioned," Liz says with a shudder, "but they didn't have anything concrete to link us to you and Eric."

"And we've hidden the films," Ben puts in. "Stashed them in one of the empty buildings in Old Town, just in case Eric—"

"He hasn't said anything," I say sharply. "He wouldn't."

"Gabe—" June begins, but I cut her off.

"How's Totes?"

"Mrs Lebbon has him." Dad nods. "Daft apeth's already torn her sofa to pieces."

A lump hitches in my throat. "You'll say goodbye to him for me? Give him a cuddle...? All right then," I breathe, "what now?"

"The plan's the same," Dad says. "Ireland. I've gone over the route with Albert."

Albert takes the backpack from his shoulder and pulls out a large Ordnance Survey map. Flattening it on the ground, he follows a faint pencil line with his finger from a point just below the city of Oxford, south-west to the northern shores of Somerset.

"The Resistance has arranged for a boat to collect you from a bay east of the town of Watchet," Dad says. "You need to be there in four days' time. That's an average of just under thirty miles a day. It'll be hard going, but it should be doable."

If I hadn't spent the past few weeks being beaten and starved, yes. But there's no point in saying anything, I can already see the doubt in his eyes.

"It's the only window the captain has to take you," he says. "It's this one chance or nothing."

He goes over to the black van and returns with a backpack identical to Albert's. Inside I find a stack of rations, Albert's forged travel passes, a water bottle, a change of clothes, a blister pack of antibiotics, a first aid kit and my old walking boots. Hunched over the bag, I take out the boots and run my finger along the initials carved into one of the soles – *E–G*.

"I've an old friend who lives out past Bristol," my dad says. "She'll be able to give you a bed for one night and maybe even… Gabe, what is it?"

I stand up, feel the world roll under my feet.

"I can't do this." The others exchange glances. "Eric. He didn't know what he was saying. You get that, don't you?" Tears prickle at the corners of my eyes as I sweep every face. "He didn't have any other choice. They interrogated him, probably for days, and…and I just can't, okay?"

"Gabe," June murmurs.

I turn on her. "If this was Liz, if she'd said this about you, you'd forgive her. Because you love her, right? Well, I love *him*. There has to be a way we can get a message to Eric. The Resistance could help with that, couldn't they? Huxley, maybe. We'd only need to wait a day. Just a day."

It's Albert who tells me. "Eric has finished at Mosley Grammar, Gabe."

"What?" I laugh. "But he's got his exams next year and then—"

"They've made an exception. He's joined the accelerated officer programme."

"No." I shake my head. "No way. He wouldn't."

None of them wants to be the one to say it. In the end, it's my dad who grips my shoulder.

"He's publicly denounced you, Gabe. Eric is now the youngest constable in the Green Jackets."

THEN

NOVEMBER – FIVE MONTHS AGO

I survey my domain. Not bad. My bed's made with fresh sheets; the last of the chipped mugs has been taken to the kitchen; there isn't a crusty sock in sight. And then the doorbell rings, and everything immediately looks terrible again.

"I'll get it," I shout, tumbling into the corridor.

There's a mirror hanging by the door, and of course my candyfloss hair looks particularly pubey tonight.

God, Gabe, get a grip, he sees your hair every day.

Still, I lick my palm and furiously pat down my curls.

"Hey," I say, breathlessly opening the door. "You're early."

"And you're…" His smile turns into a frown. "Gabe, what's going on with your hair?"

I roll my eyes. "What can I say, Dufresne? Parts of me just stand on end whenever you're around."

Grinning from ear to ear, Eric steps inside. Straight away I get the warm, soft smell of him mixed in with the breath of the forest. We spend most of our time there now, either by the river bend or at the hill overlooking the valley, climbing trees and playing tag like little kids.

"Here he is!" my dad says through the open kitchen door. "Joining us for a bite, Eric?"

"Yes, sir. I mean, thank you for having me, Mr Sawyer."

"Stop being polite," I tell him. "He'll expect it all the time." I guide Eric down the hall to my bedroom door, where I puff out my cheeks. "Okay, prepare to be seriously underwhelmed."

It's the same thing I said to him when I first showed him around Westwick, and like then, I mean it as a joke. Except of course it isn't. Eric's house is this huge gated mansion on the posh side of town, all white-gravel driveways and not a broken window in sight. I've never seen inside but I can't imagine my cramped, cluttered bedroom will be anything compared to his.

He makes a slow circuit of the room, picking up odds and ends as he goes: a snow globe containing a very mischievous Christmas elf; a swimming trophy from when I was twelve; a couple of banned books hiding behind my nightstand; the framed picture of me and my dad trying to balance his walking sticks under our noses and cackling like loons. He picks up the picture and smiles.

"You guys are so close… And I guess your dad drew all these too?"

His gaze slips across the posters tacked to my wall. Brilliant, dynamic drawings of my favourite heroes from fiction: Sherlock Holmes fighting the nefarious Professor Moriarty at the Reichenbach Falls, Captain Nemo piloting the *Nautilus*, Dorothy Gale facing down the Wicked Witch of the West. They've been up there for years, and I guess they're a bit childish, but I love them and I don't have the heart to take them down.

"Oh!" I dart over to my wardrobe and start hauling out armfuls of clothes. "Here's something you can have, if you want."

I slide out a rolled-up poster and hand it to him. He goes and sits on my bed, unfurling it carefully while I scoot up behind him, planting my chin on his shoulder.

"What do you think? I remember you said your mum liked these stories."

It's another of my dad's: a haunting, dreamy picture of the villain from the Narnia book *The Silver Chair*. The mysterious Lady of the Green Kirtle looks out at us from her enchanted throne, her jade skin scaled like a serpent.

Eric turns to me and, holding my face in his hands, kisses me. Kissing has become a regular thing since that night in the woods when he showed me his scars. That first kiss was a way for me to comfort and reassure him, and there have been many different kinds since, but this is the first he's instigated. When I look down, I see his fingers twisting his shirtfront. His fingernails aren't so red and raw any more, and he continues to promise that he isn't hurting himself, but still I place a calming hand over his.

"It's okay," I tell him. "We're okay."

As gently as I can, I pull Eric with me onto the bed, holding him so that we're lying face to face. I take a breath. "Scarecrow, do you think you might be ready to tell me?"

Scarecrow. One afternoon in the forest we started talking about nicknames. I had Monkey because of my supreme – according to Eric – climbing skills, but what about him? I tried out a few schmaltzy possibilities before he told me, *"I think maybe something like…Scarecrow?"* I wanted to talk him out of it, it seemed so hurtful, but he insisted. *"It feels like a step, Gabe. I know that sounds stupid, but maybe if I can own that name then…"* He was right. Scarecrow already means something different to us, though he still refuses to tell me about his scars.

"Not yet," he murmurs into my shoulder. "Just…not yet, okay?" He takes a moment, and then all at once he's kissing me again and the pain is gone from his eyes. "I love this," he says eventually, rolling onto his back and grinning for England.

"You mean kissing me?" I pillow my hands under my head. "Well, I suppose you're only human."

He pokes my cheek. "Your room, smart-arse. I love your room. It's just very you."

"Butch and masculine?" I flex a bicep. "You noticed my swimming trophies, right?"

"It's full of stories," he continues, ignoring me. "Like, I bet that weird snow globe has a history. And your dad's posters? He spends all that time drawing your favourite characters, even though he must be tired from drawing for work all day. My dad, he'd never even think to do anything like that... Anyway, I can see why you want to make movies."

I wrinkle my nose. "And why's that?"

"Because you'd like to be a storyteller too."

A knock at the door and we both bolt upright.

"Dinner! Come and get it while it's still vaguely edible."

Ten minutes later, we're sitting around our battered kitchen table tucking into Dad's "Mystery Ratatouille". When Eric wonders what's so mysterious about it, I cut him short.

"Don't ask. Also, don't probe too deeply into the first syllable of the second word."

Eric very sheepishly lays down his spoon while Dad and I exchange wicked glances, then burst out laughing. Eric rolls his eyes and starts tucking in again and I reach across and muss that permanently messy hair.

"Aw," I say, pouting. "Don't you just love him?"

Later, after we've helped with the washing up, I'm pulling on my walking boots when Dad takes the seat next to me. He puts down his stick and gives my knee a shake.

"Haven't seen you like this in a long time."

I scrunch up my face. "Huh?"

"Happy, I suppose."

I glance down the corridor to where Eric is tugging on his coat. "Don't be daft. Right, so I won't be back late, just going to walk him home."

My dad nods. "Be careful, yes?"

I'm about to make some flippant remark when it sticks in my throat. "I'm always careful, Dad."

Outside, there's a chill in the air and the streets are empty. We walk side by side, bumping shoulders whenever it feels natural. Once I steal a glance, and Eric's so beautiful in the lamplight, I ache to touch him.

"Tell me something new you thought today."

He grins. It's already an old game. "It isn't new," he says. "I've been thinking it for a while, but okay – Gabe, I've changed my mind."

"Yeah? About what?"

It's stupid, but I feel this nervous skitter in my stomach. *Have you changed your mind about us, Eric? About what we are to each other? And what exactly is that, anyway? Even now, I'm not sure.*

"I want to go back to the library," he says. "I want to see the films."

My heart almost stops. "You're sure?"

"I'm sure."

"But your dad. You said it would be like you were betraying him."

He makes the turn towards Old Town. "I don't feel like that any more. There's nothing wrong in what we…" He looks back at me and drapes a protective arm across his chest. "There's nothing wrong with those movies. You've shown me that."

And so we pass the smoke-scarred factories and head down to the ghostly ribbon of the canal. Even here, where no one comes, our hands only ever touch accidentally. But I'm too distracted anyway, even from holding hands with Eric.

"I saw this really good one last week," I tell him excitedly. "It's about this archaeologist who goes on adventures all around the world and fights Nazis and…" I catch him grinning. "What?"

"Nothing." We're in the alley that links the canal towpath to the town square. It's very dark, only a smudge of moonlight to show the way. "You just see so much in them," he says. "More than I think I ever will."

"What are you talking about?"

He shakes his head, and then something on the wall

behind us catches his eye. He reaches across my shoulder and traces the initials spray-painted onto the brickwork: EB and DM encased in a heart. It's so faded it looks like it's been waiting here a thousand years.

"Come on," I say.

We trot along the alley, all the way to the half-dead maple tree that stands in the bombed-out square. Eric's laughing when we reach it and only stops when I take out my pocketknife. I flick the blade and begin the downward stroke of the E.

"Don't," he says, pulling my hand away. "Someone'll see."

"Who'll see?" I laugh. "No one ever comes here. And if they did, how would they know ED and GS are boys? Or even how long the initials have been here?"

But there's that look in his eyes – the fear that stared out at me back in September. Except, not quite. It's like an echo of that old emotion – still there, but a shadow of what it was.

"Okay." I drop down to sit cross-legged on the cobblestones, then undo my laces and wrestle my right boot off my foot. "Here's a compromise."

"What are you doing, you idiot?"

"There!" I hold up my boot and show him the *E–G* freshly and finely carved into the rubber sole. "And if anyone goes searching for romantic initials on the underside of my shoe, I'll tell them it stands for Evie Glover."

"Evie-who-invited-you-to-the-Christmas-dance Evie?"
He scratches an eyebrow.

I nod. "The perfect alibi."

I pull on my boot, and he hauls me to my feet, and I entirely accidentally topple him against the wall. We stay that way for a while, our faces almost touching, giggling and catching our breath. I brush back a strand of his hair and very slowly, very gently, slip my hand under his shirt.

"Is this okay?" He nods. "Eric, it's okay for it not to be okay, but I need you to know that I don't care about your sc—"

He finds my hand and guides it to that first puckered track that loops across his belly button. I use my other hand to stroke his back, reassuring him as best I can. He lays his head against my shoulder. Whispers my name. And here, in the ruined square of a forgotten town, I realize for the first time that I love Eric Dufresne.

I love him.

"Scarecrow," I offer, "do you want to hear something new I thought today?"

"Okay."

"I thought it just now actually. Eric, I—"

A soft scratching sound cuts me dead and we both look up. Something small and dark is hobbling across the cobbles towards us. Lifting its head, it gives a half-frightened, half-hopeful yelp, and Eric and I jolt apart. But this isn't some Green Jacket Dobermann; this is a tiny, ragged dog, beaten and bleeding, pulling itself along under the single working street light. Although it doesn't have any reason to trust us, still it laps at Eric's fingers when he bends down to stroke it.

I drop beside him and let the little dog nuzzle my palm.

"Oh, Gabe," Eric says, his face stricken, "who would do something like this?"

But I can't answer him because, in a place like the Protectorate, it could be just about anyone.

NOW

19

I hold the boot in my hand and trace the initials on the sole. *E–G.* I carved these the night we found Totes. The night that I realized I loved Eric Dufresne.

Another memory: Eric's reaction after we discovered the box in the library and I made that stupid joke about him joining the Green Jackets. Then the idea had seemed to disgust him, but I suppose becoming a Filth-Finder isn't any different from the assault allegation. It's just a bit of extra insurance to protect himself, isn't it?

So why does this feel like the worst kind of betrayal?

"We do what we can to survive," I say, nodding. When my dad starts to speak, I clap my hands together. "Didn't you say we need to get moving? I'm going to change out of these clothes and then me and Albert can hit the road."

Before any of them can react, I take my backpack to the side of the van and drag off my crusty prison rags. Acres of grime and islands of bruised flesh flash in the sun as I dress into the long-sleeve shirt and worn jeans my dad has brought me. Pulling on my boots, I walk back to them, weirdly aware of those initials burning like a brand under my foot.

My dad makes me eat something before we go, popping a couple of antibiotics and painkillers into my mug of tea.

"There's something I've been wondering," I say, handing him back the cup. "Did you and Mum plan it between you?"

"Plan what?"

"The offer for me to go and live with her and the Farmer."

He takes off his glasses and cleans them on his shirt. "We were worried that something like this might happen one day, yes. You live recklessly, son, you always have. I suppose we thought you'd probably love recklessly too."

"Only maybe not this recklessly, right?"

"Gabe—"

"Have you spoken to her?"

"I have. She's..." He hooks the glasses back over his ears. "I'm afraid I didn't get a lot of sense out of her. Honestly, there's not much left of your mother now."

For the first time since I was told that Eric had joined the Green Jackets, my mind fixes on something else. All the times I rejected her, all the snide, sarcastic, hurtful comments I threw her way because I thought she was the worst kind of traitor: to my dad, to what I thought we as a family believed in. Now the urge to see her again – to speak to her myself, to say everything that needs saying – I can feel it burning inside me.

But I know it's hopeless, and so all I can do is ask my dad: "Will you tell her I'm sorry? For all those things I used to say."

"Gabe, you weren't to know," he says gently.

"No. But I don't think that matters any more."

I cinch the backpack over my shoulders and we wander back to the group. June comes straight over and frames my face with her hands.

"You're incredibly selfish, you know? Leaving me and Liz alone with the norms." She smiles over at Ben and Grace. "But don't worry, we'll look after them. G'ah!" She waggles my head. "I'm going to miss you, you know? You were always one of the least awful human beings I knew."

I nod. "I love you too, Juniper."

Liz slides in, kisses me on both cheeks, and gives a whispered promise that she'll take care of June. I make her promise she'll also keep designing incredible clothes, and that she'll save my Rebels jacket, just in case I come back for it one day. Then Ben envelopes me in a hug that seems to stretch into the next century, pulling in Grace halfway through.

"You've been good friends," I tell them. "And it's not like you had to be."

"You're kidding?" Grace squeezes my hand. "Gabe, don't you know? It was *our* privilege to be your friend."

Ben nods, serious for once, then treats me to a fierce final hug before kissing the side of my face. "We love you, mate."

They drift away to say their goodbyes to Albert, who waits on the side of the road. That precious huddle. My friends who have been there pretty much since the beginning. I'm not sure what I'm going to do without them. But at least there's one small comfort left: I'll still have Albert by my side.

"So what will happen to you, old man?" I ask when my dad touches my arm. "Will they suspect you of helping a known degen to escape?"

He laughs and waves his sticks in the air. "The Protectorate never suspect people like me of anything. And anyway, my books are gone, my house is clear, my son has vanished. There's nothing left to—"

All of a sudden Dad's eyes fill up and his face crumples. I grab him by the shoulders and pull him close.

"You're a boy out of his time, Gabe, you always were." His head shakes against my chest. "Now, I want you to promise me something, it's important. Try to leave your anger here, in this field, okay? Don't carry it with you."

He pulls back and locks eyes with me.

"Sorrow is a heavy enough burden, and you have such a long way to go."

I promise him that I'll try, but I'm not sure he believes me.

Soon enough the yellow dirt road is under our feet and, before I know it, Albert and I have covered a quarter of a mile and reached the first bend in the track. One final chance to look back. My head feels heavy as I turn, as if the metal mask is back in place.

They're still there, gathered together by the van, their faces indistinguishable against the sun. Someone waves and a breath catches in my throat. The urge to go back and repeat all our goodbyes is almost overwhelming. Perhaps reading my thoughts, Albert fishes inside his pack and brings out a pair of battered binoculars.

I shake my head. "Let's keep moving."

After a few minutes, the Resistance van passes us and turns down a side lane. No one waves from behind those tinted windows; in their minds, the favour they owed my parents has been repaid. Years of Mum's life, her sanity even, all written off with a morning's work. I watch the rooster tails of dust settle on the road and feel the old rage begin to scratch under my skin. I'm already breaking my promise to Dad, but anger has always been a part of me and it can't be exorcized with a few simple words.

I keep stealing glances at Albert as we walk; neither of us seem able to talk right now. I wonder what's going on inside that head? If it's anything like mine then there's a storm howling, thoughts and emotions battering against each other, nothing settling for long. Grief for the people we've left behind, guilt about how I treated my mum, terror at the journey ahead, and just a hint of hope, glimpsed in the heart of the tornado. Each time I try to reach for it, to hold it and make sense of it, those other emotions sweep in and snatch it away again. But as stupid as it sounds – as impossible – when I do catch sight of it, hope looks a lot like Eric.

We walk on. I try to ignore the storm. I'm pretty sure that, like me, Albert's hardly ever been out of Westwick, but he leads the way confidently enough, through fields and woodland, past the shells of jungled supermarkets and service stations, stopping only occasionally to check his map. Hours pass, we hardly see a soul, and when we do, Albert whips out his binoculars and ushers us behind some safe hiding place until the stranger passes by.

With most of the morning gone, I finally feel like I can talk again without bursting into tears. I bump shoulders with Albert.

"How are you doing?"

"I'm fine." He gives me a long look. "More importantly, how are *you*?"

I've been trying to ignore all my aches and the pains, the nagging gripe of my wasted calf muscles, the bright stabs that come out of nowhere and remind me that I'm still healing. Talking about it won't make it any better, so I change the subject.

"So where have you been hiding yourself away all this time?"

"Your dad found me a safe house outside of town," he says. "One of the old abandoned farmhouses. Not exactly the Majestic, but cosy enough. Just me and this monosyllabic man-mountain the Resistance sent to keep me safe. We played chess every night after tea. It was…"

"Boring?" I volunteer.

"Educational." He smiles. "Man-mountain beat me almost every time."

"It's crazy," I say, shaking my head. "About my dad."

"I don't know," Albert shrugs. "When we were kids, I was always pretty certain he had some big secret. That mild-mannered artist thing was just too perfect a disguise."

I manage a chuckle, dry as the dirt road. "Maybe the Resistance should've recruited you too."

"Maybe. Except then I wouldn't be here right now, escaping with you."

I turn to him. "Why did you wait for m—?"

"Can I ask," he says, cutting in. "Prison? The Filth-Finders' HQ? You don't have to say anything if you don't want to, but I just wondered… How was it, Gabe?"

I knew he'd ask, and I thought the horror of going back there in my mind would be too much. That I'd have to tell him I couldn't face reliving it. But all at once it starts spilling out of me: every indignity, every humiliation, every hurt and cruelty flowing through my lips. It isn't all horror, though. I also tell him about Mark and the other prisoners – my brothers – who offered me a tiny scrap of comfort in the dark. Albert doesn't say anything. He lets me gallop alone through my story until all at once he grabs hold of my hand, gripping it tight. I don't look at him. I don't need to. I can feel the emotion trembling in his hand.

By mid-afternoon, we've reached an abandoned town with a high tower block overlooking a huge green-scummed lake. Without a word, we drop exhausted onto the shingled shore and dig into our backpacks. The lukewarm tea in my Thermos finally shakes the question loose.

"Albert?"

He presses his hands together, clamping them between his knees. "Yeah?"

"Has anyone seen him?"

He shakes his head.

My heart sinks like a stone in the lake. These past few weeks, I'd accepted that I'd never see Eric again. That he was lost to me for ever. I hadn't made peace with it, not at all, but I'd accepted the reality. It still hurt, probably always would, but a scab had started to grow over the wound. And then, when I was rescued, I allowed myself a few sweet moments to hope: I *would* see him again, because he was part of all this.

Now the scab's been torn away and I'm bleeding.

"I'm sure he didn't have a choice," Albert says. "About becoming a Green Jacket."

I nod and try on a shaky smile. I want to believe that. So much.

"Thanks, Albert," I whisper. "I'm glad you're here."

20

Maybe it's because I'm exhausted, maybe because I feel overwhelmed by everything I've learned today, or maybe it's just because I'm an incredible idiot, but it takes a while to realize what's happening. We've left the abandoned town far behind, lost ourselves again in forest, and Albert's got his head back in the map when I let out this eureka-ish *Ohhhhh.*

"You're keeping us off the main routes."

He nods. "Yeah. I plotted it out with your dad while you were…"

"Guest of the Green Jackets? Well, I'm glad I played my part in this diabolical scheme, keeping the enemy occupied and giving you time to plan our camping trip."

"It was a valuable contribution." He smiles an uncertain smile. "Anyway, I went over the route so many times I could probably walk it in my sleep."

I grin, and then grimace. The hours of hiking are really starting to take their toll. Sweat has plastered my shirt to my back and is currently burning in the cuts and sores from the prison. I pause for a second to shake a spasm of cramp out of my calf. Albert starts to ask if I'm okay, but I wave his concern away and we move on.

"So," I say breezily, "what're you going to do when we get to Ireland?"

He shrugs. "Let's see if we get there first."

"We'll get there."

"You can't know that."

"Okay. But I do."

"How?"

"Because my movie needs a happy ending. Or as happy as we can make it anyway."

He shakes his head. "What do you mean, your movie?"

I take a breath. Why not share my dream with Albert? In fact, I think I need to. I mean, here we are, two fugitives thinking they stand a chance against a ruthless police state: next to that reality, my ambition to be a director doesn't seem all that far-fetched. And, honestly, if I want to make it happen then I need someone else to believe in it too.

"That's *my* plan," I say. "When we get to Ireland, or wherever we end up, I'm going to make movies. And for the first one, I'm going to write and produce and direct a film about everything that's happened to us. Not just the Rebels, but everyone who's gay and living under the Protectorate. I'm going to tell the entire world what it's really like to live here. Because if they knew…"

I trail off. It's hard to imagine what the rest of the planet knows about our lives – or if they know, whether they care. But one day I'm going to make them care. That's the power of movies: they can inspire compassion, outrage, empathy, the whole glorious rainbow. I learned that lesson from the librarian's gift.

"You want to be a director." Albert smiles.

"I've been thinking about it for a while." I nod. "I just didn't imagine it would ever be possible. But maybe in Ireland? It was only a daydream before, but—"

"A daydream you kept to yourself?"

"No." I hesitate. "Eric knew."

"Of course he did."

There's no edge to Albert's words, but still I feel a strange need to defend Eric. "He wanted me to tell you all," I say. "He knew you'd understand."

"Then why didn't you?"

"I just…I don't know. Maybe I had to make sense of it myself first."

"Okay. But how can you make a film about us when you don't know all our stories? Not in full."

We've emerged from the path and joined the track of a

forgotten railway. Huge bushes Eric would have been able to identify bustle in on both sides, pushing us shoulder to shoulder.

"I'd have to do some research," I admit. "Ask the right questions."

"But you can't."

"Why not?"

"Because everyone's gone," he says, his voice empty. "Because we've left them behind."

"Yes. We have." I suppose we both knew when we said our goodbyes on the roadside that it was unlikely we'd ever see any of them again, but now one of us has actually said it out loud, those words hang heavy in the air. Much as it hurts, I realize we haven't the luxury of letting them weigh us down. We have to keep moving, and so I try to change the tone. "But *we* can talk, can't we?"

Albert hesitates. "Yeah. I guess."

"Hey, I could even hire you as a consultant on the film. Or a co-writer, even better. We'll be like those old Hollywood screenwriters who stayed up late and drank stupid amounts of Scotch and hammered out brilliant scripts together. Like that movie we watched in the library that time. What was it called?"

He scrunches up his face. "*Sunset Boulevard*?"

I click my fingers. "That's it. That couple working late in their old Hollywood studio office. We'll be like that."

He doesn't nod, just keeps his gaze on the broken railway track. "I like the sound of that."

And I know I'm supposed to take some meaning from his words, but the meaning that seems obvious also doesn't ring true. Why can't I just ask him outright? Isn't it about time?

"Albert…?"

He stumbles over one of the rotten railway sleepers and I have to catch him and hold him up.

"Hey, you okay?"

He gives me this weak, watery smile. "Sorry. Yeah. Just a bit light-headed." He digs into his pack and brings out a biscuit. "I'll be all right in a minute."

"Do you think you can go on?"

He nods. "Another couple of miles. There's this little place just west of Swindon. That's our camp for the night."

And so we start walking again, and the moment's lost.

By the time we finally reach the hay barn and the millstream it's early evening, though the sun's still raging. Bordered by the stream, the building is crouched in a dip in the countryside, and if Albert hadn't guided us so expertly, I'd never have known it was there. Inside it's dry and dusty and warm. We chuck our packs onto a heap of straw and, within seconds, Albert's fast asleep.

But I can't sleep. Don't get me wrong, my body aches for it. We've covered over twenty-five miles today and I hurt right down to my bones. My injuries from the prison are really taking their toll and I'm starting to wonder whether it will always feel like I'm wearing that metal mask. As for my heart? Maybe the only reason that doesn't hurt is because of the dumb anger that throbs there. Anger at the Filth-Finders, anger at Eric for ever pulling on that green jacket, anger at myself for blaming him for something he surely couldn't help. And so I go back to what I used to do before I met him.

At the millstream edge, I pull off my clothes, down to my underwear, and dive into the blue-green waters. A delicious iciness rips across my skin, soothing as it stings. Weeks of caked-in dirt drift away on the current. I plough on, churning the surface, dragging hard, startling the wading birds from their nests.

I've no idea how long I've been swimming, and although my arms scream, I don't want to stop, but when I lift my head, I see the fuzzy shape of Albert perched on the bank. It's too deep to stand and so I swipe the droplets from my eyes and tread water. He sits with his hands on his knees, his bare feet in the stream. Ripples reflect the dying sun across his delicate features.

"Come in," I say, skipping my palm on the surface. "It's lovely."

Albert folds his arms tight across his chest. "Nah. S'okay."

When he looks up, I swim towards him, my feet finding the pebbled riverbed. I lean one elbow on the bank and waggle his foot, like I used to when we were little kids, sleeping top to tail in my bed back home.

"You okay?" I ask him.

"Yeah. I'm okay."

Birds flutter back to the water, reclaiming their nests. Stillness settles in as the shadows deepen. It's time. I can feel it.

"Albert, can I ask you something?"

He picks at a crumb of dry earth and dusts it between his fingers. "Sure."

"You don't have to tell me if you don't want to, but…" I take a breath. "Albert, are you gay?"

"What?"

I smile. "It's a better word than degen, isn't it?"

He takes a while to consider this. "It is. And I…" He grips his elbows, leans back, stares at the bruised sky. There are stars there now, smoky constellations becoming sharper by the second. "I'm sorry, Gabe, but I don't want to talk about this. Not right now. Maybe not even…" He stands, jewels of water skating down his legs. "I don't want things to change between us," he whispers.

"What? No way! Listen to me, Albert. Whatever it is you tell me, it won't change *anything*. I promise."

"But it might," he insists.

Suddenly he's turned sharply and is heading towards the barn. I pull myself up onto the bank, but turning again, he waves me back, his face tight, his expression desolate. I sink into the water. I want to go after him, I do, but I get the sense that if I push too hard right now then I'll just end up alienating him. And I can't lose Albert.

He's all I have left.

21

We're close to the end of our second day on the road. Blisters have erupted along the sides of my feet and my skin's raw from the bloodsucking insects that seem to plague every woodland pond. It doesn't help that, after my conversation with Albert at the stream, I didn't get much sleep last night.

My dreams were like walking through a minefield. Minutes of nervy stillness before I'd jerk awake at some new thought exploding in my head: the need to see my mum again, to apologize for misjudging her, burning like a bonfire in the dark; the image of her popping pills and sitting like a corpse at the telephone, talking nonsense down the line – "*Smiley. That's what we called him. Smiley in Red*"; Albert and me at the millstream while a green-jacketed Eric watches us from the bank.

I tried talking to Albert before we left the barn but he

kept shutting me down. And I guess that set the mood for the day. It just doesn't make any sense. There is nothing Albert could tell me that would make me think less of him. All through this long, hard day I've stolen glances but the words I want to speak keep dying on my lips.

At least these thoughts distract me from Eric. I've tried to hide it from Albert, but it's hard when a memory comes out of nowhere and winds you like a punch to the gut. How do I feel about Eric now? I don't even know. One minute I'm making up excuses for him joining the Green Jackets, the next I'm determined to forget I ever met him...except I know that's impossible.

We stumble upon the Grey Jacket ten miles outside Bristol. At first, because he's a bit preoccupied, he can't reach for his baton. Albert gives me a warning look as my hand slips to the side-mesh of my backpack and my old pocketknife. The same knife I used to carve E–G into my boot.

The officer zips up his fly and turns away from the bush. Meanwhile Albert's hand closes over mine. His lips are pressed into a thin line and I try to communicate with my eyes the single thought that's blaring in my head: *I'm not going back. No matter what.*

"Hello," Albert says cheerily.

The Grey Jacket's eyes go wide when he spots us, and his hand flies to his baton.

"Where the fuck did you come from? Papers!"

"Sure." Albert takes the fake travel passes from his back pocket and hands them over. "We're SEE students from Oxford, on our way to the Outrage Memorial Day celebrations in Bristol."

The young officer peers narrowly at our passes. "Why aren't you just attending the Oxford celebrations?"

"It's an exchange." Albert smiles. "Oxford kids in Bristol, Bristol kids in Oxford. Only the Transport Protectorate messed up our bus tickets, so we've had to walk the last few miles."

The Grey Jacket grins. "Those guys couldn't transport themselves into the next room without filling out five forms in triplicate." He looks like he's about to hand back the passes when a frown rumples his brow. "Why are you all the way out here? The official route is via the old motorway."

"Don't like crowds," I say. "We're country boys."

"Well, you'll have to like them," he says, shrugging. "Come on, it isn't far."

He gives back the papers and marches off.

If it had come to it, if he'd seen through the passes and tried to arrest us, would I really have hurt him? Honestly, I don't know. As it is, we cut away from the woods and descend a steep chalky hillside. Out of the trees we're suddenly aware of this low rumbling murmur and up ahead see the caterpillar shimmer of thousands of bodies moving along a wide road. A heat haze hangs above them as the crowd winds on towards the distant speck of the city.

At the base of the hill we join the motorway. There's a kind of jittery excitement in the air. Little kids sit on parents' shoulders, all waving Protectorate flags.

I turn to Albert. "It's the twenty-fifth?"

He nods. Outrage Memorial Day. Not exactly the founding day of the Protectorate, but as good as.

I glance around at the people shuffling along this broken road. Eyes occasionally flicker to faded signs on the hard shoulder, each pointing to uninhabited ghost towns: *Salisbury, Cheltenham, Bath.* At one point there's a derelict service station with rusting golden arches rising above it, like the symbol of some dead religion. There isn't an opportunity to slip away. The motorway is exposed on all sides and Grey Jackets march up and down, keeping the procession tidy. There isn't an opportunity to talk to Albert either. For now, we'll just have to play along.

By the time we reach the outskirts of the city, the sun is dipping and torches are passed through the crowd. Their light leaps in and out of abandoned hotels and firebombed restaurants as people start to sing the national anthem:

"*Save us all, O Lord Protector*

From our foes, within, without..."

We're finally turning into this big green open space when a man collecting rubbish catches my eye. He already has patches of dry phlegm staining his overalls and, as I watch, another gob launches out from the marchers. The man is about my dad's age, thin as a blade. When he bends down to collect the sandwich wrapper at his feet, the crowd showers him with picnic wrappers and apple cores.

"That's right, get on your knees and pick it up, you filthy degen."

The man does as he's told, his hand brushing against the pink cross on his overalls.

And then we're all stumbling to a halt. We're about ten rows back from the façade of a beautiful floodlit cathedral. Protectorate flags flap from its twin turrets, red crosses on black snarling in the breeze. There's an elevated stage set up in front of the vaulted doorway, where dignitaries in uniform mill about. At the sides of the cathedral stand blown-up photographs of men, women and children, all smiling, all long dead.

"Keep your head down," I whisper to Albert.

Camera crews from British Protectorate Broadcasting sweep the audience.

"When the rally breaks up, we hit the side streets," I say. "No looking back. You know the way out of the city?"

He nods and I laugh loudly and pat his shoulder.

Kids fidget and are told to keep still: *The Grey Jackets'll take you away!* Then some old crow in religious vestments struts across the stage towards a central microphone. He makes a shaky sign of the cross and we all whisper our blessings on the Lord Protector.

"On this most holy day," the priest croaks, "we give thanks to our Lord Protector and to the men of the Public Good Party, who rebuilt this nation. The heroes who took it back from the feeble, from the foreigner, from the traitor and the degenerate – from all the unworthy vermin who had weakened and imperilled it. We give thanks that the Protectorate has purified this land and we pray that it will never again become home to the outsider."

"Amen!" shout the crowd.

"The corrupter!"

"Aaa-men!"

"The FILTH!"

"AMEN!"

"Oh, they tried to stop our glorious leader and his followers. They planted their bomb at the Merripit Hotel and left their filthy note in the ruins, that alliance of traitors and foreigners and perverts. And yes, a price was paid. Look upon these good martyrs of the Outrage," the priest rants on, pointing to the blown-up posters. "Martyrs consumed by the unholy fire of the enemies of the state.

"But their deaths were avenged! After the Outrage, we fought back and reclaimed our country. Now these martyrs live on in our commitment to drive out all sin and wickedness…"

Albert clutches at my arm. "Gabe?"

I'm only vaguely aware of wrenching his hand from my wrist. Fixed on a gap in the crowd, I start to shoulder my way through. Bodies jostle against me. A voice cries out. When someone tries to block my way, I pull back my fist. Whatever he sees in my expression, the man swallows hard and stands aside. I glance only once over my shoulder, but the crowd has already closed up again and there's no sign of Albert.

Near the roadside, I wait. From behind I can hear the hate of the priest still spewing through the tannoys.

I wait…

And I wait…

Until, finally, he sees me.

Eric Dufresne in his smart green jacket. Three or four of them are gathered around an armour-plated car, a map spread across the bonnet. Rakes is among them but there's no sign of Huxley. Looming over all is Chief Inspector Dufresne. None of them is looking my way.

None except Eric.

His mouth opens, a red wound on the verge of spilling a secret.

I don't run. I walk slowly across the street and down an unlit side alley. There I wait again – in the stillness, in the dark. I'm putting everything at risk but I can't help it. Finally, I've pushed through that storm in my head, made to it to the quiet heart of the hurricane, and found him again. Whatever he's done, I can't ignore or deny what he means to me. In a world where it ought to have been impossible, we fell in love.

I *still* love him.

When Eric steps into the alley he isn't alone. I drop to my knees as he unclips the collar and Totes rushes into my arms.

"Hello, boy! Yes, I know, I know, I've missed you too." I scruff the fur around Totes's mouth before finally dragging my gaze back to Eric. "Hey, Scarecrow."

In the darkness, his eyes are impossibly huge.

"Gabe." He makes to step forward, his gaze playing over me. "Gabe, what have they done to you?"

I straighten up.

"Only what they always do to people like us. The question is, Eric, what have they done to *you*?"

THEN

NOVEMBER – FIVE MONTHS AGO

So much has changed tonight. Eric initiating a kiss. Eric rejecting the Protectorate lies he once wore like a blanket. Eric guiding my hand to his scars. And the change that strikes deepest: I love him. I love this kind, beautiful, broken boy.

But some things never change.

I sit in the library, waiting for my Scarecrow to return, and the rage I've felt ever since I was old enough to understand what kind of world I'd been born into, dances like fire under my skin. I can't even think about all the amazing things that have happened tonight. All I can do is sit here and hold the little dog's body in my lap.

"I know, I know," I soothe. "It's going to be okay."

I move my fingers gently through the dog's fur. It's matted with blood and there are wounds scored into the flesh below. His little heart thrums against my knee.

It's pretty amazing that an animal this abused would curl up like this in a stranger's lap, but I think he's too exhausted to be scared any more. I bend my head and kiss his nose.

"Who did this to you, boy?"

A second later, we hear the creak of the loose board and Eric runs breathlessly into the library. His cheeks are flushed, his hair wild.

"How is he?"

The dog looks between us, its head sagging. Eric doesn't say anything else. He empties the bag he's brought from home and starts arranging things methodically on the floor. Then he holds a water bottle to the dog's mouth and lets it drink its fill, which isn't much. From a Tupperware box, he takes out a handful of minced meat, crumbling in two white pills and forming the whole into pellets.

"Painkillers and antibiotics, though I'm not sure he'll feel like eating. You might need to hold his mouth open."

I take the animal's jaw as gently as I can and Eric encourages the pellets into its mouth.

"This might be the trickier part," he says.

But in the end the dog hardly murmurs as Eric cleans its wounds and applies antiseptic cream to the lacerations. When he's finished, he rests his hands on his knees.

"Hey." I nudge him. "You're really good at this, you know?" He looks up at me, eyes brimming, and my anger flares again. "If I could find the people who did this, Eric, I swear…"

"Gabe, don't."

For a second I don't know what to say. "Eric, aren't you angry too?"

"Of course I am." He scoots closer and runs his fingertips between the mutt's ears. "But it scares me sometimes, the way you get."

All the happiness of earlier evaporates in that moment and I feel this weird rush of shame and fear. It takes everything I have to force out the next question.

"Are you saying I scare you?"

"No," he says quickly, "I didn't mean that, not at all. I feel safer with you than with anyone, I just… It makes me scared *for* you. I can see how your feelings overpower you sometimes." It's almost like an echo of the warnings my dad has given me over the years. Finally, Eric looks up and his smile settles me a little. "You couldn't ever scare me, Monkey. But I'd like to know where this anger comes from."

Now it's my turn to look away. "Probably all tied up with my mum. How she left us…" I shake my head. Eric's laid so much of himself on the line tonight, I owe him the truth. "Really though? I guess I've always felt like this. Even before I knew who I was I could sense that I was different, and I knew this world wouldn't like my kind of difference. So, you might have noticed I'm a bit of an opinionated big mouth?"

He pokes my cheek. "Yes, Monkey."

"Well, I can never tell people *why* I'm angry, why I'm different, so my anger has to work itself out in different ways."

"You get angry on other people's behalf," he nods. "And I love that about you, I do. But, Gabe, it's dangerous. Not just because it could make them suspicious, but because I think it hurts you too. You have this huge heart and you keep leaving it open to pain."

"But not just to pain," I say.

As carefully as I can, because the mutt's sleeping now, I shuffle around and pull Eric towards me.

"My dad says things have to survive by themselves or not survive at all," he says, looking down at the little dog. "That nature's brutal. I suppose he's right. A lion who takes over a pride will kill and eat his rival's cubs, just so that the lionesses will come into heat and he can father his own children more quickly."

"Wow," I reply. "I didn't know lions were such dickheads."

"What?" He looks outraged. "Lions are magnificent!"

"Magnificent dickheads maybe. And talking of dickheads, your dad saying that about things having to survive by themselves is pretty unoriginal. I mean, that's actually a verse in the national anthem, isn't it?" I mean it as a joke, but Eric stiffens. "Sorry. Shouldn't have said that."

"It's okay," he says quietly. "But maybe you should know

something about my dad. His whole future was set when he was only a little kid. Did I tell you, his father was one of the victims of the Outrage?"

"What?"

Eric nods. "My grandpa wasn't there for the rally, so he's not technically one of the Outrage martyrs. He was just this young salesman staying at the same hotel where the Public Good Party was holding its conference. My dad told me his father even used to vote for one of the old democratic parties. He said his dad would pretty much hate what Britain has become. But although Dad loved him, he thinks my grandpa's kind of politics are the reason he was blown to pieces that day. Dad was actually there when it happened."

"Oh Jesus, Eric."

"My grandma had brought him up to the city to surprise his dad. Grandpa was in the hotel lobby and saw them waving from across the street. He was almost at the door when the bomb went off."

Much as I dislike Eric's dad, I can't help but feel for that little kid, having his hair blown back by the force of the explosion, his life shattered by the blast.

"That's why he is what he is," Eric says. "And why he hates who he hates – the liberals and the freaks and the outsiders, who all clubbed together that day to plant the bomb and destroy a group of people who only wanted to make the nation stronger. That's what he thought he saw, anyway."

"And what do you think?"

"I don't know." Eric traces his fingertips along my arm. "I only know that they lie."

"Okay," I puff out my cheeks, eager to dispel the mood. "So if I promise to be less of an incredibly sexy hothead, what do I get in return?"

"*Well*," he snakes his face left and right, avoiding my attempts to steal a kiss, "you can look forward to one of these at least once a week."

He darts in and pecks my nose. When I laugh and try to grab him, the dog grumbles. Eric settles back onto his haunches with a sigh.

"So, what are we going to do with this little guy? Can he stay at yours?"

"Sorry," I say. "My dad's allergic to anything small and hairy."

"And yet he keeps you in the house?"

"Hilarious. But you know, there might be a place. Ben and Grace told me about somewhere they found in the woods. Some old cabin. The mutt can't stay here anyway. There's no way to secure a place this big."

"And once he's better, you'll be peeing and pooping everywhere, won't you, boy?" Eric buries his head in the sleeping dog's fur. "Yes, you will. You'll be pooping *so* much."

"Okay," I say, "this is getting weird."

Eric looks up. "We need a name. We can't keep calling him 'it' and 'mutt'."

"I was thinking about that while you were getting the meds. By the way, do you think your dad will notice your first aid supplies have been plundered?"

Eric shakes his head. "Our maid Beatrice keeps it stocked. I'll just tell her I had an accident and didn't want to worry the boss. Back to names: what about Rover?"

I tilt my head to one side. "You know, it's amazing that I love someone so unoriginal."

I pause. All that build-up earlier in the alleyway, and the word just slips out. We both look down, then cast our eyes sideways, then glance up at the ceiling. Honestly, it's like choreographed awkwardness.

"It's getting late," I blunder on. "Shall we make him a bed upstairs? We can box it in for now and come by early before school."

The mutt hardly stirs as I carry him to the room beyond the broken wall. I lay him carefully on the busted sofa in front of the TV and, before leaving, drape my jacket over him.

"Won't you be cold?" Eric asks.

"Well, I may need occasional hugs."

We push the librarian's desk across the hole, then head out into the night. The first real promise of winter is on the wind and Eric puts an arm around me.

"Okay," he says, "what's your amazingly inventive name for our little one?"

"Totes."

He frowns. "Please explain."

"It comes from this old series of banned books. In the first one, *The Wizard of Oz*, there's a character called the Scarecrow." I ruffle his messy hair. "And also a little dog that belongs to the hero. He's called Toto, but I think I prefer Totes."

For the rest of the journey back to Eric's, I regale him with the tales of Oz: of Dorothy Gale from Kansas and her adventures with the cowardly Lion, the heartless Tin Man and the brainless Scarecrow. We're almost at the chief inspector's gate when my Scarecrow stops and shakes his head.

"Why were these stories ever banned?"

I shrug. "Sometimes it's difficult to work out what the Culture Protectorate finds immoral or dangerous. But if I had to guess? Near the end of the book, Dorothy and her friends discover that the all-powerful wizard is really just this sad, pathetic old man hiding behind a curtain. He's ruled Oz all these years by projecting an image of strength and power."

"But it's a lie?"

I nod. "Remind you of anyone?"

Eric's quiet for a moment. "Gabe, what you said back at the library." He looks down. "That you—"

"I do," I say quickly.

He nods. "Then I owe you the truth. About my scars."

Eric suddenly looks so lost and afraid. I want to hold him, to tell him that whatever his secret, it won't make any difference to us. But we're not in Old Town any more, so all I can do is wait.

"Please promise you'll try to understand," he says. "Because what she did, my mum... I don't know how I feel about—"

The gates clang behind us. Eric swipes his eyes with the side of his hand, straightens his back, braces his shoulders. A lean shadow stretches down the sloping driveway and, just before his father steps into the street, I see that old cage descend over Eric Dufresne.

The chief inspector casts us a hard look.

"It's late," he says, his eyes fixed on me.

"Yeah," Eric complies. "I'm sorry, but—"

"Never apologize unless there's something to be gained from it. Don't you ever listen to anything I say? Now, get yourself to bed."

I can feel my cheeks burning, but I made Eric a promise so I stomp down my anger as best I can.

Eric is starting to shuffle through the gate when he stops and turns to his father. "I told you what I was doing tonight," he says. "I had tea at Gabe's then we did some homework together. I'm not apologizing to you, Dad." He turns to me.

"I'm sorry my father's been so rude, Gabe. I'll see you tomorrow."

My heart's pounding. I want to run after him and twirl him in my arms. You told him, Scarecrow! You bloody *told him!*

I'm about to walk away when a hand clutches my shoulder and I look up into that hawkish face. It's hard to imagine the little boy who stood on the pavement outside the Merripit Hotel and witnessed the Outrage. If he is in there somewhere then he's probably buried under the same cold rubble as his father.

"My son seems different these days," says Mr Dufresne. "Certainly more willing to express his opinions. Is that your doing, Mr Sawyer?"

"I don't think so."

"Modesty's a foolish virtue, Gabriel, and I don't think you're foolish." He slips his hand down to the baton on his belt. "He seems happier too."

"He's settled in well at school," I say.

"Happiness isn't everything. It isn't even all that important. Safety is what matters. Security." He reaches out a gloved hand, as if he's going to muss my hair, then draws it slowly back. In the moonlight his face shines like statuary. "My son is sensitive, easily misunderstood. Do *not* misunderstand him."

He smiles, and it's the most dreadful thing I've ever seen. "Don't misunderstand me either."

NOW

22

I look at that heart-shaped face and all I can think of is a different alleyway in a different town. Maybe we're different now too, Eric and I… And then he speaks, and a new scar catches the light, and I feel my heart jolt in my chest.

"You're hurt," I say, my fingers tracing my jaw.

He mirrors me, touching the fresh scar at his bottom lip. "It's from when I fell," he says. "When my chin hit the wall. Gabe, I promise, I haven't done anything."

Relief washes through me and I press my hands together.

"You're hurt too," he murmurs. I try to picture myself as he sees me. I know I must be at least a stone lighter, and that my face carries the marks from my metal mask. "Gabe, I—"

"Don't tell me you're sorry, Eric. I'm not sure I could deal with that." Totes has settled down beside me. He snaps his head between us, tongue lolling. He's wondering if this is all a game. Perhaps it is. But then my anger's back, prickling under my skin. "I know," I say, snapping my fingers. "Tell me something new you thought today."

He stands there in his sharp green uniform, twining those long, nervous fingers together. Occasionally he darts a look over his shoulder, to the main square where the priest still rants and raves.

"Nothing?" I shrug. "I'm not surprised. Once you let them into your head, you become their robot. Their slave. Which is a shame, Eric, because you were *never* that. Not even when we first met."

Totes lets out a tiny whine. He doesn't like this game any more. *Nor do I, boy, but we have to play it to the end.*

"How did you find us?"

He looks at the flaking concrete walls with their almost-invisible graffiti, the rusted sign reading *College Lane*, anywhere but at me.

"Luck."

"Luck!" My laughter fills the alley. "Well, good for you."

"There are Green Jackets out looking for you all over Oxfordshire and the South West," he says. "My dad thought your only chance was to make it to Ireland, or possibly France. The wall across the Scottish border is too strongly guarded. And anyway." He casts me a pitying look and I

274

turn away. I don't want his pity. "He didn't think you could make it that far."

"What about my dad?" I ask. "Do they think he helped me escape?"

Eric shakes his head and confirms what my father said to me in the cornfield. "They'd never suspect someone like Mr Sawyer."

"So why is Totes here?"

"Dad took him from Mrs Lebbon this morning," Eric says. "I don't know why. He doesn't speak to me much these days."

"Except to give you orders, I bet."

A new speaker in the square must have said something particularly hideous because a roar of approval echoes out to us. Eric begins to pluck at the breast of his uniform. The silver buttons glint like polished teeth in the gloom.

"Please understand, Gabe. If it hadn't turned out the way it did, they would have taken him away. There would have been some kind of show trial in front of the whole Protectorate. Filth-Finder's son is a degen, so he must be a secret traitor too. You know how their minds work. Jesus, it was you who *showed* me how... I couldn't do that to him. Not after what happened with Mum."

The urge to go to him, to comfort him, is almost overwhelming. But I can't. Just seeing him in that fucking uniform. My head is howling.

"I broke," he says suddenly, his voice harsh. "Just for a minute, I broke. For a *second*, okay? That Grey Jacket who caught us at the school, he stopped hitting me when he realized who I was. I actually think I'd have preferred him to keep on hitting me and never work it out."

"That's easy to say, Eric, when you had options."

He bows his head. "I know what happened to me was nothing compared to what they did to you. When he came to collect me from the Grey Jackets, my dad didn't even... But there are other ways to make someone say what you want them to. I can't take it back, Gabe. I said you attacked me, and those words will stay with me every second of my life."

"Fuck that."

He looks at me, tears starting in his eyes.

"I understood why you said it. I signed the confession because I understood and because I wanted you to survive. But I wanted *you* to survive. That was the sacrifice I was willing to make – my life so that you could go on and be everything I knew you could be. And then you do this." I throw my hand at him, spitting the words at the uniform. "You betrayed us. *This* betrays us."

Eric takes a step forward.

"You stay there," I tell him. "You stay right fucking there."

"Gabe, please. My dad swears that if you come with us

he can put in a good word at the camp. They'll treat you with respect and he can even get your sentence reduced. But if they catch you before you surrender—"

"Can you even hear yourself?" I laugh. "You know that's bullshit, right? I assaulted his son. How could he be seen to be doing me favours without that lie crashing down around him?"

Eric looks at me, and my heart stops. Those are the same hopeless eyes I saw earlier tonight. It's like the street cleaner with his faded pink cross is staring back at me.

"Monkey..." he murmurs

That word. That stupid word. Almost at once, something unlocks inside me. I go to him. I just go, and I take both his hands in mine. They're icy cold. Trembling. Totes skips around us, yipping happily, until I tell him to be quiet. I want to hold Eric. I want to kiss him and smooth away his tears and tell him that none of it matters. But I can't.

"Come with us," I say.

He shakes his head.

"You told me once that everything good in your life started with me. Well, what do you say now? Was that the truth or is your dad right? Are we just a couple of disgusting degens? Should people like us be wiped out? Because if you stay, if you keep wearing this uniform, that's what you believe."

He cuts his eyes away. "It isn't that simple."

"It is," I say softly. "It just is. Because you right now? This is how you were when we met. Trapped and confused and repeating all their lies. So tell me, how did he get to you? Was it your mum? Did he use her?"

"No."

"Then what? Because I don't understand how your dad has undone seven months of us in a few short weeks. Is that really how much you loved me, Eric?"

When he doesn't answer, I hitch a smile.

"Well, I suppose you never actually said it back."

He tries to catch hold of me and I swat his arms aside. It can't be that easy. I won't let it be. And then I notice something, and suddenly I'm grabbing his wrists and turning his hands over. His nails are bloody, bitten down to the quick. I try to tug up the sleeves of his jacket but he pulls away and crouches over, his hands gathered into his stomach.

"You don't believe any of this," I tell him. "You never have."

"I can't..." He looks up at me from under that tumble of hair. "If I go with you then I might as well put a gun to my dad's head and pull the trigger myself."

"It wouldn't be you doing it," I shout back, not caring now who hears us. "It's *them*."

He stands and throws out his arms. "What's the difference? People still die."

"There's a difference," I insist. "Of course there's a difference. Eric, I'm only going to ask you one more time."

"All right." He nods. "So I come with you and, what? You forgive me?"

Totes presses hard against my leg. From out of the square comes a burst of applause.

"Honestly? I don't know. But don't do it for me, do it for yourself." I hold out my hand to him. "Take this one chance to be who you really are, even if that existence only lasts a single day. I think it's better than pretending for a whole lifetime, don't you?"

He reaches out his hand.

Steps forward.

And two figures appear in the gap behind him.

"Well, look who it is." Rakes grins. "Hou-fucking-dani."

Suddenly it feels as if ice water is surging through my veins. I try to ignore the shudder.

"*Dini*," I shoot back. "Did you lose a few more brain cells when the Resistance jumped your sorry arse? By the way, that moustache is still looking proper shit."

Rakes starts towards me but Inspector Dufresne's baton smacks against his chest. I back up a few paces, my gaze fixed on Eric. I'm still holding out my hand.

Please. You have to choose.

The words bellow so loudly in my head I think I've actually spoken them out loud.

Eric's hand drifts down to his side.

I nod. "Goodbye then," I say. "Eric...I'm sorry I let you fall."

23

I run.

From behind I hear his father's voice, raised for the first time.

"You better go after him. You better bring him back. You *better*. Rakes, go with him."

The inspector's order chases me out of the side street and up a flight of shallow stone steps. My footfalls echo from wall to wall, and it isn't until I start clambering over the rubble of a half-demolished church that I hear yelping behind me. Turning, I find Totes at the bottom of the brick pile.

"Stay!" I call down to him. "Wait for—"

And then I remember what Eric said: *Dad took him from Mrs Lebbon. I don't know why.* Dufresne must have linked the dog to me and Eric after my dad took Totes to our neighbour. That's not surprising; Green Jackets have probably been watching our house, but why should the inspector bother with Totes? Whatever his reason, it probably isn't good.

I skid back down the debris and gather up the little dog. A second later, Eric and Rakes appear at the top of the steps. Eric stops dead, earning him a sneer from the constable, but that slight turn of the head gives me a fraction of a chance. Cradling Totes in my left arm, I snatch up a shard of brick and hurl it at the Green Jacket.

Rakes squeals. His fingers shoot to his forehead where a large gash drips down and dyes his moustache a vibrant red. Even from this distance, it looks like a massive improvement. Meanwhile I take a firmer hold on Totes and scramble up and over the rubble.

The street beyond is empty. At the end, I jag left past a burned-out pub where sheets of spectral plastic flutter from blackened beams. Totes remains silent, bouncing against my chest as I hurtle us under the iron railings of some ancient bridge. It's in the road beyond that we run into a band of marchers. There are about a dozen of them, still waving their guttering torches.

I stop to catch my breath. Sweat is running into my eyes and my old injuries are all piercing through the adrenalin. I start to speak, when Rakes hollers from behind.

"Stop! Enemy of the Protectorate! Escaped degen!"

These loyal citizens have just spent an hour having their

brains freshly washed. They don't need any encouragement. One guy – roughly the size of a bear, but without the personal grooming skills – steps forward. My gaze skips around the group and I notice they all have almost identical facial hair, like maybe they belong to some club that commemorates history's shittiest beards.

"Lookee here, lads," laughs the high priest of the face fungus. "We've caught ourselves a mucky little faggot. What're we gonna do with him, eh?"

The street's too narrow for me to get past the beard brigade. The bear approaches and pokes a finger into Totes's chest.

"Aw and look, he's got a furry friend. Now don't you worry, champ, we'll save you from the nasty old perv." He pokes Totes again and smiles over my shoulder. "It's all right, constable, we've got him cornered for y— *Arrgghhhh! SHIT!*"

Even the softest dog in the world can be pushed too far. Another prod from the bear and small, needle-sharp teeth snap smartly around the tip of that stubby finger. The bear's eyes go round with shock. He tries to wrench his hand away but Totes isn't giving up his treat that easy.

The rest of the crew show their loyalty by falling back and hissing through their beards. When blood flashes on the ground, a guy the size of China hits the pavement in a dead faint. Meanwhile, I help things along by giving Totes a gentle tug. This just about does it. A scrap of flesh comes away and Totes seems satisfied.

For a second, I watch the bear hop around, clenching his finger and crying like a kid on its first day of school. Then I shoulder-barge us through the gap. No one seems to notice. They're all either consoling their hysterical leader or else chucking up their daily ration into the gutter.

Rakes's hand slips against the back of my jacket. I don't look round. I take the lane on the right and follow it uphill past a row of pretty, pastel-coloured houses and into an open area of withered grass. Ahead, near the summit of the hill, stands an elegant redbrick tower. I set off towards it, and reaching the far side, plant my back against its cold brickwork. A couple of huge breaths steady me. In the next moment, the clouds pull back and the moon appears, silvering a fairy-tale balcony that juts out from the top of the tower.

I'm about to set off again when Eric steps around the side of the building. My heart gives this single deep thud. We've already said our goodbyes, but maybe there's a God after all and he's allowing us a second chance. My gaze slips from those tattered fingernails to his chest. Back in the alley, I never got the opportunity to see if there were any fresh scars. I hope not, but if there are, and if we can start again…

I want to start again. Whatever I said to him just now

about forgiveness, it's bullshit. I'd forgive Eric just about anything.

"See him?" Rakes hollers from below.

I don't hold out my hand. I won't try to persuade him. Not this time.

A breeze sweeps around the tower, throws his hair across his face.

Eric licks his lips.

"No. No sign."

"Then get back here. I gotta see a medic ASAP; reckon I've lost about a pint of blood."

Eric hesitates, steps towards me, runs his fingers through Totes's fur.

And then he's gone.

I don't waste another second. If I allow myself to think or feel anything right now then I'll stay here for ever. So off I go again, dull now, thoughtless, putting one foot in front of the other. Totes whines to be let down but I can't risk him chasing after Eric, and so for the first time ever I tell the little dog to shut up.

We pass out of the park and through the grounds of a derelict hospital. Shapes move behind greasy windows but whether they're people or birds or animals, I can't tell. All I know is that I'm running again. And suddenly I'm in the middle of a road, caught like a convict in a spotlight glare. I throw an arm over my face, Totes gives a terrified yap, and something hard and metallic blindsides me. The dog jumps out of my arms a millisecond before my head hits the tarmac.

Flat on my back, I don't think I've hurt myself. At least nothing shrieks at me as I look into the grimy undercarriage of the car. A horn blares and I start to shoulder my way backwards, pulling myself up by the bonnet's grille just as the driver window whirs down.

"Get in!" Albert shouts.

I don't wait to make sense of it. I grab Totes from the pavement and, throwing my pack onto the backseat, drop into the passenger side. I barely have time to clip the belt before Albert sends us hurtling into the night. I bury my fingers into Totes's fur. We're plunging through a series of unlit streets, our headlights dazzling the windows of abandoned houses. Reaching over, Albert gives Totes a quick pat.

"Where on earth did you find *him*?" There's an edge to his voice; a coldness I haven't heard before.

"It's a long story," I say.

Albert shrugs. "It's a long drive."

"Okay," I take a breath, "but first, what the hell?"

"You mean the wheels?" He yanks the car left and I screw my eyes tight shut. "Found it in a side street after the rally broke up. Nissan Micra, 2038 model. Easy enough to get going. I've been driving around trying to find you."

"Cars. Right." I swallow, remembering how Albert fixed up that old junkyard jalopy with his dad. "Albert, I— Jesus Christ!"

At first I think he has sent the car plummeting off the edge of a cliff. Blooms of white cloud press at the windows, snatches of stars between, but then I feel the rumble of the road and glimpse these immense iron cables looping down from above. The mist parts for a moment and the Clifton Suspension Bridge – a mighty arm spanning a colossal gorge – is revealed. Lucky for us, this is one of the few great British bridges still standing.

"Okay." I take a breath. "Exactly how fast are we going?"

He doesn't answer, just toes the accelerator and plunges us on. I decide the best thing to do is clean my glasses. At least then I won't be able to see the end of the bridge rocketing towards us. Meanwhile Totes takes the opportunity to explore the backseat.

I'm just summoning the courage to put my glasses back on when Albert grabs my wrist and turns my hand to the dashboard light. I hadn't noticed the cuts in the palm before, probably from the shattered brick I hurled at Rakes.

"What happened?" he asks.

I look at Albert and feel this brutal rush of tears. It all comes spilling out: how I saw Eric through the crowd in the square; how I had to speak to him one last time; his fears for his father and his excuses for betraying me and joining the Green Jackets; my invitation for him to come with us, and that final sight of him under the tower. Albert listens to it all in total silence.

"You left me," he says finally, and the bitterness is unmistakable. "I risked everything for you back in Westwick, and tonight you just fucking left me."

With that, the truth slams into me: I've betrayed Albert. Betrayed him just as badly as Eric betrayed me. When I saw something better – something I *imagined* was better – I abandoned him without a second thought.

"Albert, I'm—"

"No," he says. "I really don't think you are. Because you don't understand, do you? My life is in your hands, Gabe, and yours is in mine. The things we decide to do right now, the secrets we decide to keep? Those are things that can get the other person killed. So no, I don't care if you saw Eric tonight. I don't care if you wanted to reason with him or save him or even enjoy one last glorious fuck in an alleyway. Because you know what? Your love makes you careless, and I won't die because of it."

I can't argue, can't justify myself. He's right about everything. I could have got us killed tonight. Because whatever Eric might think, his father will never allow me and Albert to be arrested. We'll never see the inside of a Re-Pure camp or get to wear the pink cross. We're too much of an embarrassment to the Protectorate for that.

If they find us now, they'll bury us.

And so I have to say goodbye to Eric Dufresne.

And I have to mean it.

THEN

DECEMBER – FOUR MONTHS AGO

"I am going to totally bury you, Eric Dufresne."

He skids to a halt beside me. "Um. Pardon?"

"Politeness won't save you," I add, resting my bike on its kickstand. "I am the supreme champion of ultimate hide-and-seek, and I *will* bury you."

"Okaaay."

Eric parks his own bike and joins me at the wall. From the top level of the multistorey car park we can see most of Westwick laid out below, from the factories in the east to the sweep of Hamilton Woods with its white-green hills and the valley beyond. Alone above the town, I take my boyfriend's hand.

Boyfriend. Surprisingly, it was Eric who first used that word. We were in the forest, setting up Totes's cabin, laughing about something that had happened at school, and out it popped. At first, I thought he'd try to take it back, but he didn't, and he hasn't. It's difficult to describe how that simple word has changed things, except perhaps that I have now this one space in my life that feels like a refuge from the world. A tiny corner away from all the brutality. I wonder if Eric feels this way too. I hope so.

"I thought we were here for a birthday party," he says. "What even is ultimate hide-and—?"

He's interrupted by a scrabble of claws on concrete. A second later, Totes hurtles around the spiral ramp and, spying us at the wall, yips happily. The derelict shopping centre isn't far from his home in the forest, but his little legs have had enough. Eric gathers him up and Totes receives a kiss from each of us.

"All right," Eric soothes, "good boy. Now, I'm just going to have a quick look, okay?" He parts the fur at the nape of Totes's neck, and smiles. "You know, I think a few of these cuts might not even leave a scar."

I let the word hang for a second. It's been fifteen long days since Eric promised to tell me the story of his scars. Although I'm proud of how he stood up to his father that night, Eric's secret remains a secret. But I won't push him. I know I have to be patient. There's also Mr Dufresne's vague threat to think about. *Don't misunderstand me...* Does the chief suspect what's going on with me and Eric?

Totes has got his breath back and is wriggling to be let down. We watch him scamper about the car park, chasing fallen leaves as if they're his mortal enemies. Eric shivers and I cup his hands in mine, blowing some warmth into them.

"Movie later?"

He nods. "Perfect."

Already, I can't wait. Whenever we're in the library, in the dark, it's easy to keep the promise I made him. My anger seems like a distant memory, with Eric snuggled beside me.

"So I've been thinking," I begin.

He pokes my cheek. "Do you need a lie-down?"

"You know, you're pretty adorable when you're cheeky. But, listen, what do you think about inviting the others to the library and maybe—"

Cycle tyres squeak on broken tarmac and we automatically part. Okay, so it's not like the guys don't know about us, and of course they'd never judge; I guess our reaction is just instinctive. June and Liz lead the way, followed by Ben and Grace, Albert bringing up the rear.

I puff out my cheeks. "Time to meet the gang."

"Right," Eric says. "Although I do sort of know them already."

"Trust me," I say, "you don't know these guys until you *know* them."

He laughs. "What are they, an organized crime syndicate?"

I shrug. "I wouldn't call them 'organized'."

June dismounts her bike and comes straight over. She gives Eric an appraising glance before holding out her hand. Eric actually gulps.

"I suppose you're quite pretty," she concedes.

"Oh." Eric looks between us. "Thanks?"

Before giving him back his hand, she reels him in. "Listen, I've invested a lot of time and effort into making this idiot a marginally well-rounded human being." A smile breaks out. "Just, be good to him, yeah?"

Liz slides in between them. "Hello," she says. "It really is nice to meet you properly, Eric. You've been the source of endless gossip." She casts her girlfriend an indulgent look. "But don't worry, it was all good."

Then Ben and Grace dive in with some full-on hugging.

"I'm so pleased for you guys!" Grace beams. "Although we are starting to feel a little outnumbered."

"Oh no!" June rolls her eyes at Eric. "The norms are feeling threatened. Can you even imagine?"

"Hey, guys, does this belong to anyone?"

We all turn to find Totes scrabbling wildly against Albert's chest and bestowing several enthusiastic kisses.

"Sorry," I say, coming forward and relieving him of the mutt. "He doesn't get out much."

Everyone crowds in and Totes's head starts twisting round so much I'm pretty certain it's about to come unscrewed. Honestly, he's getting an even more rapturous welcome to the gang than Eric.

"Well, what are you called, cutie?" Liz asks.

"This is Totes Dufresne-Sawyer. Or Sawyer-Dufresne?" I look to Eric. "Have we decided?"

"Both sound a little bit ridiculous," June grumbles.

"Ohhh," I pout at the pooch, "don't you listen to your Auntie Juniper. She loves you really."

"How old is he?" Ben asks, scooting down so he can receive a Totes snog.

"No idea," Eric replies, and he launches into the tale of how we found Totes in the square, beaten and starving. Everyone goes quiet for a moment. Ben looks like he might burst into tears, while Albert's lips set into a thin line, but actually it's June who looks most upset. She comes forward and lifts the dog out of my hands.

"Evil bastards," she says, burying her face in Totes's fur. "Anyone ever tries to mess with this hound again, they'll have me to deal with."

"And me," Ben mutters.

The others nod in solemn agreement.

"Anyway," I cut in, wanting to lighten the mood, "we all know why we're here. Today we gather in honour of Miss Juniper Ryerson's birthday, and for the traditional battle that has taken place on this auspicious date for the past decade. Some will stand victorious, others will fall like the contemptible losers they are." I nod at each of them in turn. "It is time for...ULTIMATE HIDE-AND-SEEK! And I nominate Eric as first seeker." Squeezing my boyfriend's cheeks together, I kiss his pouty fish-face. "So, if everyone's ready?"

They all take off towards the doors of the abandoned shopping centre. Meanwhile Eric mumbles through puckered lips, "No. Wait. What?"

"Come on, Scarecrow," I say, "it isn't rocket science."

"Okay, but hide-and-seek? Gabe, *seriously?* What are we, six?"

"Hey!" I grin. "It's tradition. I thought you were all about that sort of thing." I spin him around in a circle, then leg it in the other direction. "Count to a hundred! No cheating!"

I crash through the busted fire door in time to see the others scatter across the atrium. Spooked by our footfalls, dozens of birds screech into the iron ribs of the roof. At the escalators, I take the steps two at a time and arrive at the ground floor just as June disappears into a service cupboard. I scan the shops' glassless windows and smashed shutters. *Disney Store, Marks & Spencer, Primark, KFC* – names that might have meant something once.

I make my choice and step through a shattered shopfront. Ransacked shelves fill the store while a handful of naked dummies watch from their plinths. Although there's something eerie about those sightless stares, the mannequins give me an idea almost too hilarious to resist. But, no. If it had been just me and Eric, maybe, but there's the others to consider, and I can just picture June's face if she was the one who accidently found me, stark bollock naked on a plinth, staring into the middle distance.

Towards the back of the store I find a dusty cupboard under the customer service desk. At first I think it's too small. Then I hear the sound of Eric descending the escalator and desperation takes over. I pull back the sliding hatch as far as it will go and, after much twisting and turning, get myself into a position where my face is tucked neatly within gassing distance of my bum.

Of course, Eric finds me almost immediately.

"Hello," he says, pulling back the hatch.

"Hello," I say to my arse, "fancy meeting you here."

He stifles a giggle and helps me out.

"*Eeeeefff,*" I say, unkinking a crick in my neck. "Found anyone else?"

"Nope. You're the first."

I grab him around the waist. "Course I am. Although it's a bit unfair."

"Why's that?"

"Well, obviously you were attracted by my animal magnetism."

"Obviously."

I'm about to make my move when Eric surprises me. He very rarely initiates things but when he does…well, that old dizziness always hits. I cup the back of his head as he kisses me and then, very gently, ease my fingers under his shirt. He takes a shallow breath.

"Is this okay?" I ask.

He nods…

And an annoyed voice blares through the atrium. "Is anyone *actually* looking for us?!"

Eric sighs. "Coming, June!"

After another hour we assemble at the escalator where we crown a seriously skilful Albert as the victor of ultimate hide-and-seek. Then Grace starts handing out slices of birthday cake while Ben produces two flasks of tea.

"So, I hear your moron sister has started dating Patrick Gilligan," June says to Albert.

He shrugs. "They have custody of the same brain cell, so it made sense."

I throw Albert a grin. It's rare for him to come up with a gag, but when he does they're always worth it.

After cake we head back to the car park and I dig into my satchel and bring out the birthday girl's gift: a collection of Truman Capote short stories (very *definitely* banned). June treats me to a rare peck on the cheek, then they're all collecting their bikes and getting ready to head off.

"Before you go," Eric says, "I just wanted to thank you

for making me feel so welcome. Today…well, it meant a lot."

Ben looks like he's about to get off his bike and run over.

"Oh for goodness' sake," June says. "Ben, enough with the hugs!"

"Just one other thing," Eric goes on. "I heard my dad talking about an unscheduled inspection at the school. If you guys maybe need to hide anything?"

Grace shakes her head. "It sucks that you guys have to live like this."

"Seconded," mutters Ben.

"It is what it is." June gives me a sharp nod. "Gabriel? This one's too good for you."

And with that she leads the way down the ramp.

We stand together, Eric and I, listening until the whistle of tyres fades into the wind.

"I like your friends," he says, turning to me.

"They're your friends too now." I grin. "God help you."

A flicker of something white, maybe just the rumour of snow, begins to fall around us.

"Gabe?"

"Yeah?"

His hand steals into mine. "I think I'm ready…"

NOW

24

I'm guessing this must have been a high-ranking officer's car; it's running pretty smoothly, as far as I can tell, and the fuel cell's fully charged. Still our journey hits the odd snag: an obstacle blocking the way – a branch, a bit of broken farm machinery – and we have to get out and haul it to the side. Each time, we dust off our hands in silence before driving on, Albert focused on the road.

Dark clouds roll in. Rain patters the windscreen, a lullaby thrum that reminds me of falling snow. I think of that derelict shopping centre back in Westwick; kids playing stupid games, birds wheeling in the rafters, Eric telling me the secret of his scars. It all feels like a lifetime ago.

"I think this is it," Albert says, bringing me back to the car.

I rub my eyes and peer through the rain. Up ahead, a house stands alone on the edge of a cliff, a hint of frothing sea beyond. Albert parks up and is just turning off the engine when the front door opens and a figure emerges.

"Who is this person exactly?" I ask.

"Some friend of your dad's from the old days," Albert mutters. "Mr Sawyer didn't tell me much."

He gets out without another word. He still won't look at me. I can't say I blame him.

I'm just stepping out myself when the woman reaches the car.

"Gabriel? Albert?" She frowns. "Where did you get the wheels?"

Albert explains while I unpack our gear. Our host is holding a battery-powered lamp and, by its light, I can see she's one of the oldest people I've ever met. Sixty, maybe even seventy, although life under the Protectorate tends to age people beyond their years. Her thinning hair, curly white, stands up like tufts of cotton wool, and a few faded freckles scatter her cheeks. As Albert winds up our story, the woman laughs and pats him on the shoulder.

"Quite an adventure. And who's this?"

I'm lifting the dreaming mutt out of the backseat. "This is Totes," I say. "Sorry about the odour. He's still digesting a bit of human finger."

The woman nods as if this is perfectly understandable. "Well, welcome to my home," she says. "My name's Marsha. Shall we get out of the rain?"

We follow Marsha through the open door and into a sitting room stuffed with comfy armchairs, all arranged around a roaring log fire. I ease Totes onto the hearthrug, where he yaps and growls in his sleep, then collapse into the nearest chair. It's old and sagging and feels like heaven. Albert takes the seat furthest from mine while Marsha bustles away to the kitchen.

The last thing I see before nodding off is this framed photograph on the mantelpiece. It's old and yellowed and faded, but the beauty of the young woman in the picture shines out through the years. Coal black hair and a smile that could warm your heart. I wonder vaguely if this is someone the old woman knew when she was a girl...

"Grub's up."

The smell of food wakes me, although this isn't like any food I've ever smelled before. A plate lands in my lap and I look down at the weirdness.

"A favourite from my youth," Marsha says, taking her seat. "Slices of spiced lamb served in a flatbread. We called it a doner kebab, back in the day. Obviously too 'ethnic' for the powers that be."

Albert picks up his packed flatbread. "It looks... interesting?"

Marsha chuckles. "Just give it a try."

Even if I hadn't been surviving on starvation rations for the past couple of weeks, I'd have wolfed down every morsel of Marsha's old-world delicacy. Doner kebab is freaking delicious. When I'm done, my gaze slides to the telephone standing on the table next to Marsha's chair.

"I'm sorry," she says, catching my eye. "I tried making a call earlier but the lines are down. And anyway, I'm not sure speaking to your dad right now would be the best idea."

"Why not?"

"Because they're almost certainly monitoring his calls. Okay," she says, putting down her plate and allowing a wakeful Totes to lap up the crumbs. "I know I don't need to sugar-coat this for you boys – if this man Dufresne doesn't catch you then his career is over. It might even be worse than that – the shadow of what happened to his wife still hangs over him. And so you can expect his hunt for you to be merciless."

Albert stirs. "You sound pretty knowledgeable about this sort of thing. I'm sorry, but who exactly are you?"

"I'm a history teacher. Or I was, a long time ago."

"And now?"

"And now." The old woman shakes her head. "I don't suppose you've ever heard of the Underground Railroad? No, it isn't the kind of history they teach in schools any more. Back in the nineteenth century, when slavery was still legal in the southern states of America, abolitionists set up a network of secret routes and safe houses for escaped slaves who were journeying north into the free states. Today, I'm part of something similar. An underground railroad for degens escaping the Protectorate."

"Not degens," I say. "Gay people."

She blinks at me. "Yes indeed. Funny how even their terminology starts to infect you after a while."

"So you help kids like us get out?" Albert says.

"Kids," Marsha nods, "and even the occasional old fart like me."

"But you stay?"

"It's what others would expect of me." Her gaze flickers to the mantelpiece and the picture of the beautiful, smiling girl. "It's what I expect of myself."

"But how did you get involved in all this?" Albert asks.

"That's a long story."

The rain rattles the windows, the fire snaps in the grate. It's a night made for long stories. I sit forward in my chair.

"I grew up in a freer England," Marsha begins. "Oh, we still had our prejudices, but it felt like we were getting there. Slowly, surely, things were changing for the better. Even during my time at university, when I had my eyes opened to so much..." She smiles at some treasured memory. "You know, when you live through a time of progress it seems that progress is the only possible way. The idea that everything we'd gained, all those hard-won rights, could be taken away from us, that open minds could be closed again?"

She gives a harsh, bitter laugh.

"But then the Outrage happened," Albert says.

"That was the spark, certainly, but the fuel that helped to burn it all to the ground? We'd been storing that up for years." She spreads her hands towards the fire. "Fear did it, I suppose. Anger too, but mostly it was fear. Fear breeds hatred, you see? And there was a lot to be fearful of back then."

I stir, memories of some of the librarian's films flipping through my head. "But it seemed like such a peaceful time," I say. "At least compared to now."

She looks at me curiously for a second. "That's what we thought too. It's easy to be complacent when you think history is on your side. But things we didn't realize had any connection to us were already laying the seeds for the Protectorate. Terrorist attacks, economies crashing, environmental catastrophes, global pandemics, families going hungry. People started looking around for something to blame, but most of them weren't interested in the true, complex answers to their questions. They wanted someone strong to take charge, to explain it all to them in a few easy words. It really is amazing how people will surrender their minds, just to feel secure."

"And the Protectorate offered them that security," I surmise.

Marsha nods. "You won't find this in your schoolbooks, but in the beginning everyone thought the Public Good Party was a joke. That's how these people always start out. Just a bunch of paranoid idiots no one takes seriously. Then they start a whisper here, play on a fear there, and soon enough the joke isn't funny any more. One day we wake up and realize that our friends and neighbours – good, decent people – are starting to listen. And then this happens."

She rises creakily to her feet and moves across to an overflowing bookcase. Taking out a few innocent-looking volumes, she presses a back panel and, from a hidden cavity, retrieves a folder. She hands it to me and I divide up the photographs inside, passing a pile to Albert.

"The Outrage," Marsha grunts, slumping back into her chair. "The fuel was ready, now for the spark."

The first couple of photos are familiar from our textbooks: the Merripit Hotel, shining and whole; the next, a warped and burning shell. Bodies litter the pavement outside, so ruined it's difficult to understand them as human beings at all. The Outrage martyrs. And Eric's grandfather, of course.

"They found that note in the debris," Marsha continues. "A mocking, victorious letter from the liberals and the immigrants and the degens who all came together that day to destroy the Public Good Party. A letter saying they would never allow these fascist monsters to be elected.

Convenient, don't you think? A fully intact note surviving the blast?"

She lets the question hang for a moment and something begins to stir at the back of my mind.

Marsha continues: "Hilary Martin built his foundation on the Outrage. Despite what you've been taught, he didn't call for calm in the days and weeks following. He secretly stoked the flames of anger. And so the riots began. Homes burned out, communities destroyed, innocent people murdered in the streets. At the next election, he claimed that God had spared him from the bombing so that he could lead the British people out of their fear and confusion. A swell of anger swept him to power."

I'm flipping back through the photographs when Albert reaches for my share. I hesitate. Something is niggling at the edge of my thoughts and I keep thinking back to one of the shots – the hotel before the blast, figures frozen in time: a businessman checking his wristwatch; a teenager in a baseball cap, a grinning yellow cartoon face stark against his red T-shirt; a little girl dangling her doll by the arm, her mother hurrying her along. There's something here. It's like a word dancing on the tip of my tongue.

"As you know, Uncle Marty's first act was to create the Protectorate oaths and regulations," Marsha goes on, "then the original Declaration of the Public Good. Together these laws limited the press, the internet, free speech. A few years later, elections were abolished. Next, our rights were taken away and the Jackets were born, then the enforcement courts, then the camps.

"And so the world changed in ways my generation could never have imagined. It's *because* we couldn't imagine it that it did change. We weren't vigilant enough. Didn't realize our rights were in such danger. But those rights – to marry, to have kids, to love who we wanted to – they were young and vulnerable. They needed to be defended every day. Mostly, though, we didn't understand that people will sacrifice pretty much anything to feel safe."

Marsha sighs. "The question is, what will they do when they come to their senses?"

"What do you mean?" Albert asks.

The old woman shrugs. "The horror we're living through right now isn't a one-way street. History is a wheel and the same old spokes come up again and again. So when they finally rediscover their humanity and the Protectorate starts to crumble, will we forgive them?" She looks into the fire for a moment. "I hope I can."

"Maybe it's crumbling already," Albert says. "For a start, no one's seen Hilary Martin for years. Do you think he's dead, Marsha?"

"Perhaps. The myth of the always-watchful Uncle Marty hiding behind his curtain is a powerful one."

"The Great and Terrible Oz," I murmur.

"Yes," Marsha chuckles. "Something like that."

I return to the photograph. What is it about this image? Not the little girl with her doll; not the mother in a hurry; the businessman checking his watch, maybe? Was he waiting for something to happen? Or is it…

"What really rubs salt into the wound is that he was late for the conference that morning," Marsha says, something pointed in her tone. "Martin arrived in the street just as the bomb went off. Walked away without a scratch. Fate must have been smiling on him that day."

I focus again on the kid in the vibrant red T-shirt, the yellow grinning face so bold against the scarlet. It's as if I can actually feel it, a connection fusing in my mind, an understanding that sends shivers racing through my body. That was what she called him.

"But she was drunk," I say aloud. "Off her head on pills, and I…"

The others have stopped talking and turned towards me. Slowly, I hold up a photograph to Marsha.

"Do you know who this is?"

"Oh, him?" Marsha nods. "He's our prime suspect. The man the Resistance believe planted the bomb. Strangely, he was never really investigated at the time, but the timings of this young man's arrival and departure were always suspicious. We gave him a code name based on the shirt he was wearing."

"Smiley in Red."

Marsha stares at me. "That's right. How did you know? Did your father tell you about all this?"

"I didn't even know my dad was Resistance until yesterday."

I glance back at the photo, that stupid cartoon face staring out at me, as if mocking us all. I rise shakily to my feet. On the windowpane, my reflection shivers against the driving rain.

"I think I know who he is," I say. "And if I'm right, *if* I am, this could be the end of the Protectorate."

25

"You've been hinting at it, haven't you? The note that miraculously survived the blast, Hilary Martin arriving late for the conference." I switch my gaze from Marsha to Albert. "And I always thought we were so clever, seeing through all their bullshit. Jesus, we didn't even scratch the surface."

Marsha sighs.

"How could you? You've been brought up in their world, fed their propaganda since you were born. The Protectorate is your reality. I'm sure your dad implanted doubts about their brainwashing as best he could, but he also knew that if you questioned too much it would put you in danger. Honestly, boys, it's amazing you saw through the things you did."

Albert stands up and goes to the window. "So Martin *knew* the bomb had been planted."

My laughter is as harsh and bitter as Marsha's was earlier. "They started out as a joke, the Public Good Party. That was what you said, wasn't it? That no one took them seriously? But then a lot of awful crap started going down – economies crashing, wars, poverty, pandemics, environmental disasters. Huge, complex catastrophes that impacted everyone. So people got scared and the hateful, simple answers Martin was offering started to sound more appealing. I guess that won him some support?"

Marsha nods. "A few local council elections, nothing major."

"In other words, they were stuck," I say. "They had some appeal but not enough votes to break through. If they were going to get their hands on real power they needed something that would focus all that rage and hurt directly on themselves. They needed to be seen as *both* the victims and the solution."

Albert comes back to the table and picks up the photograph of the suspected bomber. "So 'Smiley' wasn't an assassin sent out by an alliance of the party's enemies?"

"Course not," I reply. "Immigrants, liberals and degens conspiring to kill hundreds of people? No one would even suspect such a ridiculous idea, if it wasn't for the letter they found in the debris."

"They had the fuel," Albert says. "But the spark never seemed to come. So they lit it themselves."

"Lit it *and* sacrificed some of their own people to the flames," Marsha confirms. "It's sick, but they really did see those people as martyrs to the future Protectorate."

Albert stares at the photographs taken after the bombing – a lifeless hand poking through the rubble; a bloodstained teddy bear; a tiny, crooked body covered with a blanket. They're familiar enough from our textbooks, but I don't know, it's like we're suddenly seeing them with fresh eyes. I go and sit on the arm of Albert's chair and touch his shoulder. At first I think he might pull away, but instead he grabs my hand.

"Fucking hell, Gabe. Fucking hell."

Softly, Marsha says, "We've suspected this for years, though we've never had any proof. But, Gabriel, if your father never told you, how do you know about it?"

I look up. "My mum."

That drunken phone call the night before I was arrested: "*He did tuh-terrible things… Even b-before. Way back. In the uh-early days, before any of it started. I know that now.*"

"She called me a few weeks ago," I explain. "She'd discovered something about the Farmer. I didn't listen at the time, just thought she was hammered and talking rubbish as usual. Back then, I didn't know about her being involved with the Resistance."

"What did she say?" Marsha asks. "Try to be precise."

I close my eyes. "'Smiley. That's what we called him.

312

Smiley in Red. He was there.' It was only when I saw the photograph just now that I put it together."

Marsha takes a deep breath. "Roger McCormack, aka the Farmer. He's been involved with Hilary Martin since the earliest days of the party. Joined as a youth-wing member at fifteen, rose very quickly through the ranks after the Outrage."

"A reward for his services at the hotel," I say. "My mum must have found some solid evidence that he was the kid in the smiley shirt."

"But if that's true, why hasn't she contacted the Resistance?" Albert asks. "Like you said, if it could be proved they planted the bomb themselves, then that could be the end for the Protectorate."

I flash back to what my dad told me after my rescue from the Green Jackets: *"I'm afraid I didn't get a lot of sense out of her. Honestly, there's not much left of your mother now."*

"She's not in control any more." I lock eyes with Marsha. She's part of all this; I wonder how much she knows about what my mum has sacrificed for the Resistance. "It's become a lot worse over the past six months. The drinking, the pills, the confusion. She tried to tell me that night what she'd found – but I ignored her, like I always ignored her."

Albert gives my hand a gentle squeeze. "But if your mum's right, why would the Farmer keep evidence that might implicate him?"

"As insurance," Marsha says. "The Farmer is one of the deputy protectors of England, but that doesn't mean he's safe. Whenever the Protectorate feels threatened, it will pick a high-level official and accuse him of treason. You've both seen the televised show trials. Actually, the very fact the Farmer has never been accused is suspicious. They're obviously frightened he might reveal what he did for them."

"So why don't they just kill him?" I ask.

"He must have some method for releasing the evidence to foreign press and governments, should anything happen to him."

"Okay." I try to control my breathing. This is it: the key to potentially ending all the horror and fear and misery that has textured our lives since the moment we were born. I think of the Rebels, I think of my dad, I think of Eric. This discovery could be the way out of the nightmare, for us all. "So how do we get our hands on the evidence?" I ask, my mind buzzing through the logistics. "The Farmer's country estate is just outside Taunton. That's where my mum lives pretty much full time, so she must have found the evidence there. Taunton's not far from here, right?"

"About thirty miles or so," Marsha says carefully.

"Right. So if we set out tonight—"

"No." For the first time, the old woman's voice is stern. "You've done enough by making the connection. Once the phone lines are working again, I'll report all this to the

Resistance. They will determine the best way to proceed."

Anger explodes in my chest. "But I need to be part of this! The things they've done to me, to everyone."

Marsha stands up sharply. "I'm sorry, but there are two very good reasons why you can't be involved. First, as a high-profile fugitive you would be a liability to any mission. Second, you owe it not only to yourself but to your father and your friends, who've all risked so much for you, to reach that boat. Do you understand? Gabriel?"

I turn away, my fists clenched, my eyes smarting. Yes, I understand. What Marsha's saying makes perfect sense. Of course it does. And I hate it.

"Got everything you need?" Marsha asks.

I climb wearily upstairs, joining her on the landing. "Sure. Thanks."

She pats the bannister, a rueful smile on her lips. "The apple doesn't fall far from the tree, does it?"

"So I'm told." I let go of a long breath. "Did you know my dad well, then? Back in the old days?"

Her smile becomes nostalgic. "He would've said I was his mentor. I'm not sure that's entirely true. Your father always knew his own mind, even when he was a kid. Knew it too well, perhaps. Sometimes it was only your mother who could talk any sense into him."

I don't want to ask the next question, but I have to know: "Were you involved? In sending my mum to the Farmer?"

She hesitates. "That was her choice."

"And that's a pretty shitty answer."

"It was *her* choice," she insists. "And yes, she's paid a dreadful price for it. But please don't dishonour her sacrifice by questioning it. She was a very brave and intelligent woman."

I feel the heat rush into my face. "And what is she now?"

I want to say more. I want to rant and rave and show Marsha how much I'm hurting. I want to vent my anger, my sorrow, my guilt, my despair at the idea that I'll never get to tell my mother how sorry I am for misjudging her – and then I want to let it all go. But letting go is hard.

Then Marsha says something, and it's like she's reading my mind. "Your father told me about your relationship with the inspector's son. I just wanted to say…" She stops, and I'm surprised by the crack of emotion in her voice. "You should never regret loving, Gabriel. Even if you lose the person you love best in all the world, the loving will always have been worth it. You might not feel like that now, the pain and the betrayal will be too raw, but eventually you'll realize that it was always worth the cost. You are who you are because of him."

"You don't know what you're talking about," I say.

Marsha doesn't react. She just bows her head and starts down the stairs.

I watch her go, my anger ebbing as a wave of exhaustion sweeps over me. Turning, I slip into the bedroom as quietly as I can. The house only has two, Marsha's and a spare, so we discussed the sleeping arrangements downstairs. I insisted Albert take the double bed while I crashed on a camp bed in the corner. In the dark, I quickly get undressed, place my glasses on the nightstand and inch my aching body into a sleeping bag. Staring up at the bedroom's faded floral wallpaper, blurred petals seem to float around me like falling snow.

I breathe. I count my heartbeats. But in the dark a new and awful thought jumps out at me: it was *my* stepfather who planted the bomb that killed Eric's grandfather. If Roger McCormack had failed, if the bomb hadn't gone off, if Inspector Dufresne's dad hadn't been murdered that day, how different things might be. For everyone.

There's a rustle of sheets and I glance over at the huddled form in the bed.

"Hey, are you awake?" I feel this huge lump in my throat. I don't want to be alone with my thoughts right now, and anyway, I need things to be okay between us. "Albert, I'm so sorry. About leaving you in the square. I can't even begin to—"

"I know you are." Without my glasses, I can't see his face

as he sits up. He's silent for a moment, then sighs. "Are you all right? Do you want to talk?"

I prop myself up on one elbow. Thank God for Albert. He's a better friend than I deserve.

"I can't stop thinking about my mum," I tell him. "She came for a visit last September. Offered me a chance to go live with her and I threw it back in her face. Like it was nothing. Like *she* was nothing. I thought she was being selfish, you know, uncaring towards my dad – when all she really wanted was to save me."

"Gabe, you didn't know."

"I knew she was in pain. That should have been enough. But I just loved being angry with her, so I chose not to understand what she was asking. I think maybe that was when the drinking and the pills really took hold of her. She must have been so lonely." He starts to argue, says it's not my fault, but it is. It just is. "Anyway, I want you to know, you were right," I say quickly. "Everything you said in the car about us being responsible for each other? I'm sorry I let you down."

For a long time neither of us says a word. Then Albert pulls back the bedclothes.

"It looks uncomfortable down there." He throws a pillow at my head. "Come on."

And so we top and tail, like we used to when were little kids and the world was less complicated. At first we lay there, listening to the creaks and groans of the old house settling for the night. Then I reach under the covers and waggle his foot.

"What happened to us, eh? Why did we stop being so close?"

I feel him tense. A grandfather clock downstairs chimes out a slow, musical midnight. Finally, he stirs.

"Maybe I can tell," he says. "Maybe in the dark, I can be brave."

"What are you talking about? Albert, you're always brave."

"Not always. Not ever really. So, back in school I used to watch you. Even before we became the Rebels, I liked you, Gabe. Right from when we were kids and we'd tell each other those stupid ghost stories. Even then you always knew who you were. That's pretty inspiring, you know? There aren't many people who know who they are. Or if they do, they don't have the courage to show it. You did. Just because the Protectorate and the Green Jackets never saw it, you were *always* you. And I loved you for that."

"Albert…"

"Gabe. I *love* you."

Eric told me weeks ago that Albert liked me, but I never quite believed it. We'd been friends for so long it seemed like such a leap. But now he's saying he loves me, and I feel honoured and humbled and guilty, all at the same time.

Pulling back the covers, I switch ends so that I can lie with him, face to face. His eyes are tight shut, his arms folded across his chest, hands gripping his shoulders.

"Why didn't you say something?"

He shakes his head. "Because Eric came along."

"But you said you always knew."

"I did. But the truth? It scared me. 'What if he doesn't like me the way I really am?' That was what I always thought, why I kept it secret. Why I pulled away. 'What if I show him and he doesn't understand what he sees?' Because I can deal with being on my own and never taking the risk, but if I told him and he doesn't understand? I couldn't..."

"It's all right, Albert."

He opens his eyes and a few tears spill onto his pillow.

"The truth." He lets go of his shoulders and covers his face with his hands. "I've never felt like a boy, Gabe. Not once. Not ever. A boy isn't who I am... Do you understand?"

And I do, because now it all makes sense. Albert's isolation, even within the Rebels; the reason for his sister Lana's hatred of him, a hatred so enormous it seemed insane, even by Protectorate standards. I suppose the Heck family must always have had their suspicions that Albert was a particular kind of degen. I suddenly think of us all back at the library, watching *Disclosure*. Even back when it was made, in a world a million times more accepting than this one, trans people were always the most ridiculed, most despised, even among a minority of degens themselves. It makes no sense to me, but why should it? Nothing about prejudice makes sense.

And then I remember something Albert said after the movie had finished.

They hardly ever got to be the hero of their own stories.

I realize now that she was seeing herself truly reflected, probably for the first time. What an incredible moment that must have been for her.

And I missed it.

"Say something," she murmurs. "*Please.*"

I reach out and very gently pull her hands away. Then I cup the side of her face with my palm, smoothing her tears with my thumb.

"Let me see you."

And she does. And I ask the only question worth asking.

"So what do I call you now?"

She looks at me, so much hope in her gaze. "I don't understand."

"Yes you do," I say, wiping away the last tear. "Albert's your old name, right? Okay. So I'd like to know what my best friend has chosen as her real name. Her true name."

And she smiles.

THEN

DECEMBER – FOUR MONTHS AGO

"I'm ready to tell you about my scars."

All the fun and laughter of June's birthday party has evaporated and Eric is looking at me with eyes like caverns. Meanwhile Totes scampers around our feet, tumbling through the freshly fallen snow. The sky has finally broken and thick white flakes dust the derelict shopping centre.

"Try to understand," he says. "Please, promise me you'll try."

"Eric…"

I go to hug him and he pushes me away. Then, reaching into his coat, Eric brings out the drawing I gave him weeks ago: my dad's sketch of Lady of the Green Kirtle, the Narnia villain, snakelike on her throne.

"I've been carrying this around with me. My mum would've loved—" He presses the back of his hand against his mouth. "My mum killed herself last summer, Gabe.

That's why we had to move away from London. Like my dad said, a fresh start..."

I take a sharp breath, try to reach for him, but he very gently pushes my hand away. Replacing the drawing, Eric turns to the low parapet that overlooks the town. Amidst the snowfall, houses and factories seem to blink in and out of existence.

"The day before it happened, she found me in the garage," he says. "I knew my dad was at work, that I was safe, but still, that door screeching open? That scared me to death. There was nowhere to hide, you see?

"My dad kept his garage neat as a pin. No boxes or bits of old furniture to dive behind. It was the same with our house. Everything clear and clean and uncluttered. You know I told you he was there the day of the Outrage? That he saw his dad blown to pieces? They say the bomb was hidden under a load of old bric-a-brac in the basement of the hotel. I think because of that, my dad always sees mess and untidiness as an opportunity to hide dangerous things. Well, I was hiding things that day. One thing consciously, the other..." He pats the drawing in his pocket.

"'Poor little thing,' my mum had said.

"And there was something about how she said it, Gabe. I wasn't sure if she meant me or the bird. I'd found it in the gutter outside our house. A chaffinch. They used to be really common in Britain. Millions and millions of them.

323

Anyway, I'd dug out an old shoebox from upstairs and I'd padded it out with socks and pillows and stuff, but the bird was still shaking really badly. Shock, I guess.

"'Next door's cat must have got it,' I told her. 'Its wing's broken.'

"She knelt down with me and brushed her finger across its feathers. We were quiet for a bit, then I said, 'Are you going to tell him?'

"She didn't answer. We both knew what my dad would say: 'Nature decides what survives and what doesn't. If we try to help then we're interfering with the natural order, and all that does is make *us* unnatural.'"

"I'll never understand that," I say, cutting into his story.

Eric gives me this sad smile. "I'm glad you don't. I love it that you don't.

"So, my mum went into the house and came back with the first aid kit. She cut this long piece of bandaging tape, then asked me to hold the bird while she wrapped its wing. I could feel its heartbeat against my hand." He lifts his palm and smiles at the memory. "When she was done, we put the bird back in the box and watched for a while. It walked around a bit and Mum adjusted the tape.

"'How did you know how to do that?' I asked her.

"'I might have read a banned book or two.' She gave me this look, as if she wanted to laugh but couldn't. I should've

324

known then. I *should* have. My mum always used to laugh so easily.

"'You're such a gentle boy, Eric,' she said.

"And then…" He rocks back, still clutching the wall, his face twisted with grief. "She said, 'I know, son. I *know*.'

"I asked her what she was talking about. And I tried to laugh. But I couldn't, because all of a sudden I was crying. Just sobbing and sobbing. I couldn't stop. And my mum, she put her arms around me and held me so tight. She kept whispering that she knew and that it was okay, that *I* was okay. She said she'd known since I was a little boy. That mums *always* know. She said she wished that she'd spoken to me about it a long time ago, but that she wanted me to know myself before…

"And then she stopped, right there. Right on that word. *Before.* I didn't understand what she meant. Not then.

"'There's nothing wrong with you,' my mum said. 'Not a single thing, and all those people out there who think there is? They're all just blind or confused or twisted with their own ignorance, but one day they'll see how wrong they've been. Even your dad'll see. But in the meantime, you have to stay strong and you have to play the part. Eric, you have to try…' She held my hand so tight, Gabe. 'You have to pretend. Do you promise me?'

"So I promised, and she…I could see it in her face. She could tell that I wouldn't be able to pretend. Not for ever."

Eric chokes, as if he's about to vomit, and I want to help him, but I know he has to do this on his own.

"I think maybe that's what broke her. Knowing that one day she'd have to watch as my lies came tumbling down around me.

"When my dad…when he found her the next morning, I remembered the promise I'd made. I'd be strong. I'd try. Because suicide is a crime, and being a degen is a crime, and my dad would need me to look after him now. He's never said he blames me, but I know he does, because I think he's always known too. About who I am." Eric blinks at me through the snow, like a little kid coming out of a bad dream. "That same morning, I found the bird thrown into the garbage. I don't know if it died naturally or if…"

He shivers. Hugs himself. Looks out onto the ghostly town.

"So now you know why."

I grab his hand. "Eric."

"If I could've pretended, if she'd believed I could, then—"

"You don't know that," I say. "You don't know why your mum did what she did. She was probably unhappy for a lot of reasons. And anyway, she told you that being who you are is okay, didn't she?"

"It's not only that," he says. "Gabe, I was angry with her. I *am* angry with her. For giving me those consoling words and then just abandoning me. For leaving me alone in all this shit. And when I think stuff like that, my head, it's like all these thoughts screaming over each other. The anger and the grief. And the only way to stop all the noise is…"

His fingers drift across his torso, tracing hidden loops and whirls, white-hot highways of misplaced shame.

I won't let him do this to himself any more.

"Your mother would never want this," I say. "And, Eric, I don't ever want to see you hurt yourself again." He sobs and I pull him towards me and wrap my arms around him. "It's okay. I'm here. I'll always be here."

NOW

26

Her name is Alice.

That's what she tells me and straight away – no doubts, no hesitations, that's who she is. My best friend Alice. Because it's who she's always been, and yes, because at last there's no more awkwardness or distance between us. It just feels right.

"But why would you ever think I wouldn't accept you?" I ask.

"Because although you're gay and you know what it's like to be different, you can't understand what it's like to be trans, Gabe. Not completely. It's like those people said in *Disclosure* – sometimes even those who count themselves as allies get it wrong. They can be guilty of insensitivity and misrepresentation too. And even worse, some gay people can be prejudiced. Remember what I said at the millstream? I knew that if, when, I told you, things might change between us."

"But, Alice—"

"I knew it wasn't likely, but they *might*. And let's forget about me liking you for a second – I couldn't risk everything changing. Not now. Not with so much on the line. If we stopped trusting each other, stopped caring about each other, that could have put both of us in danger."

Alice continues to talk and I continue to listen. I hear about how she tried to understand her identity from an early age but, with no cultural references or role models to guide her, it had taken her a long time. Then, when at last she had begun to realize who she was, the doubts about how even her closest friends would react started to overwhelm her. And so in order to protect herself, she pulled away from us. Just a little, just enough. It devastates me that this is how she felt, but listening to Alice, I understand her fear.

It isn't until the grandfather clock downstairs chimes one that we finally come to it. We lie face to face, and her smile falters.

"I said I love you, Gabe."

I nod and take her hand. "I know."

"But if I'm honest, I always knew you didn't feel that way about me."

"Alice..."

"It's okay."

I squeeze her hand and when she looks away, I duck my head to meet her gaze again.

"You're right, I don't think of you that way, and it hurts more than you can imagine to say that. Because you're just about the kindest, bravest person I've ever met. But here's the thing. Hey." I lean in and kiss her gently on the forehead. "You're my best friend. You always were. And I will *always* be there for you, okay? I promise."

We go on talking for another hour or so, reliving old memories in a way that makes our drifting apart these past few years seem somehow unreal. But finally exhaustion overcomes us. Still holding Alice's hand, I plunge into the best night's sleep I've had since my arrest.

Someone rocks my shoulder and my eyes snap open. As gently as I can, trying not to wake Alice, I reach for the dressing table and my glasses. Over by the black rectangle of the window, Marsha waits with Totes anxiously twisting between her legs.

"Three cars on the road," she mutters. "They've found you."

I go and stand beside her. The rain has stopped but the wind still shrieks around the clifftop house. Far out in the distance, pinprick headlights tumble towards us.

"Still quite a way off," Marsha says. "That's one of the advantages of living in the middle of nowhere – you can always see trouble heading your way."

"How do you know it's them?" I ask. "Could be the Resistance."

"Nice thought, but the phone lines are still down. I haven't managed to tell them about your discovery just yet."

"But how do the Jackets even know we're here? Have you ever been under suspicion, Marsha? Maybe Dufresne's checking out any possible Resistance sympathizers in the area."

"No one's ever suspected me of anything," she says. "I've made sure of that. You see, it isn't only your mother who's made sacrifices, Gabriel. I knew right from the beginning that, if I wanted to help people escape, I could never draw the attention of the Green Jackets."

Her meaning hits me hard. "You mean you've always been alone?"

She turns and heads for the door. "Best wake your friend."

Alice opens her eyes with a start when I shake her and, after a few words of explanation, we're both frantically pulling on our clothes. Downstairs, we find Marsha at the open front door. The sky is moonless, the landscape hidden. Only those six headlights shine out, like spider eyes homing in on the house. We grab our backpacks from the hall and follow Marsha into the little kitchen. As soon as she opens the back door, the wind wrenches it from her grasp and the smell of the sea crashes against us.

"Here," she bellows, handing over a pair of torches. "Follow the path to the edge of the cliff. There's an old iron stairway that leads right down to the beach. It's high tide, so you're in for a paddle, but if they're bringing dogs with them, that should be enough to confuse the scent. Once you're on the beach, turn off the torches and head west."

Alice glances round as a blade of illumination cuts through the house. Over the roar of the wind we can just about hear the approaching engines. I reach down for Totes.

"No." Marsha blocks me. "The dog stays."

"What? No way! I told you last night, Marsha, Dufresne took Totes from my neighbour. We don't know what he's planning, but if he finds him here—"

"But I do know," Marsha says. "And the inspector's plan has already been successful."

She crouches down and parts the fur at the nape of Totes's neck. A couple of the old scars from when Eric and I first found him last November are still just about visible, but there's another that looks brand new.

"Tracker chip," Marsha grunts. "Should've thought of it last night. That's why the inspector wanted you, isn't it, Totes? This was Dufresne's insurance policy."

"If Eric ever decided to desert the Green Jackets and make a run for it, he'd take Totes with him," I say. "Implanting the chip, Dufresne would be able to locate

332

Eric and bring him home before too much damage was done." I kneel down beside the little dog. "Maybe if we can get this thing out of him…"

Totes whimpers as I press my fingers against the hard square under his skin.

"There's no time," Marsha insists.

"There has to be—"

"Gabe," Alice snaps. "Gabe, stop!"

She pulls my hands away and Totes darts behind Marsha's legs. I try to make a grab for him, then slump against the doorframe while the wind screams at me.

"I'm sorry," I say, looking around at each of them. "I'm sorry."

Totes pads towards me and licks my outstretched fingers.

"You have to leave him here," Marsha insists. "It's the only way."

"And when Dufresne gets hold of him?"

There's no answer to that, and so we stand in silence for a second or two and try to push away all the dark possibilities. But the engines are louder now, the lights brighter.

"Come with us," Alice says, turning to Marsha. "Even if we have to leave Totes, you don't have to stay. They'll know you've helped us. You'll be taken to a Re-Education camp, maybe worse. It'll be the end of the Underground Railroad."

"It'll be the end of my part in it," Marsha replies. "But there are always others waiting to pick up the reins. Anyway, there's no chance an old fart like me could make it down those stairs and along the beach. I'm better use to you here, keeping them busy as long as I can."

Alice and I exchange an anguished look.

Finally, I crouch down and let Totes snuggle up to my chest. I always used to tease Eric about those simple tricks he tried to teach this doofus-y dog, but maybe I misjudged our mutt. Totes laps the tear from my cheek and whimpers. I think he understands.

"You be a good boy now." I gather him up and kiss his nose, then hand him quickly to Marsha. "Thank you. For everything."

There's nothing else to be said. We flick on our torches, give Marsha a nod, and head into the night.

Our boots crunch the gravel path that leads arrow-straight to the cliff. Reaching the precipice, I think Marsha must have made a mistake, or else we've somehow misunderstood. There's no stairway here, only a few tufts of yellow grass clinging to the brink. I plant my feet close to the edge and peer down. Far below, I can just about make out the pointed white hoods of the waves, while all around, the same exposed landscape that warned us of the approaching cars now threatens to give us away.

Lights bloom against the little house behind us. Engines

die and doors snap open. Voices shout commands into the wind while dogs bark, harsh and full-throated.

Alice looks at me. "Gabe…"

A stupid thought comes into my head: is Eric with them? I tell myself I don't care.

And then a sound like a cracked bell echoes from below. Metal tolling against stone. We look at each other and dip our torchlight over the drop. Hugging the cliff, a ladder of switchback iron jags down into the darkness. It's possible that Marsha hasn't checked the stairway in a while because, from the few empty bolt-holes in the rock face, it looks as if the topmost level has fallen into the sea. The remaining steps begin five feet below.

"I'll go," I grunt. "If it holds me, you follow."

Alice shakes her head. "Too dangerous."

I open my mouth to argue and catch sight of the dog. It races around the side of the house, stopping dead when it sees us, ears sprouting like demonic horns. It's alone, but that's not much comfort. Not when you could pretty much fit your entire head inside those slick black jaws. After a second's indecision, the Dobermann sets off again, bounding towards us.

"Change of plan," I shout. "We go together. Now!"

I tear off Alice's backpack and throw it, together with mine, over the ledge. There's no time to check my aim; I turn around, my back to the precipice, and drop to my knees.

The wind rushes against me as, flat on my stomach, I slither backwards until my legs are hanging over the brink. Alice moves with me, shoulder to shoulder, our bodies pivoting between one kind of death and another.

I grasp tufts of sodden grass, working them hand over hand, shuffling further into thin air. My feet dangle in the void. Now my chest is scraping against the cliff edge, now my elbows are planted on the last scrap of stone, now it's only my fingers clinging to those final few inches. Loose pebbles rain down, scratching my face, chinking brightly against the waiting stairway.

It's time to choose.

Closing my eyes, I let go of the cliff.

27

I hit the stairway and the whole structure groans like a dying giant. The impact collapses my legs under me and I instinctively grab for the handrail. Clutching the rain-slick metal, it feels as if every organ in my body has been thrust into strange new positions, my heart rammed up into my throat, my stomach cycloned around my ribs. I'm panting, spitting copper onto the stairs, when Alice slams into the step below.

I see her reel against the dark, hands grasping the air, her face long with terror. Behind her, the stairs spiral down, a hundred glinting teeth ready to crush and tear. Her boots teeter on the step, her mouth yawns into a scream, and I throw myself sideways. Wet fingers slide through mine, I think I've lost her, but in this split second I decide that, unlike with Eric, if Alice falls, she won't fall alone. I lunge again, grab her shirt, and somehow haul us both back onto the level.

"You're okay," I grunt. "We're—"

Something thick and treacly winds down onto my shoulder. I flick it away, disgusted, and we both glance up. The Dobermann is straining over the drop, its doll-like eyes fixed on us, a thread of drool dribbling from its lower lip. Staggering backwards, I push Alice against the rock face and then press my own body tight to the cliff. Over the wind, I can hear footsteps.

"Get away from there, Diana!"

The dog's head jerks around and a torch beam flashes down. I hold my breath. In that moment, the pain from my landing rips through the adrenalin in my bloodstream and saws a path along my left leg and across my hip. I bite the inside of my mouth against it.

There's no outcrop to shelter us, the cliff is sheer. If the Green Jacket looks directly down then he *will* see us. But that would mean he'd have to stand on the very edge, and with the wind tearing at him, he might not chance it. I reach out, place the flat of my palm against Alice's shoulder, count my heartbeats.

"C'mon," the voice mutters at last. "Let's get back to the house."

Diana barks her complaint as the torchlight swings around.

We wait for a few breathless moments, then peel ourselves away from the rock. Luckily our packs have landed more or less at our feet. We exchange a quick glance and then start our descent. I go first, taking it slow, gripping the icy rail. When we reach the first switchback, I have to snatch my fingers away and flex some warmth back into them. Alice does the same.

At the third turn, we're forced to stop. The gradual vibration of our steps has set off shock waves throughout the structure. Even over the wind I can hear the weeping of the rusted bolts while through my feet I feel the teasing give of the stairway. Any second now it could shear away from the cliff, mangling itself and us as it falls, hitting the water like some blood-soaked sculpture. We wait, eyes locked, until the shudders subside. Then down again. Down, down, down. There's no light now, only the bellow of the night and the rush of the sea.

Spray whips up, drenching my glasses. It doesn't matter, there isn't anything to see in this starless dark, but there is plenty to imagine. As we spiral on, I wonder what's happening in the little house high above. I start to picture Dufresne, angry and desperate, Marsha crumpled beneath him. Totes whimpering in a corner of the lounge as another boot strikes the old woman. I thumb the water from my glasses and glance upwards. I *want* to go back, want to tear those bastards to bits, but I know how impossible that sounds, and anyway we need to get the evidence that will destroy the Protectorate for good.

My boot plunges off the final step into a freezing tide. Reaching into my backpack, I take out the torch and risk a snatch of light. In both directions, a foot of seawater is lapping against the base of the cliffs.

"West," I say, nodding left.

Alice's face shines, pale and worn in the torchlight.

Marsha was right: it's a nightmare walk. The wind howls around us and our feet keep slipping in the pebbled sludge. We both fall at least once, slicing our hands on rock and stone and shell, salt water smarting our cuts. When I take my tumble, I lose my glasses in the swell and this suffocating panic almost overwhelms me. I plunge down to my knees and start thrashing at the waves.

"What's the matter?" Alice shouts.

"My glasses! I've lost them!"

She drags me to my feet and I try to fight against her. Doesn't she understand? My glasses... Facing me, pinning me to the cliff, Alice lifts them very gently off my nose.

"It's okay," she says. "They're right here."

She hooks them back over my ears and I shake my head. "What's happening to me?"

"You're exhausted," she says. "But look."

Back the way we've come a red-hot wire is singeing the sky. Dawn. And just a few hundred feet ahead of us, a bay with a gentle slope to the headland.

By the time we reach dry land, the wind has fallen and

the sun is blazing. There's a cave halfway up the beach with a circle of stones where others have made a fire before. We quickly gather up driftwood and some of the marram grass that grows in the lee of the cliffs. Alice hunts in her pack for matches; luckily, they're still dry.

We huddle close and watch the fire paint phantoms on the walls.

"Can't stop thinking about Marsha," Alice whispers. "What do you think they'll do to her?"

I shake my head. I've already imagined all the nightmares the old woman might be going through.

Alice spreads her hands to the flames. "Should only be another twenty-five miles or so to the meeting point. Less, if we can find a way to cross the River Parrett. Then we just need to—"

"We can't."

She turns salt-stung eyes on me. "What do you mean?"

"Sorry," I give her a weak smile, "I shouldn't have said we. I can't."

Her voice trembles. "You're not making any sense."

"The phone lines were still down when we left," I say. "Marsha never got the chance to call the Resistance. Only we know about the Farmer's involvement in the Outrage."

"You don't know that," Alice objects. "Maybe your mum already told your dad."

"He would have mentioned it," I say. "That garbled

message she gave me? That all happened weeks ago. Alice, my mum found evidence that the Farmer was the Outrage bomber. The whole Protectorate is built on that lie."

She's quiet for a moment, her hands bunching together. "Marsha said you owe it to your dad to escape."

"I know, but I owe it to *everyone* to get that evidence. This isn't just about freeing ourselves any more. If we can take it to the Irish government, if we can prove the Protectorate planned the Outrage, then perhaps everything changes." I take her fire-warmed hand in mine. "My dad told me that the beauty of freedom sometimes demands a great sacrifice. I think the librarian's films taught us the same thing. That was their most important message, wasn't it? Whatever the risk, the fight is always worth it."

She shakes her head. "I'm scared, Gabe."

"You don't have to be. The boat will be there tomorrow morning. You can still be on it."

She stands, facing the mouth of the cave and the sea.

"No," she says. "I can't."

28

It might sound crazy, but one of the hardest things to bear when you live under the Protectorate is their claim to own every inch of this country. Sometimes that doesn't seem like a big deal. Let them keep the poisoned skies and polluted streams, the abandoned ghost cities and the bombed-out houses: that's *their* legacy. But when you're walking through hills and heathlands like these, their right to fly a red-and-black flag over it all is the sickest kind of joke.

I glance at Alice and the anger cools in my chest. It's almost funny, two teenagers limping like an old couple through the wilderness. She catches my gaze and smiles. I'd like to stay in this moment, just the two of us, but the same dark thoughts roll in again. She shouldn't be here. She should be halfway to the bay by now, comfortably ahead of schedule, confident that she'll arrive to meet the boat at dawn. She definitely should *not* be marching in the opposite direction, towards fuck knows what.

Part of me wants to start the argument again. This is my decision, my fight. But we've already spent the whole morning going round in circles. She won't leave me, and that's that. And anyway, a smaller, more selfish part of me is glad that I have Alice by my side.

I scramble up onto an old dry-stone wall and Alice climbs up after me. It's a narrow shelf and the bits of slate and slab see-saw under our feet.

"Look over there," she says. "I think that's Wales." She points excitedly, way out to the northern horizon where a hint of land rises above the gleam of the Bristol Channel. "Still Protectorate, but technically a different country." She sighs. "I'd like to walk in a different country one day."

"You can," I tell her. "If you go back."

She looks at me and smiles. "Right here. This is where you should set the penultimate scene of your film. A moment of peace and beauty before the finale. Before the happy ending."

And suddenly Alice's smile becomes something else. I don't know how to describe it. It's like she's seen something between the cracks of the universe, and what she's seen is sad and comforting all at the same time. Those moon-grey eyes dance across the landscape. Far down the hillside, a flock of wild ponies cut loops and whirls in the heather.

"We'll make a film like no one's ever seen," I promise her. "And it won't just tell the world the literal truth, it'll get into their hearts and minds. It'll dig deep and it'll stay with them. That's how you change people, I think. You have to touch their soul."

"And you'll do that, Gabe," she says. "I know you will."

"*We'll* do it. You and me."

"That sounds nice."

"And what about you?" I ask. "What do you want to do when we get to Ireland? You never answered me before."

She takes a moment, her fingers twined together. "I want to be me. Finally, I just want to be *me*." I put my arm around her shoulders. "I'd also quite like to be a car mechanic." She laughs. "And help you with your movie, obviously."

"Obviously."

An hour later, we stop for lunch in the shelter of an old shepherd's hut and I warm some tea over a fire. Then, sitting beside her, I peel off my boots. The odour is not pleasant.

"Sorry."

Alice shrugs. "Mine are just as bad."

I take some of the leftover water from the tea and slosh it over my blistered feet. The pain makes the space between my eyes sing.

"Here." Alice dusts off her hands. "Let me."

"No," I gasp. "It's disgusting."

"Well, you can do mine after. Deal?"

All I can do is nod. Alice digs some antiseptic ointment out of her bag and hands me a couple of painkillers. I swallow the tablets quickly and look away. It's weird, I've lived through some pretty brutal beatings these past weeks, but those blousy, white-bellied blisters are the worst kind of agony. I close my eyes, ready to hold back a scream.

"What do you reckon the guys are doing right now?" Alice asks.

"The Rebels? Let me think. I'm picturing June grappling Ben into a headlock after her no-hugs policy has been ignored for the thousandth time. And Grace is in the back office helping Liz with her latest fashion masterpiece. I don't know." I laugh. "I hope they're back in the library again, watching movies."

"That's how I like to think of them, too. Snuggled up on that ratty old sofa, quiet for once."

"Hey, maybe they'll watch our movie one day. Imagine years from now, when the Protectorate's only a memory – we'll invite them to the premiere. Black limousines and red carpets, the whole deal."

"Brilliant." She grins. "Aaaaand…we're done."

"Wait. What?" I look down at my feet. They're both neatly bandaged and I haven't felt a thing. "You know, Alice, they'd have burned you as a witch a few centuries back."

"I suppose so." She picks up my boots and works them gently onto my feet. "Course, they kill us for different things now." She holds out the ointment. "Your turn."

Afterwards, I kick over the ashes of the fire and we drift out into the sunshine. Ahead of us, mile after mile of the same beautiful hills.

"I miss them, you know." She blinks up at me, hesitates. "I miss *all* of them."

"Me too," I say, cutting my eyes away.

The sun arcs overhead and shadows lengthen in the valleys. Colours change around us, purple heather stained red, streaks of green leaping out of the sandstone. Alice checks her map and points south-east, towards the outskirts of Taunton. At last we slope down from the hills and, after another mile or two, I start to recognize familiar landmarks: a church with a wall full of old bullet holes; a toppling, fire-bombed pub; and in the distance, just visible above the trees, the chimneys of Roger McCormack's country estate.

I gesture for Alice to follow me into the woods. So many school holidays spent here, so many rows with my dad about whether or not I had to go. *"She's still your mother, Gabe."* At least that sullen, stupid boy made good use of his time. The hideout I dubbed Castle Sawyer is still standing, more or less. Pretty amazing considering it's six years old and is basically just a few nailed-together crates half buried in the undergrowth. Crouching low, we throw our packs inside then worm our way in after them, feet first. In my memory, Castle Sawyer is gigantic, but this is a tight squeeze. Shoulder to shoulder, I point through the bracken.

"The Agriculture Protectorate isn't much of a target for the Resistance, so the Farmer's never needed top-notch security. All he gets is a couple of guards who sleep in an outbuilding. They've got pretty lazy over the years and tend to knock off right after he goes to bed, but it's a weekday, right?" Alice nods. "Which means he's probably in London. My mum too."

I get this hollow, aching, desolate feeling as I say it. Ever since I found out what my mother has sacrificed for the Resistance, the urge to see her again, to apologize, has haunted me. Now I'll never get the opportunity.

Something flashes between the trees and we shuffle further back into the fort.

"Grey Jacket patrol," I whisper. "There should only be one of them. He'll make a continuous circuit of the whole outer wall; probably take him twenty minutes for each pass."

We watch the officer stroll by the back gate, head down, yawning.

"What now?" Alice whispers.

"Now we wait."

Hour by hour, the darkness deepens. After a while, the injury to my hip from landing awkwardly on the stairway starts to spasm and I have to dig more painkillers out of my pack and chew them fast to take off the edge. When the Grey Jacket makes his eighteenth pass, I give Alice the signal. It's time.

At the treeline, we pause. The path that separates the wood from the high, wire-topped wall of the estate is empty. Turning to Alice, I lick the pad of my thumb.

"This is the residence of a deputy protector," I whisper, rubbing a smudge from her nose. "Have to make you presentable."

It's a jokey thing, something to ease the tension, but still my heart jolts.

"Ready?"

She nods, and we step out onto the path.

29

We move quickly to the iron gate and the keypad attached to the wall.

"Remember me saying how lazy they've got about security?" I say. "Well, they never once changed the code when I visited. I suppose the numbers might mean something to the Farmer or maybe—"

And suddenly it hits me, and I think I might vomit. Alice watches as I punch in the digits with a shaking finger.

"Is that…?" She stares at me. "Jesus, Gabe, is that the date of the Outrage? Like the bastard's proud of it or something?"

I glance up at the red-and-black flag that cracks in the breeze beyond the wall.

"Of course he's proud of it."

The gate buzzes open and we move into the coal-dark shadows of the garden. Again, I'm thankful for all those miserable summer holidays; I guide Alice smoothly through the maze of shrubs and fruit trees and huge topiary animals that tower along every path. The night's silent, still, and we're almost at the patio steps leading up to the house when one of the Farmer's bodyguards emerges from the side of the building.

I grab Alice and pull her behind a bush shaped to resemble a sleeping lion. Through gaps in the greenery, I can see the flare of the man's cigarette as his head snaps in our direction. Did we make a sound? We must have. He's coming towards us.

Boots crack the gravel. An angry flash as the cigarette hits the ground. The bodyguard's hand reaches around to the back of his jacket. I remember when these guys played Frisbee with me in the courtyard and I'd catch glimpses of the sleek black weapons they kept holstered in their belts. Is this one of those men? Will he remember me? Will it make a difference even if he does?

I glance back down the path. It runs dead straight, the hedges either side tall and impenetrable. If we make a break for it, it'll be a bullet in the back. If we stay? Well, it's a degen's grave either way. I look at Alice and see the same thought reflected back at me. She squeezes my hand.

"Holy crap!"

Through the hedge, I see the bodyguard hit the brakes, three feet from our hiding place. With a wry smile, he bends down and scoops something up into his arms.

"Was that you making all that racket? You're lucky you didn't end up as target practice. Stupid animal."

He turns and walks back to the house, the Farmer's ancient tomcat peering at us over his shoulder.

Alice and I glance at each other and almost burst out laughing. It's a weird, giddy moment, and we soon pull ourselves together. Breaking cover, we sweep up the steps and head for the veranda doors that lead to the Farmer's study. My guess is that he'd want to keep the evidence of his involvement in the Outrage somewhere private, and this is the one room in the rambling Elizabethan mansion where no one, not even the housemaid, is allowed to enter unsupervised.

A keypad identical to the one by the gate guards the veranda doors. I punch in the same combination and the lock clicks. Evil is so unoriginal. We step over the threshold and I close the doors behind us, pulling the long green curtains to. The room is in darkness but I can smell the fresh stench of the Farmer's cigars. My heart leaps into my throat. He's here, which means *she's* here… I push the thought away; I don't have time to think about my mum right now.

Alice stands watch at the main door while I check all the most obvious places: bureaus, desk drawers, filing cabinets. I'm thorough, but as nothing is locked I already know I won't find the evidence here. I look up from the desk and scan the vast, shadowy room. In mystery novels, there's always a safe hidden behind a picture. It's worth a shot.

A decade or so after the Outrage, Hilary Martin and his cronies began to close down England's great art galleries and museums. Each artefact, sculpture and painting was assessed by the Culture Protectorate to see if it might pose a risk to public morals. Those that failed the test were piled onto colossal bonfires in city squares where loyal citizens were encouraged to dance around the flames. Only a few very famous, very expensive pieces were spared. Some of these now hang on the walls of the Farmer's study.

I grab a chair and start pulling down paintings: a striking, smoky portrait of William Shakespeare; a swirling wheat field under big billowing clouds; a hazy riverbank, sailboats, children playing in the water, a little dog like Totes in the foreground; a wrecked ship with a ghostly sun dying fast in the sky. Behind each there's only blank wall.

Alice comes over. "Nothing?"

"Could be anywhere," I whisper. "It might not even be in the house at all."

"It's here," she assures me, "you just have to think. When your mum called you, did she say anything else?"

"No. Just the stuff about Smiley and that she'd found the evidence and…" I stop dead. My eyes flick to one of the paintings, now resting on the floor, then to the place where it had hung. "The swimmers. She said it was hiding behind the *swimmers*."

That dreamy painting of kids enjoying the river on a summer day. I'm sure whoever painted it was very famous and that my dad would probably have heard of them. The image certainly sparks a lot of memories from my own childhood, swimming at the river bend back in Westwick. I go to the wall and press my hand against the plaster, hoping there might be some secret catch or cavity.

"Gabe…"

"I don't understand," I mutter. "There's nothing."

"Gabe."

I turn to find Alice sitting cross-legged on the carpet. In front of her, the picture is turned upside down and the cardboard backing has been removed. Taped to the inner side of the backing is a thin A4 envelope.

"Hiding behind the swimmers." She grins.

"Alice, you genius!"

She hands me the envelope. I tear it open and pull out the contents. My hands are shaking. Even in the darkness of the room, I can see that we've found it. The evidence that will destroy the Protectorate.

The first item is a crystal-clear photograph of the Outrage bomber in his smiley T-shirt, baseball cap turned backwards, his face easily recognizable. There's no doubt that this is a teenage Roger McCormack. The second item is even more damning. I turn it towards Alice.

"The original draft of the letter they found at the bombsite. The letter that implicated the enemies of the Public Good Party. See this underneath? Instructions for Roger to copy out the letter and then leave it in the debris. It's even signed."

Alice stands up, her eyes bright.

"Hilary Martin."

And then the grin falls from her lips.

The study door has opened and Roger McCormack has stepped into the room. He turns on the light and those small, mean eyes dart from under the slab of his brow, first to me, then to Alice, then the painting. His mouth flaps open and shut like a landed fish. He comes forward a step or two, leaning heavily on his stick. He's only eight years older than my mum, but all that rich food has given him agonizing gout. So at least there's some justice in the world.

At first I think he's going to call for his bodyguard. Then a look of stark terror washes over his face. He knows he can't involve them. Not while we have the letter and the photograph.

"Gabriel," he says, forcing a chuckle. "This is a surprise."

"I bet," I reply. "Sorry about the mess."

He closes the door and moves to his desk, planting his backside on the corner.

"You always did like to make a scene. Last time we met it was some drama at a hotel, I remember."

"As far as dramas at hotels are concerned, I think you've got me beat." I hold up the evidence. "How many people died that day? Do you even know?"

"How many children?" Alice snaps.

He shrugs. "They were a means to an end. The problem with this country, boys, has always been its unwillingness to look an ugly fact in the face. Oh, we call it tolerance and values and whatnot, but really it's just squeamishness. We don't like to get our hands dirty. We have to be pushed and bullied into making a stand. And, honestly, you have no idea what it was like back then: foreigners on every street, traitors in every government, queers parading their perversions in front of our... Oh, I'm sorry. Have I offended you?"

"You offend me, yes," I reply. "Murderers tend to."

"I got my hands dirty," he retorts. "I did my duty and I made my stand." He taps his silver-handled cane lazily against his foot. "But all that's ancient history. You have my secret, I want it back. I'm not even interested in how you found out about it. In fact, I'm quite impressed. I always knew you were a clever little faggot. But now you've found yourself in a – how shall we put it? – *delicate* predicament. You must have calculated that, although I could help you, I probably wouldn't, unless perhaps there was some way to force my hand." He gestures towards the letter and the photograph. "So, what can I do for you, my boy?"

Alice looks at me, her mouth set firm.

"Nothing," I say. "We're taking this with us, that's all."

Roger bursts out laughing. "And you expect me to just sit here and let you go?"

"What else can you do?" I shrug. "The two of us are more than a match for you."

"I have a house full of security guards," the Farmer laughs.

"Then call them. Except…if you do and one of them saw this evidence, well, they could easily end up blackmailing you. So, I guess this is a catch-22 situation." I click my fingers. "Actually, it's one of my favourite banned books." I start shoving the evidence into the envelope and put the envelope into my backpack. "At least this way you've got a day or two before the story gets out. Enough time to escape the country, if you're lucky." I head towards the veranda doors. "Come on, Alice, I think we're done h—"

I never would have believed he could move so quickly. One second, he's propped on the desk, smiling his fake smile, the next he's lunged forward, raised that heavy stick over his head, and smashed the silver handle against Alice's skull. The sound of breaking bone is bright and clean and devastating. Standing near the desk, she had been his easiest target and, as she spins around to face me, I know I'd give anything to have switched places with her.

Her lips stretch into a surprised "O" and her hand goes to her hair, fingers sweeping through the pale strands above her temple. She takes a step, draws a sharp breath. When she pulls back her hand and looks at her stained fingertips, a puzzled expression crumples those delicate features, as if she can't understand why her palm is so red. She holds it out to me and says in a wondering voice: "Gabe, I think something's wrong."

THEN

FEBRUARY – TWO MONTHS AGO

I'm just thinking about Eric when there's a knock at the door – his trademark *rat-tat-a-tat-tat*. Skipping over the usual carnage of my bedroom into the hall, I find him on the doorstep, planted there like some gorgeous garden gnome. Honestly, with his red bobble hat and the striped scarf wrapped around his chin, all he's missing is a fishing rod and a pipe.

"Hello, boyfriend." I grin at him.

He shoots a quick glance over his shoulder. "Hello, boyfriend."

I take his hand just as my dad wheels out from the kitchen. "Eric, this is a pleasant surprise. Are you hungry? I think there's enough in the pot if you fancy some mystery ratatouille?" He tips Eric a wink. "Guaranteed rodent-free."

"No thanks, Mr Sawyer. We're going out."

I frown. "We are?"

He prods my cheek. "We are."

Edging past me, he grabs my coat from the hook and starts pulling my arms through the sleeves, like I'm a toddler who hasn't quite mastered the complex physics of dressing myself. When I insist on changing into my walking boots, he starts to hop up and down on the spot.

"Comeoncomeoncomeon!"

I dangle a boot in front of his nose, sole turned up so he can see the initials carved there.

"I never leave home without my lucky footwear."

After a quick goodbye to Dad, we head out into the night. It's bitterly cold and I'm immediately jealous of my gnome's fetching red hat.

"No Totes?" I ask, puffing warmth into my hands.

"We'll visit that rascal later. This is a humans-only date night."

He doesn't even whisper it. Occasionally in the past couple of months, Eric's surprised me like this, with a phrase, a gesture, a glance that seems like an extraordinary leap. I think he surprises himself in these moments too because they're often followed by a few days of extreme caution. But still I sense it in him, like I've sensed it in myself ever since I was little: the almost irresistible urge to announce who you are to the world.

We walk side by side through puddles of street light, our breath steaming, hands clamped in our pockets.

"So where are you taking me?"

"Old Town," he says. "I've found something I think you might like."

"Oh God. It isn't another badger sett, is it? Because I love that you love badgers, Scarecrow, I really do. I mean, Badger is the only character in *The Wind in the Willows* who you think might actually do the reader a favour and kick the ever-living shit out of Mr Toad. But, man. I have now spent half a millennium with you sitting outside badger holes and I have not yet seen a single bloody badger."

He pouts. "I thought you enjoyed our midnight badger-watches."

"Okay," I grimace. "One of us really needs to stop saying 'badger'."

"Gabe, the surprise isn't badgers."

"G'arghhh!" I give him a long look. "So, you've been out to Old Town by yourself?"

We're now walking through the factory district, not a soul in sight. The gnome leans in and kisses the frozen tip of my nose.

"Yes. I'm a big boy now."

He means it as a joke, but it isn't. It's wonderful. Back in December, after he told me what had happened to his mum, I thought Eric might close down completely, maybe even start hurting himself again. Those first few weeks, I barely slept for worry. I knew that no matter what I said,

Eric would probably always believe that he was responsible for his mother's death. That's just the way people are sometimes; you can't always logic them out of their convictions. But my boy didn't go back to hurting himself, and now when I look at him, I hardly ever see the cage, and I'm just so freaking proud.

We head through the alleyway where we found Totes, running now, Eric leading the way. Passing the square, I look over to the library. It makes me smile to think of us arriving here on our bikes back in September, on the cusp of something unimaginable. And then we're out of the square and down a side street I've never explored before. Eric skids to a halt.

"Ta-dah!"

He sweeps his hand across an old dark building that sways out into the street like it might tumble at any minute. There are steps leading up to the broken doors of its foyer, above which *The Electric* is spelled out in dangling neon.

"A cinema?"

"The Palace of Dreams," Eric tells me, reading from the sign above the ticket booth.

Dead leaves rustle under our feet as we mount the steps, and Eric hauls open one of the busted doors. I take a sharp breath before following him inside. It's ridiculous, but my eyes are suddenly blurry. Maybe it's the idea that there are ghosts pressing in behind me; queues of happy, chattering, excited people ready to see the show.

Eric takes a couple of torches out of his pocket and passes me one. I click the switch and the foyer, cold and damp and brilliant, is revealed. A long concessions stand with a popcorn machine and dusty drink dispensers runs along one wall, and here again I imagine ghosts casually ordering their Cokes and hot dogs and sweets, as if such treats aren't wonders to be savoured. We move on, Eric guiding me around the walls. Behind plastic frames, rows of posters for films no one's seen in a lifetime: *The Shining; Mary Poppins; Ghostbusters; The Godfather; Jaws; Toy Story; Back to the Future; Pinocchio; The Princess Bride;* and there, right by the doors to the auditorium, four friends arm in arm, dancing down a yellow brick road.

"*The Wizard of Oz.* I didn't even know they'd made it into a film." I turn to Eric. "Thank you. This is just so…"

"You ain't seen nothing yet." He grins, and opens the swing doors.

It must have been magical. It *must* have been. To sit here in the dark, that silver beam flickering overhead. I walk slowly down the central aisle, my hand playing over the backs of empty seats, my gaze fixed on the huge blank screen. A silent canvas, a doorway to other worlds. I love watching our films in the library, but this? Who would ever give this up? I think I'd die first.

There's a small stage in front of the screen. I clamber up onto it like a little kid at Christmas and run my fingers across that enchanted wall.

"Hey. Hey." Eric crawls up beside me and places his own hand on the screen. "Are you okay? Gabe, I'm sorry, I thought this would make you happy. God, you're shivering. Are you cold?"

He wraps his arms around me.

"I'm not cold," I say. "Not one bit."

I glance over my shoulder at the watchful seats, and for just about the first time in my life, I *don't* feel watched. Or if I do, then the ghosts here are friendly and only wish us well. Maybe Eric feels something similar.

"Do you remember that first time you took me to the valley," he says, "and we climbed up into the oak?"

"Our first date? Of course."

"And I said we couldn't stay up there for ever? That one day we'd have to go down because it's what the world expects – we'd have to get married and start families and live good Protectorate lives?" He uses his thumbs to wipe away the tears in my eyes. "I don't want those things any more, Gabe. They don't matter. I have you."

"And badgers!" I grin, holding him tight. "Badgers count too!"

He laughs and leans back, his hands in my hair. "Do you ever take anything seriously?"

"You." I hold both his hands. "I take you seriously, Scarecrow."

His eyes are so dark in the shadows. His voice rises and falls, excited and nervous.

"I think I'm ready," he says.

I move my fingers across his chest, over his shoulders.

"Are you sure?"

We've talked about it for a while, but the time has never felt right, and the talking was important anyway. So I'm not some know-nothing kid, I've had experiences before, and my dad has always been there if ever I had questions. Still, I suppose all this was easier before the Outrage – before all sex, and especially degen sex, was seen as something dirty and sinful. But yeah, I know the mechanics and I also know that's only part of it. Talking has helped me understand what Eric might enjoy and what makes him nervous. It's also made us both understand that this first time probably isn't going to be perfect, and that's okay.

I kiss the well of his throat.

"You blush so easily." I smile.

"Sorry."

"Don't be sorry." I trace the blooming island with my finger. "I love your blushes."

I pull off my jacket and start to unbutton my shirt. At the third button, Eric takes over. He kisses my chest and I lean backwards until I'm almost lying on the stage. Eric sits astride me and I move my hands slowly under his clothes. I feel the tightness of his stomach and the downy hair and that first looping scar.

"You're beautiful," I tell him. "Eric, you are *so* beautiful."

He closes his eyes.

Afterwards, I wrap my coat around him and we sit together on the edge of the stage.

"Okay?"

"Yes." He smiles. "You?"

"Very okay." I nudge my forehead against his. "So...I've been thinking. Ah-ah-ah!" I cover his mouth. "No smart-alec comments. I can think without smoke shooting out of my ears. Anyway, you remember that old sci-fi movie we watched last week?"

He furrows his brow. "*Space Wars*?"

"*Star Wars*." I flick his nose with my finger. "It was an absolute classic."

"If you say so."

"Well, what do you think about maybe sharing these movies with the guys? June and Liz and the others. We could be like the Rebel Alliance in the film. A small band of resistance fighters secretly undermining the evil Empire."

"By watching movies?"

"Hey, it's a start… Unless you want to keep it just the two of us?"

Eric's quiet for a moment, those long nervous fingers twisting together. "Part of me does," he admits. "But I know that's selfish. I think the librarian wanted these films to be shared. All right, so how do we do this?"

He actually looks excited.

"Maybe we should have a test run," I suggest.

"What do you mean?"

"Try the idea out on one of them."

"Okay, who?"

"I was thinking, Albert?"

"Albert Heck?"

"Do you know any other Alberts?"

He swats me. "All right, but why him? He always seems so…I don't know. *Albert*."

I nod. "But there's something about him, don't you think? Personally, I think Albert Heck sees a lot."

NOW

30

I'm holding on tight to Alice, guiding her to one of the armchairs by the veranda doors, when the Farmer makes his second move. I sense him behind me, a blur of silver out of the corner of my eye. The impact knocks me forward, shock waves of pain electrifying every nerve in my body. He's missed the base of my skull by inches, the cane striking between my neck and shoulder. Stumbling over my own feet, I manage to hold onto Alice long enough to help her into the chair. Then I turn to face him, no anger, no fear, no emotion at all right now, just the instinct to survive.

He stands there, panting, the weapon in his fist, its head flecked with Alice's blood. A sheen of sweat sparkles his brow as he draws it back.

I don't waste any time. I underestimated him before and Alice paid the price. He's just started to swing at me again when I step inside the arc of the cane and land a hard punch against the crook of his elbow. His eyes go wide and a startled grunt escapes his lips. His fingers automatically open. The stick has barely hit the floor when I land a second punch under the Farmer's jaw and he joins it, collapsing onto the plush cream carpet.

While he writhes about, I take a quick glance at Alice before moving to the desk. I know she's badly hurt but I have to secure him before seeing to her. Ransacking the drawers, I find a roll of parcel tape and, kneeling over my groaning stepfather, wind several strips around his wrists and mouth. He isn't going anywhere, at least for the time being.

Back at the armchair, I try to ignore the agony dancing along my spine; try to ignore the dread curdling in my stomach.

"I'm here," I say. "Alice, I'm here."

She flails for my hand and I take it. She doesn't seem to be in any pain and her pupils are focused. Still her words make my blood run cold.

"Something's broken." She reaches for her head. "Something's broken."

"Don't." I draw her hand away. "Just let me see first."

A scarlet trickle skates down from her fringe. I snatch up my bag, tear open the first aid kit and find the bottle of rubbing alcohol inside. Dousing my hands with disinfectant,

I very gently part the hair around the wound. I swallow hard. It's a red and a white mess, her scalp split. Not knowing how deep the break goes, I can't risk cleaning the wound and so I pull a wodge of sterile padding from the kit and start to bandage her head.

"Is it bad?" she says, her voice slightly slurred.

It's difficult to tape the layers of gauze in place, my hands are shaking so much. When she looks up at me, I force a smile. "Just a scratch. Don't be a baby."

She smiles back. "I thought you said I was brave."

"You are."

"Gabe?" She clutches at my shirt, suddenly frantic. "Take my bag. T-take the map."

"What? Don't be ridiculous."

"I'm not the one being ruh-diculous. Do you know why you always lost when we used to play ch-chess? It's because I can see right through you. I always know what you're thinking, Gabriel Suh-awyer and r-right now you're..." She shudders, head to toe, as a stark, insistent blot begins to seep through the bandages. "You're scared. Because I can't do this any more and you know I c-can't. But I'm telling you, you need to leave me. Now. You have to go on. Alone."

I drop to my haunches and take both her hands in mine. They're cold, clammy, trembling, but her gaze remains clear. Just the beginnings of pain there now as the shock and adrenalin start to wear off.

"You listen to me," I say. "There's no way I'm going on without you."

"But the ev-evidence."

I shake my head. "No way."

"Getting it out. Bringing them down. Duh-destroying it all." She tries to sit forward and another spasm shoots through her body, making her teeth clench. "It's all that matters."

"If that's true," I say, "if that's *all* that matters, then what have we been fighting for? *You* matter, Alice. Your life, your hopes, your dreams. Your chance to be who you are. That's what we've been trying to do, isn't it? To achieve that freedom for ourselves, for everyone?" I lean forward and kiss the cold plain of her brow. "So here's the truth – you're hurt, and it's bad, and you're coming with me, and we're going to make it to Ireland, and you're going to be fine. Have you got that?"

A single tear tracks down the side of her face. She nods. "Got it."

"Good."

I quickly repack my bag and throw the strap over my shoulder. Then I thread my arm around Alice's waist and, as gently as I can, raise her from the chair. Straight away, the stain grows against the pristine white of the bandages, a shocking red star that cannot be denied. Her lips set into a thin line. When we lock eyes, I try my best to hide my fear and doubt.

Over twenty miles of hill and valley separate us from the bay and the boat that will be waiting to collect us at dawn. We've walked ourselves ragged these past few days, hardly slept, and my injuries, old and new, are constantly sapping what little strength I have left. With every move, pain from the Farmer's attack crackles across my back and already Alice can barely stand. Those were fine words just now, but here's the reality: there's no way either of us is going to make it to Ireland. No way we'll deliver the evidence that will destroy the Protectorate. No way we'll get to live out our hopeless dreams. Best case scenario, we manage to limp half a mile before we collapse in the forest, unable to move until the Farmer's guard dogs find us.

As if echoing these thoughts, I hear a wet, sarcastic chuckle.

"Give it up, Gabriel. You know very well you're not getting out of this alive. You haven't got a chance, and I will personally see to it that you and that little faggot never—"

I'm turning towards him, Alice already heavy in my arms, when the Farmer's words are cut short.

He's still lying there on the carpet. The tape has come loose from his mouth but his wrists remain bound and now there's a fourth person in the room. Kneeling behind him, my mother checks for a pulse in the folds of his neck. She gives me a quick, dull-eyed glance, staggers upright and places a small metal sculpture back on the desk. Then she goes to the door and turns the key, locking us inside the study.

I haven't seen my mum since last September, when I threw her offer of a new home back in her face. She looks at me now as if from the bottom of a deep well. There's something of her old self there, I think, but it's very far away. When she comes over and kisses the side of my face, I can smell the alcohol on her breath. She doesn't seem surprised to see me but, in her present state, I'm not sure anything could surprise her.

"Poor boy," she says, her words even blearier than Alice's. "My poor boy."

"Mum…"

There's so much I want to say, so much I need to tell her – *I'm sorry, I didn't know, forgive me* – but Alice's head is drooping against my shoulder and I can feel her breath, shallow and stuttering on my neck. I know there's no hope of us escaping, but while we're free, while we're together, I'm going to try.

I have to hold onto Alice and so I can't even give my mum a hug, but she seems to understand. As we move to the veranda doors, I feel her hand rubbing the small of my back. I remember her doing this when I was little. I'd run into my parents' bedroom, the fragments of a nightmare chasing after me, and she'd pull me into their bed and tell me not to cry. *"There are no ghosts, Gabe, no monsters."* I look back at the Farmer, unconscious but still breathing. She was half right, I suppose.

If only we had time. After all, I don't owe Eric any promises now. Finally, I could be who I really am. I could pick up that silver-handled stick from the floor and give in to the anger raging in my heart; the anger I've suppressed throughout my entire life. I could take revenge – for Alice and Liz and June and Marsha and Miss Calloway and Mum and even Eric. Why not? They made him what he is, didn't they? They made us all who we are.

And the Farmer, he would deserve it more than anyone. If he hadn't planted the bomb, if he hadn't killed Eric's grandfather, if he hadn't started it all. Isn't he every officer who ever arrested a frightened kid? Isn't he every guard who marched a trembling boy into a castration cell? Isn't he every hangman who threw a tortured body into its degen grave?

Wouldn't this be justice?

"Gabe," my mother whispers. "You need to go."

She pulls back the curtains and opens the veranda doors. Before stepping through, I touch the back of her hand.

"I'm sorry I didn't listen to you when you called that night. I'm sorry I didn't understand what you were trying to tell me. I'm sorry for everything." She looks at me, her expression puzzled. "Mum, do you remember when you asked me to come and live with you? You and dad had planned it so that you could save me. Maybe so that we could save each other."

She smiles. A smile I haven't seen in a long, long time.

"We tried to change the world." She nods. "We tried."

I look back at the Farmer. "Did he see it was you?"

She shakes her head and points to the darkened garden and the gate beyond.

"Hurry now, both of you." She says it so casually, as if we're late for school. "You need to fly."

31

The doors close behind us. Looking back, I see my mum staring out, her brow furrowed as if I'm a stranger on a street who reminds her of someone she used to know. Then the curtains meet and she's gone. Gone again. I try to imagine some way in which she could come with us, but I'm already carrying Alice, and my mum can barely walk without stumbling. I have to leave her, I know.

And it kills me.

Alice grips my shoulder, a touch so weak it's frightening. "I'm suh-so sorry, Gabe."

One look at her is enough to refocus my mind. I can deal with my feelings about losing my mum later. Right now, I have to get Alice out of here. That scarlet star has grown against the bandages and her lips look almost blue in the moonlight. She manages to shuffle with me down the veranda steps and into the avenue of topiary animals before bending almost double and retching onto the path. The pain in my spine explodes as I bend with her and I have to bite the inside of my mouth against it.

Turning her head, she gives me a rueful look. "Are you d-done being heroic? This is impossible."

She's right. We've covered maybe ten yards and already ground to a halt. What's the point in continuing to push through my pain and her agony? There's no way we can ever make it to the bay. If only we hadn't had to abandon the car at Marsha's, then

A memory strikes out of nowhere. The first time I had to say goodbye to my mother: uniformed men carrying her cases out of the house, my dad sitting helpless – *seemingly helpless* – at our kitchen table. *"Talk to her! Make her stay!"* My hand on her arm. *"Mum, please, don't."* Her eyes cutting to the figure in the backseat of the waiting Bentley…

Alice shivers against me, her gaze cloudy.

"Hey!" I shake her. "Stay with me. Alice, I'm going to need you."

Gritting my teeth, I lift her into my arms and start to make my way down the avenue. She tries to protest again, asks me to hide her in the bushes so that I can get a head start before she's discovered. I tell her, very gently, to shut the hell up, and finally she nods and tucks her head into the crook of my shoulder.

I'm moving at a slow jog, careful as I can so as not to

jostle Alice. I can feel the warmth of her blood seeping into the fabric of my shirt. No time to stop now, no time to check on her. Shut out the pain, shut out emotion. I narrow my thoughts on our destination. Not far now.

At the end of the avenue, I turn and plunge us into a little copse of trees that lead to the estate's western gate. My boots pound the hard earth and some startled night creature scurries for cover. I sympathize. With the full moon out, it's a night made for hunters. Over to my left, the monstrous hulk of the house sits against a tapestry of stars, just a slit or two of light at its windows.

We come out of the trees and find the gate looming before us, the garage set to one side. Apart from the Farmer's study, this was the only bit of the estate forbidden to me. I guess because the old bastard didn't trust me around his pride and joy.

Probably wise.

I lower Alice to the ground and rest her back against the side wall while I go around to the front of the building. I grip the handle of the garage door and pull upwards, wincing at the screech of metal hinges. A shaft of moonlight grows as the door folds into the ceiling, illuminating the winged logo and blunt face of the Bentley. The car that took my mother away, the Farmer's favourite.

Now it's mine.

I open the passenger door before returning for Alice.

No one locks their cars these days – with working vehicles so rare, it's almost impossible for thieves to sell them on. When I place her carefully in the passenger seat, Alice reaches out and runs an appreciative hand over the interior.

"Wow," she says, her voice almost a whisper. "We tr-travelling in style, Gabe?"

"Only with your help."

I close the passenger door and race to the gate. Same key code again, of course. Evil isn't only unoriginal, it's epically stupid. The gate begins to jolt open, every clang like a gunshot in the stillness. Scanning the garden for movement, I start back towards the garage. Now I have the car, the possibility of rescuing my mother from this darkness, of making amends for despising and misjudging her all those years...

But suddenly the decision is made for me. Through the copse of trees, I see a dozen lights blaze in the windows of the house. Somewhere a radio squawks. Elsewhere a voice shouts. Barks erupt across the estate.

I run to the car, throw my bag into the backseat and drop behind the wheel. "They're coming."

Alice nods and reaches a clumsy hand for the ignition button on the central console. Like most ancient cars, this beast has been converted to run on a fuel cell and, at her shivering touch, the twin turbo engine purrs into life. Quiet, but not quiet enough. Alice's face shines bloodless in the glow of a dozen dashboard readings, all of them a mystery to me.

"Thank God it's an automatic. You wuh-won't be able to stall it." Her shaking finger flicks along the console and disengages the parking brake. "No lights until we're on the r-road. Okay. Fastest driving luh-lesson in history." She slips the gearstick into drive. "Now, gently press down on the throttle." She points at my feet. "Pedal next to it is the brake."

"That easy, huh?"

"That easy. And, Gabe. Hurry."

I follow her gaze through the open garage door.

The gate is closing again.

I grip the steering wheel, depress the throttle. As we creep forward, I can feel the raw power of the machine striving against my hesitancy. I remember us last night, rocketing across the Clifton Suspension Bridge, my eyes tight shut as Alice plunged us on. There's no time now to overcome my nerves, no time to learn whether or not I can do this. We have seconds.

My foot sinks against the pedal and the Bentley leaps out of the dark.

"Hold tight."

I flex my fingers around the wheel. Resist the urge to release the throttle. Push down my fear as far as it will go. Force my eyes to stay open. Push us on towards that narrowing space between the arms of the gate. Feel the judder of metal meeting metal. See the sparks fly against my window. Imagine the gouging paintwork all along the panels on either side as the car screams its way through. And, spinning the wheel as we hit the lane beyond, smile at the idea of the Farmer seeing what I've done to his treasure.

Now I'm thankful for the moon. It lights the lane ahead, picking out the usual potholes and debris that litter every road. At first, I swerve wildly, almost crashing us through the forest on one side or into the wall that rings the estate on the other. But it doesn't take long to appreciate the sensitivity of the steering and, by the time we've left wall and forest behind, I'm confident enough to push the speedometer to forty.

I try to concentrate while also checking on Alice and the rear-view mirror. No sign of any pursuers yet. Alice has studied the maps so much she doesn't need to refer to them any more and she guides me in a thin, haltering voice. When I look over, her face is tucked up tight with pain. I start to say something but she just shakes her head and reaches for a switch. A pair of powerful headlights splash out across the blacktop.

"Doing f-fine," she says, her voice heavy and thick. "Only twenty miles to go. Be there in no…" Her eyelids close and she slumps to the side.

"Alice!" Taking one hand off the wheel sends a skitter of

fear through me, but I know she can't lose consciousness. I shake her roughly by the shoulder. "Wake up!"

Her eyes snap open and her hand automatically goes to her head. That red star has stopped growing but still her fingers come back sticky.

"Stay with me," I tell her. "We've almost made it."

Minutes crawl by like hours. We sweep through sleeping countryside, through empty villages reclaimed by nature, past buildings that might once have been homes. Every time I look in the mirror, I expect to see headlights tumbling over the hills behind us. Every time I glance at Alice, I expect to find her passed out, or worse. Locating the window controls, I open hers a crack and she stirs in her seat, breathing in the fresh night air. A tiny scrap of colour creeps into her cheeks. Her directions come in a surer voice.

Suddenly, she's breathing hard, a little blood foaming from her nose. I begin to reach over, to check if she's okay, when a series of lights flash across the dashboard. Then the rhythmic purr of the engine falters and, with a low-pitched whine, dies completely. At the same moment, Alice starts to shake – sharp, ragged movements. As the car trundles to a stop, I unclip my belt, throw open the driver door and rush round to the passenger side.

She lies back in her seat, calm again. Her entire body is a picture of agony and exhaustion.

"Sl-orry. Suh-orry."

"No." I half collapse against the open passenger door. "No, Alice. It's okay. We're going to be…"

The lights on the dash flicker out.

"Fuel cell's uh-empty." Her gaze switches to the road ahead. "Three miles to go. Thereabouts. Time to st-stop dreaming. Time to start walking, Gabe."

"Yeah, I guess it is." I return to the driver's side and reclaim my pack from the backseat, then I go back and unclasp her belt. "Come on, then."

"Don't."

She sobs, pushes against my chest as I lift her out, not an ounce of strength left in her.

"You can't. Please. Leave. Muh-ee. *Please*."

I take the first step and my back roars.

"Don't you understand?" My voice hitches in the dark. "You carried me all this way. You carried *me*. I would have never made it this far without you. Never. So let me carry you now."

Alice doesn't argue. I don't think she can. She just rests her head against me.

Leaving the road, we're back into the hills now, where the night wind stirs the heather. I stumble. I stagger. I hold her close. Feel her heart against my ribs, light and skittish like a bird's. Feel her wrist against the side of my thumb, cold as stone. Her chest barely rises when she breathes, but still she breathes, *still she breathes,* and so I carry her.

Occasionally, I have to rest. I lie Alice gently in the heather, whisper to her, tell her we're going to make it. She doesn't open her eyes any more, but sometimes she nods. Her hands are so cold. I sit beside her, cross-legged, warming them in mine, staring up at the stars. Through the pain that beats inside my head, I see my friends in the curve of a tree and in the hollow of a hill.

Keep going, Gabe, the Rebels whisper to me.

Keep going.

And I do.

I cradle her again and we move on.

On.

On.

On.

I walk in a field of red poppies. In a field of tattered scarecrows. I walk through scorch marks in library floors. I fall through cardboard treasure boxes and old television sets and cabin doorways and air-conditioning vents.

I walk.

I carry her.

And light creeps into the dark. It's only a watery trace at first, edging the blue-green cliffs. Then, as I lurch down into the bay, the sky begins to bleed. It spreads like a red star against the pale bandage of the sky, and I feel the warmth of the dawn on my face.

It's difficult to see. The sky's so bright and the pain in my spine makes my vision jolty. But I think there are boats waiting in the mist. A small rowboat at the water's edge and a larger vessel anchored out of the bay.

"We're here, Alice," I tell her, smiling. "Look, we're here."

She doesn't look.

She doesn't move.

I run. There's no pain now, she's so light, I could carry her for ever. The stones that pebble the beach fly beneath me, offering no resistance. I crash into the shallows, numb to the touch of the sea, fight my way through the waves, all the way to the woman in the boat, who holds out her arms to take Alice. She looks at me as if I should know her but my thoughts feel slow and thick.

"He's alive," the woman says, as she cradles Alice into the boat. "He's breathing."

"She," I murmur, my heart full. "She. Her name is…"

And then a distant voice is calling *my* name, and I turn to see them closing in.

"Stay where you are! And you in the boat, don't move! By order of the Protectorate!"

Three shapes wind down the pathway into the bay, the lead pair running hard. Sweat jewels their faces; the inspector and the grinning constable. Dufresne points his gun at the woman in the boat and she freezes, Alice still in her arms. Then the gun sweeps around and focuses on me.

"It's over, Gabriel. There's nowhere left to run."

I let out a huge breath.

We tried, didn't we, Alice?

We tried.

And I'm just so tired.

A dark-eyed boy steps between the men. The small dog at his feet comes bounding across the stones. I wade back to the shore, my pain returning with every step. At the water's edge, I bend down and lift Totes into my arms. He doesn't bark, just licks the dirt from my face. I kiss his nose and look over at Eric. His father takes Eric's gun from its holster and hands it to him.

"Bring him in," he says. "This is your last chance."

Rakes's grin is almost as bright as the dawn.

Dufresne watches patiently as Eric moves towards me.

Eric lifts the weapon and points it at my head.

"I'm sorry," he says. "I'm so sorry..."

32

The gun trembles in his hand. That red mouth, so like a wound, twists with pain.

Maybe this was how it always had to end between us. Me so full of rage at the world the Dufresne family helped to create and Eric, raised by his father to loathe and doubt himself. There was never much of a chance for us, was there? So no, I won't blame him any more.

"How did you find me?" I ask.

"The car," Rakes calls out, delighted. "After the Farmer recovered, he called us. Said you'd broken into his house. You and two other degens. The Heck boy he dealt with, but this mystery kid knocked him out and you all got clean away. So we went there last night, interviewed the Farmer and your dear old mum." He chuckles. "Poor cow was so out of it, she didn't have a clue what was going on. But then we found the empty garage and located the Bentley via its GPS. We guessed you'd be heading for the coast and, knowing you were both injured, there were only a few bays you could possibly have made it to. Then we intercepted a call from the local Grey Jackets – two strangers sighted in the area, making for the beach."

I'm sure that wasn't all they were told by the Farmer. I'm pretty certain he would have mentioned some private document to them as well – a document we'd stolen. Nothing to do with their case, of course, but if the envelope was found and returned to him unopened? Well, Roger McCormack would be eternally grateful. My fist tightens around the shoulder strap of my bag.

"What about the third kid?" Rakes asks. "Where is he?"

"Gone," I say. "Vanished back into the Resistance. You'll never find him."

The constable shrugs. "We'll see."

I turn back to Eric.

He shakes his head. With his free hand, he plucks at his shirt and I see his fingernails, raw and bleeding.

"Hey." I reach for him, my palm a few inches from the mouth of the gun. It seems to yawn before me, a Protectorate emptiness that's always been there, waiting to swallow me whole. "You need to listen. I don't blame you, not any more. None of this is your fault. Whatever happens now, I want you to remember that."

Snuggled against my chest, Totes looks between us and whimpers.

"I'm sorry," Eric says. "I'm so—"

"Don't be sorry," I say. "I forgive you."

His grip flexes around the gun. He nods.

And a moment before it happens, I know what he's going to do.

"I'm so sorry, Dad."

Eric spins around and points that waiting emptiness at the Filth-Finders. I see Rakes and Dufresne over Eric's shoulder. The constable immediately trains his own weapon on Eric, wetting his lips like a jackal, while the inspector cries out. It's a dull, stupid sound, and I think it comes from the same hopeless place as my anger.

"You'll stop this now!" he roars. "Do you understand me, Eric? I told you this was your last chance, and I wasn't joking. You've been given every opportunity to make things right with the Protectorate, but if you continue down this path, I can't save you."

Rakes speaks up. "It's gone too far for that anyway, sir. This counts as aiding the enemy, threatening Protectorate agents, high treason—"

"Shut your mouth!" Dufresne snaps.

The constable falls silent but his grin remains. Dufresne steps forward, holstering his own gun. Waves clatter the pebbled shore while seagulls squall above the surf. Cresting the sea, the sun throws our darkness against the cliffs, a shadow play with puppets whose strings might be cut at any moment.

"Dad, stay where you are," Eric shouts. His finger, bleeding from the pressure of that raw, bitten nail, trembles on the trigger. I step to his side and catch the desperation in those huge dark eyes.

"Don't do this," I say. "Eric, don't. You won't ever forgive yourself."

Dufresne shoots me an uncertain glance. His lips tighten over the words, but he speaks them just the same. "Listen to him, Eric. Listen to Gabe. He..." We lock eyes, me and the man who ordered my torture. "He cares for you. I know that. And if you stop this now then maybe we can all sit down and talk, just the three of us."

"That's close to treason, sir," Rakes warns him.

Dufresne ignores him. "I'm owed favours by important people. There are solutions here."

"Then why weren't there before?" Eric screams.

He brings up his free hand to grip and steady the gun.

"Why did you let them interrogate and torture me if there were solutions? Why did you let them break me down until I told the worst lie I could ever, *ever* tell? That Gabe would do *that* to me." His arms shake, the weapon flashes in the morning light. "That he'd hurt me in any way. In *any* way. It was Gabe who saved me, Dad. Don't you even understand that? After Mum, I needed you to tell me that it was okay. That I was—"

"Eric, stop." Those regulation black gloves come up to cover the inspector's mouth. "Please, son, just please, stop."

"I needed someone to give me their hand and tell me it was going to be all right. But you wouldn't. And you won't. Because you know, don't you? You've always known, just the same as Mum knew. And if you offered me your hand then it would be real. You'd have to admit who I was."

Dufresne throws Rakes an imploring look and the constable shakes his head.

"Why won't you, Dad? Why won't you admit it?"

The inspector's arms drop to his sides. "Eric. Let me help you."

"You *can* help me. You've always been able to help me. Just say you love me as I am." He turns to me, tears starting in his eyes. "Because I love *him*. I've failed him and I've betrayed him, but I will always love him, and there isn't a single thing you or the Protectorate can do that will ever change that. We belong together." He refocuses on the Filth-Finders and spits his words at them: "But your world won't let us. *You* won't let us, Dad."

"Scarecrow." My heart hammers. Very gently, I set down Totes onto the stones. "Listen to me. I don't want this."

"I know you don't," he says, the tears streaming down his face. "But we don't always get the luxury of the right choices, do we? Not here. Not now. It has to be this way." He steps closer to his father. "Go, Gabe! Run!"

"No." I grab his arm. "Eric, they'll kill you for this."

I stare at the inspector. "They'll kill him. Your son. You know they will. Whether I get away or not, they'll try him for treason and they'll hang him for it. Mr Dufresne, Eric told me that you'd watch the whole world burn to save the Protectorate. Are you willing to watch your son burn too?"

Dufresne casts his gaze at the pebbled shore, at the blood-red sky.

"I let him fall once," I say. "Don't you let him fall now. Help me save him."

"Gabe, can't you see? He doesn't care." Eric pulls my hand from his arm. "Just go!"

"I can't…" My voice hitches. "I won't leave you behind again."

"How touching," Rakes sneers. "But come now, Eric, stop your pansy heroics. We all know you would never shoot your father."

"You're right…" says Dufresne flatly. "He wouldn't."

I hear the click of the gun, as the inspector turns and fixes his weapon on the suddenly unsmiling constable.

"But he wasn't aiming at me."

Eric starts forward. "Dad, what are you—?"

His father waves us back. "You're right. Your mother knew. The night before she… She tried to talk to me about it and I wouldn't listen. I pushed her away, told her to stop imagining such…" His shoulders tense. "Such filth." The gun remains steady in his hand, but all at once that proud face gives way to unimaginable grief. And in that moment, I think again of the little boy who saw his father blown to pieces. "It was the last thing your mum ever said to me, Eric – 'Love him. Just love him'… And I do.

"Now take him, Gabriel. Take my boy and go."

I don't wait. I grab Eric's wrist and haul him backwards into the surf, away from the Filth-Finders, towards the little rowboat. He stumbles; there's a splash as he drops the gun into the shallows. Up ahead, I see the old woman grip the oars and wave a signal to the boat waiting out at sea. Totes hurtles along beside us, skipping the waves as the seagulls take flight. Across the cliffs, our shadows scatter.

"Gabe, we can't leave him," Eric cries.

He grabs my shirt, tries to struggle.

"It's his choice," I say, echoing some words that were said to me a lifetime ago. "You have to honour it."

I shoot a quick glance behind as we reach the boat. Two figures with guns drawn, frozen like characters in a movie still. I think they're speaking, but the wind and sea drowns their words.

Hands reach out and pull Totes and then Eric into the boat. I clamber up after them, my soaked boots sloshing the baseboards, and stow my backpack containing the evidence that will destroy the Protectorate under the seat at the prow. Then I turn, ready to thank our saviour. It takes me a second to recognize the white-haired lady at the oars. She gives me a quick nod before heaving away.

"You're not the only one who can escape a Green Jacket prison, Gabriel. I'm very glad to see you."

Marsha pulls hard against the tide, sending the little boat rocking towards the mouth of the bay. Huddled in a blanket at the old woman's feet, her head cushioned by her coat, Alice stirs. Eric crouches beside her. His fingers hover over her blood-soaked bandages and he looks up at me, his expression bleak. He touches the back of his hand to her cheek and her eyes flicker open. Seeing him, she manages a tiny smile, and I feel my legs give way. I catch hold of the side of the boat for balance and manage to kneel beside Eric. We huddle over Alice, arms around each other, Eric telling her that he's sorry while I explain everything he should know.

"Alice," he says. "Alice, I'm…"

She whispers something and he bends down to catch her words.

"I will," he murmurs, looking back at me. "Always."

Before she closes her eyes again, she reaches out to me and I lean forward. "L-looks like we'll be starting that f-film script. Soon?"

I nod and wipe my eyes. "Very soon. I promise."

And then Totes is snuffling in between us. He lets out a low whine and curls up against Alice's chest, giving her some of his warmth.

"You should rest," Marsha tells her, never missing a stroke. "There are medics on board the ship and I've taken a look myself. I've patched up more than a few fractured skulls in my time. Believe me, you're going to be okay."

My hearts fills as Eric and I move towards the stern. There, I pull him into my lap.

"I won't let you go," I whisper to him. "Not this time."

"You never did," he says. Then, "Where *are* we going, Gabe?"

I smile. "To the Emerald City, far across the sea."

He smiles too, though his eyes are raw with tears. I pull him up and we both look back to where two figures remain on the beach, tiny and unmoving. That's the Protectorate, I think: a world of people locked together in fear, blind to the tide that rushes in to drown them all.

I hug Eric to me. As we pass out of the bay, I feel it: my anger, drifting with the tide. Because if even Eric's father can change, then there is hope, isn't there? And that's what our film will be about – not just what hate can destroy but what hope can achieve.

Eric rests his head against my shoulder; I hold him tight.

Together, we look out to a place beyond the dawn.

THREE YEARS LATER

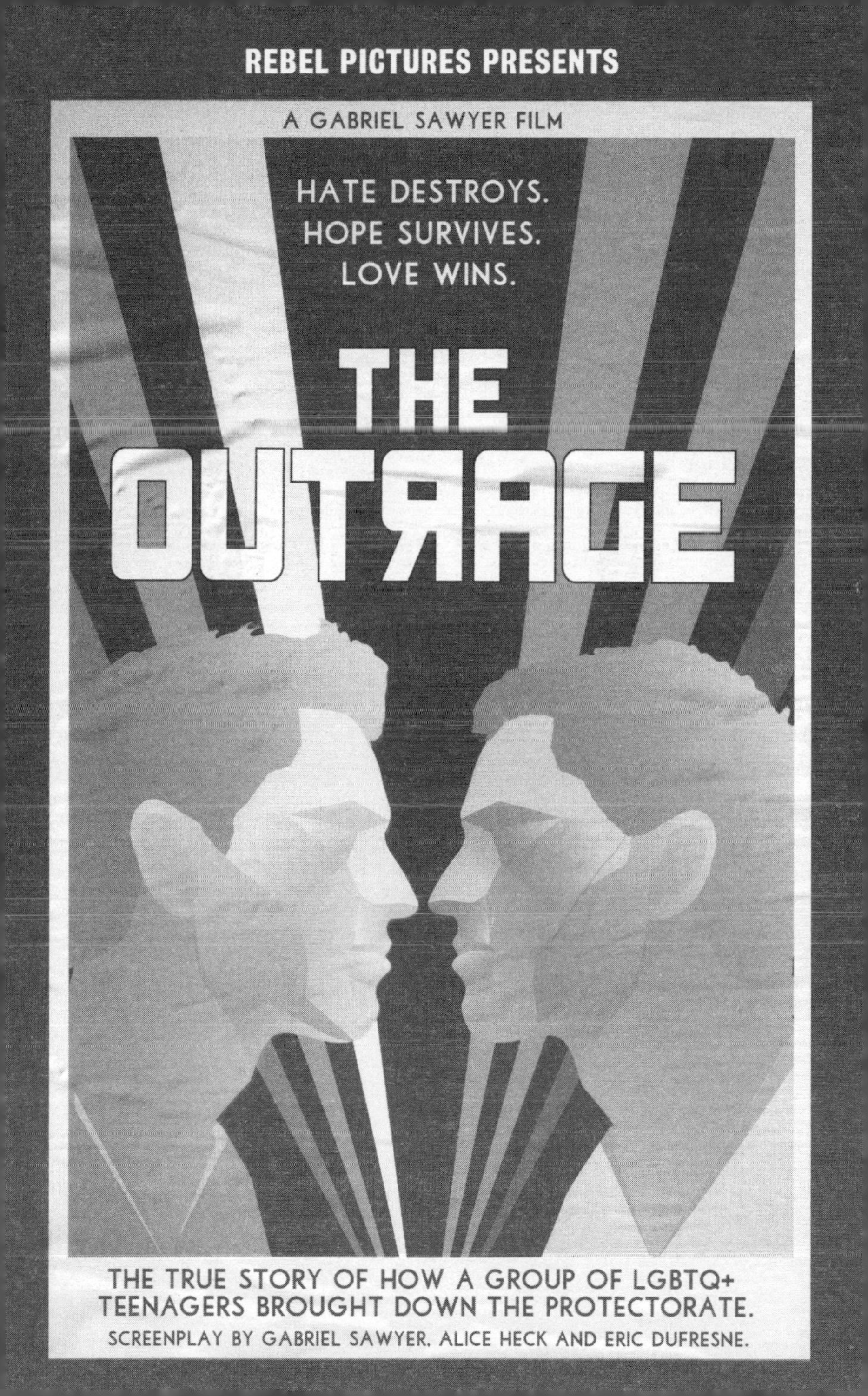
REBEL PICTURES PRESENTS
A GABRIEL SAWYER FILM
HATE DESTROYS.
HOPE SURVIVES.
LOVE WINS.
THE
OUTRAGE
THE TRUE STORY OF HOW A GROUP OF LGBTQ+
TEENAGERS BROUGHT DOWN THE PROTECTORATE.
SCREENPLAY BY GABRIEL SAWYER, ALICE HECK AND ERIC DUFRESNE.

"We cannot be a better society until we see that better society. I cannot be in the world until I see I am in the world."

Yance Ford, filmmaker (DISCLOSURE, 2019).

We use the law to defend
the human rights of
LGBT people globally

The Human Dignity Trust is the only organisation
working globally to support strategic litigation to
challenge laws that persecute people on the basis of their
sexual orientation and/or gender identity.
We provide legal and communications assistance to
lawyers and activists who are defending human rights in
countries where private, same-sex, consensual sexual
activity is criminalised. At the same time we also work
with governments wishing to reform outdated,
colonial-era laws that discriminate against LGBT
people and other marginalised groups.

For more information and resources visit
www.humandignitytrust.org

If you have been affected by some of the issues raised in this book, the following organisations can help or provide further info:

 Stonewall is a charity which supports equality for all LGBT people and prevents discrimination – at school, at work and in communities. We produce education materials and information and have an advice line. Find out more at www.stonewall.org.uk

 Gendered Intelligence is a national trans-led charity that works to improve the lives of transgender people in the UK, specialising in supporting young people up to the age of 21. GI delivers trans youth programmes, support for parents and carers, and educational workshops for schools, colleges and other educational settings. www.genderedintelligence.co.uk

AFTERWORD

Dear Reader,

Representation is important. Particularly, as a member of a marginalised or minority community, to see yourself reflected in books and movies as a real human being, with worth and dignity, can be a transformative, empowering, revolutionary experience. It can even save lives. But representation in these forms is a constantly evolving thing – a flawed process that is striving always to do better. No piece of art is perfect in this regard. It can't be. It is created by writers and filmmakers who are shaped by their own times, culture and particular life experiences. The LGBTQ+ films the Rebels watch and take inspiration from in *The Outrage* are all imperfect in terms of representation because each one is part of that evolving effort. But before we get too picky about their defects maybe we should take a moment to reflect on how far we've come?

When I was a young kid growing up in a conservative community in rural England in the 80s and 90s, I did so under the shadow of Section 28 (of the Local Government Act 1988). This vile piece of legislation forbade, among other things, local authorities to "promote the teaching... of the acceptability of homosexuality as a pretended family relationship". In effect, this meant that books about LGBTQ+ people were banned in British schools and teachers could be prosecuted for even discussing the acceptability of gay lives (having read *The Outrage*, you can possibly see the many parallels from my own childhood experiences). Sadly, this also created a culture in which anything that could be deemed as "promoting" homosexuality was suppressed, inevitably leading to negative attitudes around LGBTQ+ people in wider society. Another consequence of the legislation was that we received no sexual health and relationship education, right at a time when the AIDS epidemic was still at its height. You can imagine how many lives might have been saved had this not been the case.

At the same time, the only queer people I saw on television and in film were either "comic" stereotypes to be ridiculed and despised or else sinister serial killers and spreaders of deadly disease (as the Rebels reflect after watching *Disclosure*, until very recently this was the only representation of trans people as well). As a consequence of this, I wasted many years of my life consumed with needless misery and self-loathing. If I had seen just one positive representation of someone like myself – however imperfect that representation might later be judged to be – then things could have been very different.

This is why I think it's important to look at queer literature and cinema as an evolving thing. Yes, individual representations might be flawed at the time of their creation, but the motive behind creating those stories must also be interrogated and appreciated. So let us reflect on our cultural history with this in mind and see it, like every part of the LGBTQ+ struggle, as part of an ongoing effort to do better.

I'd also like to take a moment here to say a word about the importance of remembering our past more broadly. I'm acutely aware that the nightmare future faced by Gabe in *The Outrage* is a current reality for millions of queer people around the globe. In the UK and many liberal Western democracies, we are incredibly fortunate to have benefited from the work of those protesters, freedom fighters and organisations who came before us – from the first bystander shout of "Gay power!" at the Stonewall Inn during that oppressive June night of 1969 to the advent of equal marriage and LGBTQ+ adoption rights in the past few years in Britain.

But the fight is not over. Is never over. Which is why I wrote *The Outrage*.

We stand with all LGBTQ+ people who live under

oppressive regimes. We call for their liberation and, while doing so, we must be vigilant about the fragility of those rights we have won.

In a gay bar in London during Pride 2019, I was asked by a group of very polite young men what my Stonewall Inn anniversary T-shirt was all about. It seemed incredible to me at the time that these men had attended Pride, waved their rainbow flags, enjoyed the party, without having any idea of the weight of history behind the day. So we sat down in a cramped corner and I told them the story of their freedom: the freedom to sit in that very bar, openly and without fear of police raid and arrest, of trial, of chemical torture and social disgrace. They hadn't heard a word of it before. For them, Pride was just a party, its hardscrabble political roots unknown.

Complacency is our enemy and ignorance of our past means we might well be doomed to repeat it. Already within Europe and beyond, debates we thought were settled are being opened up again. Have no doubt, our very right to exist – and to love who we choose – is under attack.

And so let's always remain vigilant and, if necessary, be ready to wage battles, old and new.

At the very least, we owe that to our history.

Your ally in the fight,

William x

DISCUSSION QUESTIONS

- Think about the terminology of the government in the world of the novel, such as the Protectorate, the Outrage, the Public Good, degenerates, Re-Purification. How is language used to reinforce the message of the Protectorate? Do you see any parallels with how language is used in real life to try to promote a particular agenda?

- Look at pages 51 and 52, where Gabe describes the posters circulated by the Protectorate. Discuss the use of visual propaganda within *The Outrage*, and how it compares to examples you know from real life, both present day and historical.

- How has England changed under the Protectorate, and how has the author threaded these details through the narrative? Who and what else has suffered under the new regime?

- In this novel, William Hussey has played with time – moving between chapters set "now" and "then". What effect did this have on your reading experience? Did knowing what was in store for Gabe and Eric change the way you felt as you read about the early days of their relationship?

- Think about the idea of allyship, in the Protectorate and everywhere that prejudice exists. What is the role of people like Ben and Grace, who stick by their LGBTQ+ friends when it would perhaps be easier not to?

- "Without the absent character of the librarian, none of the events of *The Outrage* are possible." Discuss. How does the discovery of the box of DVDs in the abandoned library act as a catalyst for the events of the book?

- Make a list of all the films mentioned in the book. What do they have in common? In what ways are they different? Why do you think the author decided to include these films?

- After the Rebels watch the documentary *Disclosure*, they come to realise that not all representation of LGBTQ+ people in films is positive representation. Think back on the films the Rebels watch, and any films you have seen recently. How have characters from marginalised or minority groups been represented in those films? Is bad representation better than no representation? Discuss.

- In the Protectorate, officers have powers under Section 28, named after a real British law from the 1980s, which forbade the discussion of homosexuality in schools. Did you know about the real Section 28 before reading *The Outrage*? Why do you think the author chose to reference it in this book?

- Many people across the world still live under restrictions similar to those depicted in *The Outrage*. What are some ways in which fiction can help us to navigate issues that exist in the real world? Do you think there are limitations to its use?

- Consider Gabe's mother and father. How did your view of them change over the course of the book? What do you think about some of the choices they made as members of the Resistance?

- Why do you think the author chose to include Alice as an important character in *The Outrage*? How does her experience differ to that of the other Rebels? Were you surprised when she revealed her true self to Gabe, or had you noticed places where the author had foreshadowed this moment?

- Marsha tells Gabe and Alice that she used to be a history teacher, before the Outrage. Look at the passages on pages 302-307 where she describes the origins of the Protectorate. What role do you think historical knowledge can play in protecting human rights?

- Throughout *The Outrage*, we are told that Mr Dufresne "would watch the whole world burn to save the Protectorate". Why do you think that ultimately he decides to protect his son, at great risk to himself, and at the expense of the Protectorate?

- How did you feel when you saw the poster for Gabe's film at the end of the novel? Why do you think the author has chosen to frame the story in this way?

ACKNOWLEDGEMENTS

As ever, my undying thanks go to my agent, Veronique Baxter of David Higham Associates, for seeing potential in this story and for all her early encouragement and continued support. My foreign rights and media agents Allison Cole and Clare Israel are also owed a huge debt of gratitude.

Massive thanks to my dear friend and editor Stephanie King, for giving inspiration when it was needed, a listening ear when it was very badly required, and the occasional well-timed (and gently delivered) kick up the backside. This book would have been so much poorer without you, Steph.

Thanks also to the team at Usborne: editors Sarah Stewart and Rebecca Hill, copyeditor Tilda Johnson, proofreaders Alice Moloney and Gareth Collinson, cover designer Will Steele, designer Sarah Cronin, marketer Stevie Hopwood and publicist Katarina Jovanovic.

Gratitude, as always, to my friends (too numerous to mention – but especially Trevor Bettison for helping me devise the structure of the Protectorate, Joshua Winning for all the long chats, and to Debbie Scarrow and Dawn Andrew for reading early drafts and keeping me enthused) and my family: Dad, Georgia, Carly, Jon, Jamie, Johnny, Lyla, Jackson and Charly. And to Mum – we miss you every day.

Some special mentions: performance poet and activist, Jay Hulme, our incredible sensitivity reader, who not only reassured me that I was doing right by Alice but was kind enough to help me steer her story in a different direction. I can't thank you enough for this, Jay. Alice owes so much to your influence.

In the middle of editing this book, I was forced to take three months out to have life-saving open-heart surgery. The fact I'm here today is down to the care and skill of Dr Stephen Hoole, Mr Ravi De Silva and his surgery team, Alison Ames, Suzanne Ward and all the brilliant nursing staff at the Royal Papworth Hospital. Thank you for keeping my heart beating so that I could see Gabe, Eric and Alice take their bow!

William x

How well do you really know the people you love?

Dylan falls for Ellis the moment he meets him,
although deep down, Dylan sometimes wonders if
Ellis is keeping secrets from him.
When a tragic accident rips them apart, Dylan begins to
discover just how little he knows about the boy he loves,
and that Ellis isn't the only person with secrets…

"This tender, poignant evocation of first love is warm and profoundly thought-provoking."
The Guardian

"A heart-breaking love story steeped in a thrillingly dark mystery for teens."
Attitude

"The UK finally has an answer to Adam Silvera."
@ elfcouncillor

"A touching tale of LGBTQ+ identity with an intense, emotional mystery...poignant and powerful."
@bradleybirkholz

"Beautifully written and unpredictable." *@faridahlikestea*

"Had me completely hooked in a way that only the likes of Adam Silvera and Karen McManus have managed." *@LoofyJ*

"I love love love this book. Buy it, read it, support it. Brilliant, realistic characters; excellent queer representation; thrilling mystery; important themes; beautiful writing. Essential reading." *@nocaptainreuben*

"A mystery with same sex kissing. Lots of kissing. Heartbreakingly good." *@PewterWolf*

"Finished HB. Dude. I'm in awe." *@empireofbooks*

Love this book? Love Usborne YA

Follow us online and sign up to the Usborne YA newsletter for the latest YA books, news and competitions:

usborne.com/yanewsletter

@UsborneYA

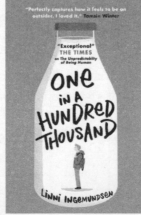

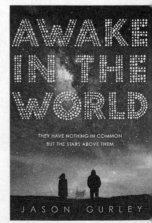